"Lianne, come home with me."

Gabe murmured the words against her mouth, the stark statement more an order than a request. Then he drew her into the shadows of the sheltered portico to await the arrival of his Jag, and pulled her roughly into his arms, his mouth ravishing hers, his body pressed impossibly close.

But the fiasco of their Sunday date was still painfully clear in her memory. Doubts returned, crowding in, cooling the fever of longing. What if they indulged in another night of passionate lovemaking and he simply walked away from her as he had done once before? She was ready to admit that what she felt for him was more—much more—than simple sexual attraction. But Gabe didn't seem ready to admit any such thing.

Could she trust him enough to open herself to the possibility of yet another rejection? Worse yet, if they ended up in bed together, was she ready to cope with the emotional consequences of having sex with a man who didn't seem to like her?

Weddings by De Wilde

Weddings by DeWilde™

Since the turn of the century, the elegant and fashionable DeWilde stores have helped brides around the world turn the fantasy of their "special day" into reality. But now the store and three generations of family are torn apart by the separation of Grace and Jeffrey DeWilde. As family members face new challenges and loves—and a long-secret mystery—the lives of Grace and Jeffrey intermingle with store employees, friends and relatives. For weddings and romance, glamour and fun-filled entertainment, enter the House of DeWilde....

ISBN 0-373-82537-4

SHATTERED VOWS

Jasmine Cresswell
SHATTERED VOWS

Harlequin Books

TORONTO • NEW YORK • LONDON
AMSTERDAM • PARIS • SYDNEY • HAMBURG
STOCKHOLM • ATHENS • TOKYO • MILAN
MADRID • WARSAW • BUDAPEST • AUCKLAND

Dear Gabe,

I've been trying to call you all evening——and a small, cowardly part of me is almost glad that you weren't at home. Some things hurt too much to talk about, even with someone you love. One day you may understand how intimidating it is——as well as wonderful——to have a son whom you love and admire so much that you're afraid to disappoint him.

I'm sorry, I meant to keep this letter reasonably brief and to the point, with no self-pitying digressions. For the past twenty-four hours, I've been rehearsing ways to break the news that your father and I are separating. Separating. What a bland word to cover such a terrifyingly bitter tangle of hurt, anger and bewilderment! But however hard I try, however much I search, I can't find any words to make the truth seem less brutal: after thirty-two years, my marriage to your father is over. Permanently over? Yes, I'm very much afraid so. To be honest, I don't see any way to heal the wounds we've inflicted on each other over the past couple of months. The events of this past weekend have brought everything to a rushed and explosive end, but I can see now that the end itself was inevitable. A marriage can endure only a certain number of blows before it simply gives up and dies.

I realize that I shall be in San Francisco before this letter reaches you, and I'm afraid you'll be very upset, and perhaps even angry, that I didn't take you into my confidence weeks ago. Please understand how difficult all this has been for me, Gabe, and remember that although my marriage to your father may have ended, I will always be your most loving and affectionate Mother.

CHAPTER ONE

GABRIEL DEWILDE STORMED into his father's office and slammed the door shut behind him. "What the hell is this all about?" he demanded, thrusting the solicitor's letter onto his father's desk. "If this is your idea of a joke, I don't find it funny."

Jeffrey DeWilde continued to stare out of his office window, apparently fascinated by the view of gray slate rooftops awash in spring rain. "It isn't a joke," he said finally. "Grace has left me."

He sounded no more than mildly regretful, as if he were commenting on the fact that this morning at breakfast he'd run out of his favorite brand of marmalade. Gabe ran his hands through his long, light brown hair and paced the room. He felt as if he'd walked into the familiar surroundings of his father's office only to discover himself free-falling into an alien universe.

"Left you?" he repeated, the simple words incomprehensible when applied to his mother. "She can't have left you. You've been married for thirty-two years!"

"But she has left me." Jeffrey's stark response reverberated in the oak-paneled quiet of the room. "She moved out to a hotel on Friday night. I don't know which one."

Gabe shook his head, trying to restore his sense of reality. "None of this makes the least bit of sense! You and Mother always seemed to have the ideal marriage. Neither of you ever gave any of us the slightest hint that you were having problems."

Jeffrey still didn't turn around. "Some things are too painful to discuss, even with your children. And perhaps the hints were there if you'd been willing to look for them."

"No, of course they weren't. We didn't have a clue—" Gabe broke off, suddenly remembering the Sunday morning last month when he'd arrived unexpectedly at Kemberly, his parents' home in Hampshire. He'd found his mother red-eyed and alone. She'd insisted her problem was nothing more than allergies, caused by the spring pollen. Wanting to be convinced, Gabe had accepted her explanation without pushing very hard for another. In retrospect, he cursed his willful blindness.

Angry with himself, he took out his frustration on his father. "Your children aren't supposed to be mind readers," he said. "Damn it, Dad, you should have warned us what was going on."

"What would you have expected me to say? I wasn't sure how . . . the situation . . . would be resolved."

"Well, I certainly didn't expect you to wait until Mother had left and then order the family solicitor to send us an official announcement that the two of you had separated! Ramsbotham's letter reads like an announcement from Buckingham Palace about another royal marriage on the rocks. We're your children, for God's sake, not company employees! How do you think Kate and Megan are going to feel when they get their copies of this bombshell? They're miles away. They can't even come and talk to you."

"I'm sorry." Jeffrey's apology was clipped. "In the end, everything happened rather suddenly. I tried to phone you last night but you were out, and I suppose I felt a somewhat cowardly sense of relief. I did manage to talk to Megan in Paris early this morning, but you know I've never been good at explaining emotional...things. That's your mother's department. She always does this sort of thing so much better than I do. I rely on her—''

Jeffrey got up abruptly but didn't seem quite sure what to do next. He opened the heavy drapes to their fullest extent, then pulled them back to their original position. He sat down in his chair once more, his back to Gabriel, and resumed his contemplation of Bond Street in the rain.

He cleared his throat, started to speak, stopped and started again. "Grace has returned to San Francisco. She left yesterday morning, so I expect she's there by now and settling in to...wherever she plans to stay. I'm quite sure she'll be in touch with you soon, Gabriel. It's me she wants to divorce, not you or your sisters. You know how much she loves you all.''

Divorce? Good God, were his parents really talking about getting a divorce, not just separating for a while? The more his father explained, the less Gabe understood. This entire conversation would have been ridiculous, a splendid example of black comedy—if it hadn't been so sad. He knew deep in his bones that his parents had once been happy together. Children didn't need to understand adult emotions to be aware they existed, and Gabe had always known his parents had not only liked and respected each other, they'd been deeply in love. Awareness of his parents' love for each other suffused all his childhood memories. Where had all that love gone? If Jeffrey and Grace couldn't make their marriage last, Gabe wondered if any couple could.

"How can you let Mother divorce you?" he asked. "Can't you fight this? Surely you can work out your problems, whatever they are? Good Lord, after thirty-two years there must be some groundwork left to build on. You love each other!"

Jeffrey didn't answer, didn't even move, and Gabe pleaded, "Dad, look at me, for God's sake! Make me understand what's happened. The two of you have always been so happy together!"

"Obviously not happy enough to persuade your mother to remain here in England," Jeffrey said.

"But why has she gone to San Francisco? What in the world is she going to do there?"

"I don't know." Jeffrey shrugged. "San Francisco is her home, after all. And Kate is there."

"Kate's only there until she finishes university," Gabe said tightly. "Mother's home is here in London, with you. Her work is here, her friends are here. Her whole adult life. Why is she doing this to you? To us? How could she just... walk out?"

Jeffrey finally swung his chair around and faced his son. An outsider might have thought his thin, aristocratic features expressionless. Gabe knew better. His father's hazel eyes normally gleamed with laughter, displaying a rueful appreciation of the world's follies, and his own. Today his gaze was cold and bleak, his mouth compressed into a tight line. Whatever the reasons for this stunning rupture in his parents' marriage, Gabe could see at a glance that his father hadn't wanted it and was shattered by Grace's abrupt departure. Jeffrey might sound cool and collected, but inside, Gabe suspected, his father smoldered with feeling.

"A marriage involves two people," Jeffrey said with the same unnatural calm. "When it ends, you can safely bet that both partners contributed to the breakup."

Had he misjudged his father's mood, after all? Gabe wondered. "Are you telling me this was a mutual decision? That you both wanted your marriage to end?"

"I'm certainly not blameless in all this, but the truth is that your mother seems to feel our marriage was a mistake from the beginning." Jeffrey drew in a sharp breath. "At the moment, I think she wants to be as far away from me and from London as possible."

Gabe noticed that his father hadn't quite answered the question. No doubt because he was too honorable to throw all the blame on his wife. His estranged wife, Gabe thought bitterly. "If it's taken her thirty-two years to discover she made a mistake, couldn't she have waited for a couple of months to see if things got better again?"

"Apparently not."

Gabe felt a flash of white-hot anger on his father's behalf. And on his own. He'd always felt a deep affection for his mother, admiring her boundless creativity and the light, whimsical touch she injected into the most mundane aspects of life. Her abrupt departure felt like a personal betrayal. Whatever her reasons for leaving his father, they didn't excuse her flying out of the country without a word to anyone. Why hadn't she called him to say goodbye? To explain why she needed to abandon everything she'd spent a lifetime working to build?

For the past couple of years, Gabe had been the only one of the three DeWilde children living and working in London, and the respect he felt for his mother had increased as he grew to appreciate the heavy workload she carried and the importance of her unique contributions to the DeWilde organization. Her abrupt departure left him disoriented, with the reliable boundaries of everyday life suddenly fluid and uncertain. Her silence left him feeling both rejected and oddly bereft. And if he was feeling bereft, Gabe reflected, it was hard to imagine what his father must be suffering.

"My mother has responsibilities," he said harshly. "Even if she's decided to throw away her husband and family, there's the business to think about. She does remember that she's executive vice president of DeWilde's, doesn't she?" He picked up the solicitor's letter and stabbed his forefinger at one of the many obscure sentences. "What does this mean, for heaven's sake? 'Various financial matters of a personal and business nature continue to be a subject for discussion between your parents.' Elaborate, please."

Jeffrey steepled his fingers and stared down at them as if he weren't quite sure that they still belonged to him. "Grace says that she has no interest in the future success or failure of DeWilde's." He realigned his fingers and stared at them again. "Her official letter of resignation was waiting on my desk this morning. She wants to sever her connections to the stores, as well as her marriage to me."

Jeffrey's voice remained uninflected, but Gabe realized that his cool, courteous and seemingly calm father was hanging on to his control by the merest thread. Not only was Jeffrey personally devastated by his wife's flight, he was fully aware of the serious implications for the business. Stock market analysts might admire his firm control over the bottom line and his ability to cut costs while maintaining the highest levels of service in all the DeWilde stores, but anyone who'd been closely involved in the day-to-day running of the company's five international stores knew how vitally important Grace was to their success. She was recognized throughout the organization as a creative whirlwind, swirling around the solid pillar of Jeffrey's business acumen, breathing life and color into her husband's fact- and number-oriented decisions.

Grace's retailing instincts were unsurpassed on either side of the Atlantic. She had a sixth sense that told her months ahead of the competition what sort of weddings next year's brides would be planning, and she also seemed blessed with a seventh sense that told her exactly how to display and market DeWilde merchandise so that it fulfilled every bride's fantasy of that perfect wedding—and glamorous honeymoon. With a sense of definite foreboding, Gabe realized that his mother's hasty departure had not only destroyed a marriage but could also have a devastating effect on the continued success of the DeWilde stores. With the current upheaval in the retail market worldwide, this was not the moment to have stock market analysts raising questions about DeWilde's capability to remain an industry leader.

"How do you want to handle this with the management group?" Gabe asked. He glanced at his watch. "We have a few hours before the store will be open in New York. But somebody needs to call Ryder Blake in Sydney right away. And we have to talk to Paris, too. Or is Megan handling things over there? And Monaco. Who else have you spoken to here in London? How many people already know that Mother has gone?"

"Nobody," Jeffrey said.

Gabe bit back a frustrated expletive. Grace's departure must have thrown his father for an absolute loop. In normal circumstances, the departure of a key executive would have meant that Jeffrey had spent most of the weekend on the phone, making sure that his managers were fully aware of the situation, discussing tactics and strategy, preparing his people so that they would be ready to hit the ground running on Monday morning. Gabe began to realize the enormity of the problem he was facing. Losing Grace was bad enough, but DeWilde's couldn't afford to lose Jeffrey's input, as well, not when they had major expansion and renovation plans in the works.

He drew in a deep breath. "If nobody knows about Mother's resignation, you need to call a management meeting right away. You'll need to start assigning people to cover her current areas of responsibility. Mother has four department heads reporting directly to her in London, and she acts as the merchandising consultant for all five stores." It was ridiculous to be reminding his father of such basic information, but Gabe was afraid that at this precise moment Jeffrey needed all the help he could get. "Do you want her people to report to you for the time being? And if not, how do you want to structure things?"

"I haven't thought about it," Jeffrey said. "We don't have to deal with that today, do we? At the moment, all anyone needs to know is that Grace has left the company and won't be coming back."

"Dad, I'm sorry, but that's not true and you know it." Gabe's shock was beginning to fade, and he decided that perhaps the most immediate and effective way to help his father was to ensure that Grace's departure had as little negative impact as possible on DeWilde's. "This insane decision of Mother's doesn't just affect the family, it affects the company, too. If word about her leaving leaks out in the wrong sort of way, it could have a disastrous effect on company morale, not to mention our share price. Quite apart from any problems with the stock market, we need to handle the internal announcements just right or we're going to have a hell of a lot of unhappy employees."

"Grace is gone," Jeffrey said, his voice icy. "How do you propose we dress that fact up to make it sound positive?"

"I've no idea, but perhaps someone else in the management group will have something constructive to offer. At the very least, we ought to take steps to avoid having the news spread by whispers and rumors. You need to call our PR consultants and institute some instant damage control. Have them draft an announcement about Grace's departure, emphasizing in as upbeat a way as possible that we have people ready and waiting to step into her shoes. And you need to be ready to field the blizzard of phone calls we'll start to get as soon as the press release hits the financial wire services. You also need to decide who's going to take over the international merchandising functions. I can handle things here in London, but I have no international experience to speak of. Adam in Marketing is good, but he doesn't have any of Mother's natural—"

"I can't do this," Jeffrey said, standing up and gripping the edge of the desk. His face was white. "Gabe, I'm sorry. I thought I could handle coming into the office today, but I can't. I have to get out of here for a while. Please, take care of things for me." He strode to the door of his office and walked past his secretary's desk to the lifts, ignoring the astonished stare of Monica and Gabe's plea for him to wait a minute, or at least to take an umbrella.

"Is he going out in this downpour?" Monica asked, tapping a pencil against her computer keyboard without any awareness of what she was doing. "Oh, dear, I do hope he hasn't forgotten that Sir Walter Kenyon is scheduled to arrive in twenty minutes."

"He may well have forgotten," Gabe said. "Either way, it's probably best to cancel Sir Walter, at least for today. Try to postpone the meeting until next week, will you?"

Monica picked up the phone to make the call. She grimaced faintly as her conversation ended. "Sorry, Gabriel, but Sir Walter left fifteen minutes ago. There's no way to reach him and put him off."

"Damn. Do you know if my father arranged for anyone else from DeWilde's to attend the meeting?"

Monica glanced at her desk calendar. "Rupert Findlay was supposed to join them," she said.

"Makes sense. Rupert's the chief financial officer and Sir Walter's a banker. Well, Rupert will have to take care of things. Since he was scheduled to attend the meeting, anyway, he probably knows what my father planned to discuss. Call Rupert and warn him he's going to be on his own with Sir Walter, will you?"

Gabe started to leave, but Monica called him back. Normally the perfect model of the circumspect executive secretary, she couldn't hide her concern. "I hope you won't think I'm pushing into private places, Gabriel, but your father hasn't seemed himself for the past several weeks. Is something wrong?"

It was humiliating to learn that Jeffrey's secretary had noticed something amiss when he hadn't, Gabe thought. He'd been a damn sight too caught up in his own affairs these past two months. While he'd been running around London with Julia Dutton, trying to convince himself he'd found the woman who would make him the ideal wife, his parents' marriage had been crumbling into ruins right under his self-absorbed nose.

There seemed no point in attempting to hide the truth from Monica. Grace would soon be conspicuous by her absence. "My parents have separated," he said. "Grace has already left England and gone back to San Francisco. She has family there." He tried to make it sound rational, as if a brother and a smattering of cousins were sensible reasons to abandon a husband of thirty-two years and a dazzling career with one of England's most famous and successful stores. "And, of course, Kate's at Stanford, finishing her residency," he added lamely.

"I don't understand." Monica flushed with distress. "Isn't Grace coming back?"

What was the point of pretending? "No," Gabe said. "At the moment, she isn't planning to return."

"Oh, no! I'm so sorry. I never dreamed..." Monica smothered a murmur of distress. "Poor Jeffrey!" She straightened, visibly squaring herself to face the uncertain future. "Well, I can see this is going to be a difficult day for everyone. How would you like me to help?"

"I have to inform the members of senior management that Grace has gone," Gabe said. "Would you call everyone and ask them to meet me in the boardroom in half an hour?"

Monica looked at the clock on her desk. "That'll be nine-thirty. Yes, everyone should have arrived by then. I'll start notifying people right away. I'll make sure they realize this is a must-attend session."

"Thank you." Gabe walked back to his office at such a fast pace he was almost running. He didn't manage to outpace his worries. Life had an annoying habit of creeping up behind you and grabbing you by the throat to make sure you were paying attention. At eight o'clock this morning, he'd thought that the biggest problem he faced was extricating himself from his relationship with Julia Dutton without hurting her feelings. Now, an hour later, his problems with Julia seemed little more than a footnote to the stunning news of his parents' separation. He reflected wryly that he would have preferred a less painful and dramatic lesson on how to put his problems into perspective.

Perhaps he'd originally been attracted to Julia just because she was so different from his mother, he thought, pushing open the door to his office. Julia was sweet, calm, even-tempered and—restful. The contrast with the bubbling, high-speed energy of his mother had seemed irresistible. But why had he needed the company of someone restful? Because he'd subconsciously sensed the note of strain behind Grace's habitual effervescence? Because he'd felt the high-wire tension suddenly stretching between his parents? Why else had it seemed so important to spend his leisure hours with a woman who was the antithesis of his mercurial mother?

The phone rang and he snatched it up, dealing swiftly with a call from a supplier. When he hung up, he started sketching out some alternative management reporting structures. This was his father's job, of course, but since Jeffrey wasn't available, somebody had to reassign Grace's duties, at least on a temporary basis. He worked intently, his concentration rigorously focused. For the next few hours, he wouldn't allow himself to think about the personal aspects of the split between Grace and Jeffrey. He needed to keep his attention fixed on the impact their separation was likely to have on the DeWilde organization.

To put it mildly, this was not proving to be the most enjoyable Monday morning he'd ever lived through. Gabe hoped like hell that the day had exhausted its store of unpleasant surprises.

CHAPTER TWO

WHEN SHE REALIZED there was going to be no letup in the unrelenting downpour of rain, Lianne Beecham decided to blow her week's lunch money on a cab. After all, she was about to become a gainfully employed woman, with a real job and a regular income. Once her first month's salary was deposited into the bank, she'd be rich. Or at least solvent, which was a great deal more than could be said about her situation over the past few months. Freelance designers didn't have it any easier in London than they did in New York, Lianne had discovered, and she was heartily sick of being a starving artist.

When she won the prestigious Garnet Award last December, she'd hoped that commissions and honest-to-God work for pay would result. Instead of work, she'd received accolades. The *Guardian* had assured its readers that she was a costume jewelry designer with "flair to spare." The *Times,* more soberly, had announced that her creative talents "showed astonishing technical competence and promised to develop into genuine originality."

Lianne was suitably grateful for the positive reviews and rather liked the experience of being a minor celebrity in the incestuous world of high fashion. She just wished that the critical praise could have been accompanied by a few checks, since even artists with flair to spare occasionally needed to do mundane things like eat and pay their share of the rent. If Julia Dutton hadn't been such a sympathetic friend and flat mate, Lianne wondered if she would have been able to hang on in London long enough to land a job.

But her life, not to mention her bank balance, was about to undergo a marvelous change. Lianne paid the cab driver, giving him such a generous tip that he actually smiled. She hauled her portfolio out of the cab and looked up at the imposing entrance to DeWilde's, oblivious to the rain pelting down. Her heart pounded with emotion and she felt hot all over, despite the chilly spring breeze. She was so excited to think she was about to start work behind those hallowed blue doors and elegant Queen Anne windows that she would have danced a jig of sheer delight if the pavement hadn't been so wet and muddy.

The rain wasn't letting up, even for a minute. Lianne made a dash for the store and ran inside, tossing back the hood of her raincoat and letting the streams of water drip off her sleeves onto the iron grates set into the marble floor. After a year in England, she really ought to have learned never to leave the flat without her umbrella, but it seemed that she still retained her stubborn American optimism that, however terrible the weather right now, in a moment the sun would be shining.

Unfastening the buttons of her sodden raincoat, she pushed through the second set of heavy doors and squinted into one of the mirrors positioned on the cosmetic counter just inside the store entrance. She sighed. Yep, she looked just the way she'd feared. Her hair was always unruly. On a rainy day it became a tyrant with an uncontrollable will of its own. She'd tried every hair length known to woman, from a short crop to her current shoulder length. Her hair had defeated the best efforts of stylists on both sides of the Atlantic. Before leaving the flat this morning, in honor of her new job, she'd scraped it into a severe French twist and sprayed every obstinate strand into submission. What she had now, a mere thirty minutes later, were the tattered remnants of a French twist and a riot of chestnut curls framing her face. Before informing Grace DeWilde's assistant that she was here, she'd better find the ladies' room so that she could try to re-create her original elegant style. She wasn't holding her breath, though. From past experience, she knew she probably wouldn't achieve anything more sophisticated than flattened curls at the front and a frizzy knot at the back of her head.

But there was no point in agonizing over her hair, which was simply one of those intractable laws of nature, like English rain, or the vile taste of fat-free ice-cream. On this, the first day of her new job, she had plenty more important things to worry about.

Lianne had decided to enter the corporate offices by way of the store itself. Grace DeWilde had given her an extensive tour during one of their preliminary meetings, but Lianne needed to internalize the atmosphere of the display floors so that she could develop her own intuitive sense of who the customers were and what fantasies they carried with them as they walked through the imposing gilded doors and into the Edwardian grandeur of the ground floor. From her own brief experience as a bride-to-be five years ago, Lianne was quite sure that brides, even more than most shoppers, were buying a dream right along with their dress and lace veil.

She looked around her, breathing in a subtle scent of lavender polish, sandalwood and rich satin. The overwhelming impression of dignified, traditional splendor would have been out of place in most retail stores, but DeWilde's had proven that, even on the cusp of the twenty-first century, British women enjoyed planning their weddings in surroundings imbued with the solid virtues of permanence and understated elegance. A woman who had shopped at DeWilde's for her trousseau in the thirties could come back today with her granddaughter and be comfortably aware that she was in the same store. And come back they did, bringing new generations of brides with them. In an ever-changing world, customers seemed to appreciate this oasis of tradition.

Still, despite DeWilde's successful track record, Lianne understood why Grace wanted to introduce certain changes. The dawn of the new century was likely to presage an increase in nontraditional wedding ceremonies, and DeWilde's needed to be prepared for the shrinking of their market base. Magnificent as the hand-crafted mahogany counters were, they didn't allow for dramatic or inviting displays of merchandise. The lighting was in desperate need of updating. Space wasn't utilized to its maximum advantage. Lianne wholeheartedly agreed with Grace that the famous ground floor could be given a modest face-lift without destroying its beauty and architectural integrity. Still, change wasn't going to come easy. Lianne smiled to herself, glad that she wasn't the one who would have to fight all the stuffy old die-hard conservatives in the upper echelons of management.

In the years following the First World War, DeWilde's had gradually expanded until it sold everything the bride-to-be might need for her wedding and honeymoon. For the past twenty years, most of the store's profits had come from the sale of wedding gowns, lingerie and high fashion clothes for romantic honeymoons. Whether you planned to spend the first few days of your married life sunning on tropical beaches or climbing ice floes in Alaska, DeWilde's had the outfit you needed. But for all this recent emphasis on clothing, the business had built its reputation originally as a jewelry store. Four generations of women had felt their hearts beat a little faster when the young men in their lives pulled out one of the famous dark blue leather jewelry boxes and opened it to reveal a ring, nestled in velvet, with the flowing gold letters of the DeWilde name stamped on the puffed peach satin lining of the lid.

In the nineties, of course, men and women were more likely to come and select an engagement ring together, but the tradition of the real leather box and the real velvet lining persisted. It was one of the luxurious touches that distinguished DeWilde's from its rivals and kept the store ahead in the cutthroat world of modern retailing.

Lianne lingered for a few moments, admiring the dazzling display of engagement and wedding rings, all set with the finest quality gemstones. Although her own interests lay in the realm of costume jewelry, which was considered an offshoot of the fashion industry rather than the world of gemologists and goldsmiths, she often drew her inspiration from the creations of Victorian jewelers, particularly those who had worked at the sumptuous courts of the Indian maharajas. In addition to a line of exquisitely crafted rings set with semiprecious stones such as amethysts and aquamarines, she noticed that DeWilde's had a small display of antique rings for couples who wanted to bring a touch of nostalgia into their marriage. One in particular caught her fancy, an exuberant floral design with tiny diamonds at the heart of each flower, the pink gold a much deeper color than was currently fashionable.

"Is there any way I might help you, madam?"

"No, thanks." Lianne gave the formally dressed man standing behind the counter a cheerful smile. "I'm just looking, but some of these antique engagement rings are so pretty it makes me wonder if marriage might not be so bad after all. That floral design is especially lovely.''

He returned her smile, his warm manner belying the high, starched collar of his shirt. ''It is lovely, although the diamonds are smaller than we'd use nowadays. My wife always says it takes a lot of diamonds to make up for sharing your bathroom with a man.''

''She's right, I'm sure. Your wife sounds like a wise woman.''

''With many diamonds,'' the salesclerk agreed with mock solemnity.

Lianne laughed and walked on. Making her way around the scattering of early-bird customers, she finally stopped in front of the trademark centerpiece of DeWilde's London store, an exquisitely mounted display of a tiara from the DeWilde family's famous jewelry collection. Protected by an octagon-shaped case of bulletproof glass, the tiara glowed with subdued radiance against its cushion of navy blue velvet. Beneath a cleverly focused spotlight—and a dozen electronic security devices—the strands of diamonds and pearls twisted in serpentine opulence. A descriptive note explained that the provenance of the tiara had never been reliably established, but it was reputed to have been worn by the Empress Eugénie of France on the day of her wedding to Louis-Napoléon in 1853. The empress had lived to a ripe old age after her husband lost his throne, and she'd died in England during the 1920s, so it was quite believable that on some occasion when they'd needed ready cash, Eugénie's heirs had quietly sold the tiara, and it had eventually made its way into the hands of England's most famous family of jewelers.

Lianne stared at the piece for several minutes. She'd seen it before, of course, on previous visits, and she found the subtle mixture of color and texture enchanting, the diamonds imparting brilliance, the pearls offering a rounded, milky contrast to the glittering facets of the gemstones. The overall effect should have been absolutely breathtaking. For the umpteenth time she wondered why there was some tiny part of her that felt disappointed, as if this glorious—and priceless—piece didn't quite live up to the allure promised by its design and history.

Turning away from the famous tiara, Lianne glanced at her watch. Ten-forty-five. Time to make her way upstairs to the corporate offices. The last thing she wanted was to create a bad impression by being late. For her first day, Grace DeWilde had suggested that Lianne should arrive at eleven, two hours after the official opening of the corporate offices and an hour after the store opening at ten.

"There's always so much for me to do on a Monday morning," Grace had said, her husky voice an intriguing contrast to her elegant appearance and blond, classic good looks. "And May is such a hectic month for us. All those June weddings coming up, and all the brides wondering if their dresses are going to be ready on time. And, of course, at the corporate level, we're already making major buying decisions for the following year. I'm usually at my desk by eight-thirty. Give me a couple of hours to catch up on the weekend faxes and get a head start on the crisis of the week—whatever it might be!—then I'll be able to give you my undivided attention for the rest of the morning. I'd like to take you around and introduce you personally to everyone. They've already heard all about my plans to revamp the layout of the ground floor and introduce boutique settings for the first-floor bridal salon. They'll be thrilled to know that I've recruited someone as talented as my first in-house designer. Then, after lunch, I'll hand you over to Personnel, and they can take care of all the paperwork.''

Lianne could hardly wait. Even filling out forms in Personnel had sounded appealing, since it would be the final, official stamp on the reality of her new job. She found the ladies' room and made a valiant stab at fixing her hair, then set out to meet Grace DeWilde. Tapping her foot and humming beneath her breath—she absolutely had to find some outlet for her creative energy or she would explode—she took the lift to the sixth floor. After a year living in England, she was finally remembering not to say "elevator." The doors opened into a pleasant lobby, decorated in beige and moss green, with a large reception desk straight ahead. A receptionist, not the security guard Lianne had seen on previous occasions, greeted her with a somewhat flustered smile.

"Hello, may I help you?"

The receptionist was young and she sounded very unsure of herself. Lianne gave her a friendly smile. Perhaps she, too, was a new employee. "I'm here to see Grace DeWilde. Would you let her know that I've arrived? My name's Lianne Beecham."

If she'd announced that she was the Grim Reaper come to cull excess workers, the receptionist couldn't have looked more horrified. "M-Mrs. DeWilde?" she stammered. "You're here to see Mrs. DeWilde?"

"Yes, that's right." Lianne tried another smile, but the receptionist seemed too distraught to respond. Definitely a new hire, she decided. "If you're busy, why don't you just point me in the direction of her office? I seem to remember that I have to turn left at the end of this hallway."

The suggestion that she might intrude into Grace DeWilde's inner sanctum jolted the receptionist into recovering her voice. "Oh, no! I'll have to ring through first. Someone must, um, escort you. So if you'll just take a seat, Miss—"

"Beecham," Lianne supplied patiently. "Lianne Beecham."

"Yes, thank you, Miss Beecham. Please take a seat for a moment, would you, and I'll let Mrs. DeWilde's assistant know that you're here."

It was clearly an order rather than a request. On Lianne's previous visits, Grace DeWilde had come out to greet her in person, a dynamo in human form. Lianne had secretly been hoping that Grace would be waiting to meet her the moment she stepped out of the lift. Foolishness, of course. Grace was much too busy a woman to hang around the lobby, waiting for a relatively insignificant new hire to show her face.

The receptionist seemed to be having trouble locating the person she needed. Lianne hoped it wouldn't take too long to get through all these preliminaries. She wanted to sink her teeth into her new job and get started. She'd been working twelve hours a day ever since Grace made the final offer, and she was itching to get some of her ideas approved. She wanted to find out where her office was, who'd been hired to design the boutique that would showcase her bridal headdresses, how long it would be before her first designs could be put into production. After waiting nine endless days since her final interview, she had exhausted what little patience she had. She wanted everything to happen now, this very second. Amused by her own zeal, Lianne forced herself to sit decorously in one of the comfortable wing chairs situated at the side of the lobby. As an exercise in self-control, she propped her portfolio against the occasional table and flipped through the glossy pages of *Country Life* magazine. She leafed

through a gossipy article about who planned to stay with
whom for Ascot week and shook her head in disbelief at
a photo of a woman called Lady Emmington, who looked
like a New York bag lady and had created a garden of
such surpassing beauty that even the magazine pictures of
it had the power to bring a lump to Lianne's throat.
Sometimes she wondered if she would ever understand the
English. Every time she started to think she might at last
have a handle on what made them tick, she needed only
to pick up a journal such as this to know that her mid-
western American soul had barely begun to grasp the in-
tricate weave of history, genes and circumstance that had
made the citizens of her temporary homeland what they
were.

The receptionist finished her hushed conversation,
presumably with Grace's assistant. She looked over at
Lianne, her earlier uncertainty replaced by a distant, off-
hand courtesy. "Mrs. DeWilde's personal assistant will be
with you in just a few moments, Miss Beecham. We
apologize for keeping you waiting."

Lianne found the formality of the receptionist's manner surprising, as well as off-putting. Grace had implied
that the DeWilde corporation was run rather informally
by British standards, and she'd suggested at their second
meeting that Lianne should call her Grace. The receptionist clearly adhered to a different set of guidelines.
Restless and suddenly on edge, Lianne gave up on reading the magazine and rose to her feet, pacing nervously.

A handsome, middle-aged woman, neatly attired in a
tailored gray suit, came into the reception area. "Good
morning," she said to Lianne. Her smile appeared polite, but her body language conveyed the same odd wari-
ness as the receptionist. "I'm Fredda Halston, Mrs.
DeWilde's assistant." Her voice thickened, and she

cleared her throat. Lianne had the crazy impression the woman was choking back tears. "I'm sorry that you've been kept waiting, but Mrs. DeWilde didn't make any notation on her calendar that you were coming today."

"Isn't Grace in the office?" Lianne said. "I know she was expecting me. She arranged the time herself."

Fredda's smile became a little strained around the edges, then slipped away completely. "Did she? I'm so sorry, but I'm afraid Mrs. DeWilde has been, um, called away this morning."

How strange, Lianne thought. She ignored the flicker of alarm in the pit of her stomach and mustered a smile. "Well, never mind. Here I am, and anxious to start work. Grace and I can get together this afternoon."

"Work?" Fredda repeated. "What are you supposed to work on?"

Lianne began to feel as if she were trying to communicate in a foreign language. Not just American versus English, but something obscure like Pashto or Swahili.

"Bridal headdresses," she said.

She picked up her portfolio, trying not to appear visibly impatient. "Grace explained how busy she is at this time of year, so if you'll show me to my office, I'll get settled in and Grace can introduce me to everyone later on in the day. Perhaps you could point me in the direction of Personnel once I've seen my office? That way, I could get all those boring forms filled out while we're waiting for Grace to get back."

Grace's assistant and the receptionist exchanged what looked like a totally horrified glance. Fredda Halston cleared her throat. "Miss Beecham, this is rather embarrassing, but am I correct in assuming you're expecting to start work here today?"

The flicker of nerves in the pit of Lianne's stomach swelled to a giant, three-alarm blaze. "Grace DeWilde offered me the job over a week ago," she said tightly. "She said she'd get my contract drawn up and ready for my signature when I arrived for work today. I assumed that you would know all about it since you're her assistant."

Fredda Halston's cheeks flushed an agitated pink. "I'm sorry. I'm afraid there's been some sort of mix-up. . . ."

The three-alarm blaze died an instant death. Lianne froze. She could think of only one explanation for Fredda's flustered behavior. "You mean Grace has rescinded her offer of a position as in-house designer?"

"In-house designer?" Grace's assistant sounded like a Victorian maiden hearing a gentleman swear. "Oh, dear. I hadn't realized—" She stopped abruptly. "Look, Miss Beecham, this clearly isn't the place for us to be discussing this. Why don't you come along to my office? At least I can offer you a cup of coffee."

A cup of coffee didn't sound like much of a substitute for her very own office, a permanent job and an in-store boutique dedicated to the display and sale of her bridal headdresses. Lianne trailed behind Grace's assistant on feet turned suddenly leaden. What had happened? Where was Grace DeWilde? She had seemed such a friendly, efficient, reliable person. Lianne just couldn't visualize her casually offering an important job, then equally casually withdrawing the offer. It was especially hard to imagine her leaving a flurried assistant to handle the resulting mess. Had she misjudged Grace so badly?

Fredda Halston led her into a small, cheerful office, with a computer humming on the desk and shelves stacked high with sample fabric books, catalogs and photos of brides, dating back to the 1930s, all outfitted by De-

Wilde's. "How do you like your coffee, Miss Beecham? Cream and sugar? Black?"

"Let's skip the coffee, shall we?" Lianne suggested. "Frankly, I'm anxious to clear up this muddle and start work."

"This is very awkward," Fredda said, removing a pile of bridal magazines from a chair so that Lianne could sit down. "I'm afraid I've no idea what Grace hired you to do, so I don't quite know who to call. Since she isn't here, perhaps you could tell me what you do...." Her voice tailed away.

"I'm a costume jewelry designer," Lianne explained. "I studied at the London School of Design here in England and at the Pittsburgh School of Art in the United States."

"You're an American, then?" Fredda shrugged apologetically. "Of course you are. Silly question."

"Yes, I am an American, but my father was an officer with the U.S. Air Force and I spent four years in Hertfordshire, near the U.S. military base, when I was a teenager. I've always loved England, and when I finished my courses at the London School of Design, I decided to take a stab at establishing myself on this side of the Atlantic while I was still young enough to take the chance of falling on my face."

"And that's what Grace hired you for? To design costume jewelry for DeWilde's?"

"No, not exactly. Recently, a friend was thinking about getting married and I played around drawing bridal headdresses for her. I became intrigued with the concept of designing for a bride, and I worked up an entire collection, some of it very traditional, some of it anything but. I submitted my designs to Grace, who liked them so much that, instead of just buying those designs, she decided to hire me with a specific mandate to create a line of bridal headdresses that would be presented as a signature collection—*Lianne for DeWilde*. Now I'm here, ready to start work. As we agreed."

Fredda Halston's gaze narrowed. "This is very difficult for both of us, Miss Beecham, but to be honest, I don't quite understand how you had all these discussions with Mrs. DeWilde without my ever meeting you or even being aware of what was going on."

Lianne decided she was becoming more than a little irritated by Fredda's attitude. "As to why Grace didn't mention our discussions, naturally I'm not in any position to comment on that. I'm as puzzled as you are. As to why we never met, that's easy to explain. Grace arranged our interviews for the evening, after the offices were closed. She said it was the only way we'd be able to talk without constant interruptions. I actually went around to her flat in Chelsea in order to make my final presentation and iron out the last kinks in our agreement."

Fredda's phone rang. She pressed a button and cut off the ringing noise, but Lianne saw that the light went on flashing, presumably meaning the call remained unanswered. "And when was that, Miss Beecham?"

Lianne was watching the phone light blink. It stopped, then started again. Fredda studiously ignored it. "I'm sorry. When was what?" Lianne asked, distracted by the unanswered phone. This was a very strange office. She was highly sensitive to moods and atmospheres, and something about the atmosphere of the DeWilde offices was all wrong. In efficient offices, ringing phones didn't get left unanswered.

"Your final presentation to Grace DeWilde," Fredda said. "The one you made at her home. When did it take place?"

"A week ago on Friday. In fact, that was the interview when Grace specifically mentioned your name. She said that you were an administrative marvel, who kept her flighty feet tethered to reality. She made copious notes about the terms of our agreement and said that she would arrange with you to take care of all the paperwork connected with my new job, and that you would notify Personnel and so on."

Fredda's fingers drummed on the desk. When she realized what she was doing, she stopped at once. "I had a raging toothache that weekend, and when I saw the dentist early on Monday morning, he discovered an abscessed tooth that needed immediate surgery. I had a bad reaction to the anesthesia and was out of the office for three days. Then Grace was in Paris on Thursday and Friday of last week, so we only dealt with absolute essentials. I would have thought, however, that Grace would consider it essential to tell me about a major new hire." Fredda's fingers started drumming again.

Lianne began to wonder if working at DeWilde's would be the dream come true that she'd been imagining, even when Grace put in an appearance. She hoped to goodness that the receptionist and Fredda Halston weren't typical of other DeWilde employees. They both seemed— to use a good old Yankee phrase—several cents short of a dollar. Lianne knew only two ways to work. One was in absolute isolation while she created her designs. The other was at top speed as she interacted with her colleagues to refine the designs into maximum commercial viability. If the remaining DeWilde employees were as dithery and slow as Fredda and the receptionist, Lianne would blow a gasket before the end of the first week. She tried to jolt the assistant into action without being downright rude.

"Look, Ms. Halston, I don't quite see what your problem is. Naturally I'm sorry that Grace isn't here this morning, but I'll see her this afternoon, and if not this afternoon, then tomorrow morning. All you need to do is find me a desk, even a temporary one, and let Personnel know I'm here. I'm sure everything else can be straightened out once Grace gets back to the office. When do you expect her, by the way?"

Fredda Halston's face took on a hunted expression. "I'm going to call our merchandising manager," she said. "I'm sure he'll be able to help you, Miss Beecham. I think he's the proper person to handle this."

"Yes, please do." Lianne's enthusiasm for meeting the merchandising manager was genuine, even though he wouldn't be her direct boss. Since her employment was in the nature of an experiment, with implications for all five of the DeWilde stores, Lianne would be reporting exclusively to Grace for at least the first six months. Consequently, they hadn't spent much time talking about the specific management structure of DeWilde's London store. However, London would be the laboratory for their tests, and the cooperation of the merchandising manager would make Lianne's life a great deal easier. In fact, in many ways it would be essential to her success. She could only hope that the merchandising manager would turn out to be someone with a bit more oomph than the two DeWilde staffers she'd met so far.

Fredda tapped a few numbers on her phone and sighed with audible relief when someone answered. "Thank goodness I caught you at your desk," she said, spinning her chair around as if she wanted to look out of the window. Her voice immediately dropped to such a low pitch that Lianne suspected her real purpose in turning around had been to muffle the sounds of what she was saying.

Good grief, what was the matter with the woman? How much secrecy did you need to convey the information that a new employee had just arrived and that Grace had screwed up on the paperwork?

Her mood hovering somewhere between disappointed, annoyed and fearful, Lianne stood up and roamed around the room, staring aimlessly at the bridal photographs and absentmindedly arranging a collection of beads and feathers into an impromptu bridal headdress, vaguely reminiscent of a court headdress of the 1920s. She was stepping back to adjust the angle of one of the ostrich plumes, when she realized that Fredda had hung up the phone.

"Gabriel DeWilde will be with us in just a moment," Fredda Halston said. "His office is only three doors down."

"Gabriel DeWilde?" Lianne spun around, still clutching the ostrich plume. "*He's* the merchandising manager? Grace never said." She had no time to gather her wits, no time to do anything, before Gabriel walked into the room.

For a split second they stared at each other in weighted silence. Then Gabriel closed the door behind him and the spell broke. "Miss Beecham?" His voice caught slightly as he said her name, but he collected himself so quickly Lianne was sure Fredda wouldn't have noticed a thing. He advanced toward her, his features schooled into an expression of careful blankness. His eyes, an unusual color somewhere between green and hazel, displayed nothing beyond normal courtesy. She envied him his capacity to contain explosive memories behind such a neutral facade.

She found her voice. "Hello, Gabriel." No way was she going to pretend they'd never met.

He answered her with a bland smile. "Goodness, Lianne, it really is you. I wondered if it might be when Fredda mentioned your name."

"Yes, it's me." She realized she was waving the ostrich plume like an idiot and hastily set it back down on the shelf. "How are you, Gabe? I haven't seen you in several weeks."

"No, we always seem to just miss each other, don't we?"

"You two obviously know each other already," Fredda said, sounding overwhelmingly relieved. "What a coincidence!"

"Yes, Lianne shares a flat with a good friend of mine, Julia Dutton. But she always seems to be out when I call for Julia." If Gabe made his voice any smoother, it would slide away. "Why don't you come into my office, Lianne, and we'll try to straighten out this muddle. I apologize for the way you've been kept waiting."

She'd known Gabe worked at the London branch of DeWilde's, of course. She just hadn't reckoned on meeting him the very first morning she set foot in the place. She certainly hadn't reckoned on meeting him without the moral support provided by having Grace DeWilde standing right next to her. Still, the job she'd been offered was a great deal more important to her than the memory of a sexual encounter that should never have happened. She would concentrate her thoughts on seeing him as merchandising manager of DeWilde's rather than the man she'd found so stunningly attractive that they'd made wild, passionate love the first and only time they'd met.

She followed him out of Fredda's office and into his. Her heart was pounding like an overworked trip-hammer, but that was worry about her job, she assured herself, and had nothing whatsoever to do with any lingering sexual attraction toward Gabriel DeWilde. She wasn't allowed to have sexual feelings for Gabe. Julia Dutton was deeply in love with him. Julia wanted to marry him. And Julia was her best friend in the whole world. End of story.

He sat down behind his desk and gestured to the leather chair on the opposite side. "You're looking...well," he said, his voice curt.

"Thank you." Gabe wasn't looking well, Lianne realized. He looked strained and oddly weary. Beneath the veneer of self-control, she sensed a simmering tension that was perking close to a boil. But it was going to be a lot easier for both of them if she stopped looking beneath the surface and accepted whatever face he chose to present to the world, so she said nothing more. Casual acquaintances weren't supposed to sense each other's moods, and that's all she and Gabe were. Casual acquaintances who'd lost control one night and shared the most incredible, fantastic, wonderful sex Lianne had ever dreamed about, let alone actually experienced.

Gabe met her gaze with no hint of embarrassing memories of sweat-sheened bodies writhing ecstatically on cushions in front of the fire. He sure was doing a better job of pretending cool indifference than she was, Lianne thought. Except, of course, he wasn't pretending. He actually felt nothing more for her than cool indifference. Their one-night stand had been one of those meaningless flings men always seemed to handle so much more easily than women. Presumably he loved Julia and planned to be faithful to her from here on out. She sure as heck hoped he planned to be faithful to Julia, who was the world's sweetest person and deserved only the best.

"You must be thinking you've walked into a madhouse," Gabe said. "The fact is, we've all been thrown for a loop this morning." She saw him draw in a deep breath, as if steeling himself to impart unpleasant news. "My mother has just announced her resignation from De-Wilde's and we're all trying to recover from the shock."

"Grace has left DeWilde's?" Lianne repeated stupidly. "But where has she gone to?"

"San Francisco, apparently." This time, the weariness in Gabe's voice was unconcealed. "The financial press has already heard the news, of course, and every journalist in London seems to be hounding us for a statement that we're not ready to give. We can't access half the files on Grace's personal computer because we don't know her access codes, so we're frantically trying to reconstruct her work schedule for the next month, and my father has disappeared, God knows where—" He stopped abruptly, shoving his chair away from the desk as he stood and began pacing restlessly. "I'm sorry, this has nothing to do with you, and I've no idea why I unloaded it onto you. I apologize again."

Lianne had to sit on her hands to resist the entirely inappropriate urge to walk across the room, put her arms around Gabe's waist, rest her head on his shoulder and absorb some of the electric tension crackling from him. With Grace gone, she realized she could probably kiss her fabulous new job goodbye. But bad as the news of Grace's departure was for her, Gabe seemed to be finding it even worse.

"I can understand how upset you must be," Lianne said. "I hope this doesn't mean your mother has discovered she has health problems?"

"No," Gabe said bitterly. "Unless it turns out she's suffering from a sudden attack of insanity."

Lianne decided she wasn't understanding a tenth of what was seething beneath the surface news of Grace's departure. "Where exactly is your mother, Gabe? If she isn't sick, why can't you reach her? Even if she's resigned from the company, she must realize that you need to access her files and records. Can't you call her and ask some of these basic questions?''

"You'd think so, wouldn't you? She's my mother, after all, as well as my boss, so you'd think she'd give me some idea of where she's flown off to."

"You mean you don't know?" Lianne was genuinely appalled. "I thought you said she'd gone to San Francisco?"

"So the rumor has it, but I don't have anything as helpful as an address or a phone number." He laughed without mirth. "God alone knows why she's chosen to flit off to San Francisco. Or maybe my father knows, only we can't find him, either, so it's a bit difficult to ask." He caught himself in midbreath, running his hands through his dead-straight light brown hair in a gesture that Lianne found both erotic and sympathy-inspiring. Since neither emotion was appropriate to their situation, she decided to focus on the only thing that seemed relatively suitable as a topic of conversation with Gabriel DeWilde. Her job. Or rather her vague hopes of salvaging what had once promised to be her job.

"Gabe, this is obviously the wrong time for you to be worrying about taking on a new employee. Would you like me to come back later in the week, when things have quieted down a bit?"

"No," he said, sounding calmer. "I'd like you to stay. Having you here will give me something halfway rational to think about. I thought I would be able to take charge of things and control the way events unfolded this morning, but I've realized I can't do that. I could cover for my mother's absence, perhaps, or for my father's, but I can't cover for both of them. It's not even appropriate for me to try to step into their joint shoes. DeWilde's isn't a family company anymore, it's a public company, with thousands of shareholders, and there are people working here with a lot more experience and seniority than I have. I should leave them to do their jobs, and I should get on with mine. Which happens to be merchandising manager of the London store. And since Grace isn't here anymore, and we have nothing in writing about the terms of your employment, I'm the person who has to decide whether or not to go ahead and agree to the terms she negotiated.''

Obviously energized by a new sense of purpose, Gabe sat down in his chair and leaned back, pushing against the arms. "Okay, Lianne, give me the presentation that sold my mother on your ideas, and I'll see if I agree with her.''

If she'd been asked to describe the least favorable combination of circumstances she could imagine for selling her creative ideas, this was it, but Lianne would be damned if she was going to lose the chance of working at DeWilde's if there was any way to salvage it.

She got up and propped her portfolio in the chair where she'd been sitting. "I didn't come prepared to make a formal presentation," she said. "What I have here are the ideas and sketches I've been working on since Grace offered me the job of in-house designer. I'm happy to show them to you, Gabe, but before both of us waste our time, I need to know if you agree with your mother's plans for creating in-store boutiques. If that idea's going to be scrapped now she's gone, then there's no place for me in the DeWilde organization. I'm a designer, not a retailer.''

"I not only approve, I was the person who first suggested the boutique idea," Gabe said. "Grace built on it and developed the concept of hiring our own signature designers for the boutiques. She told me a couple of weeks ago that she'd begun interviewing designers.'' He frowned slightly. ''It's odd, come to think of it, that she never brought me in on the discussions she was having with you.''

Grace DeWilde seemed to have been doing a lot of peculiar things over the past couple of weeks, but Lianne kept that observation to herself. Maintaining a tactful silence, she simply unzipped her portfolio and pulled out the first sketch. She used the back of the chair to make an impromptu easel, feeling the familiar sensation of her surroundings fading to gray as her attention focused on her work. Peripherally, she was aware that Gabe had walked around his desk and was leaning against it, eyes narrowed, attention as sharply focused as her own. She felt a huge wave of relief when she realized that, like her, he was one of those rare people able to close his mind to his personal problems while he made decisions connected with his work. Turning back to her designs, she led him with renewed confidence through a concise and lively presentation of her concept for a line of bridal headpieces that would inspire misty eyes and beautiful memories in women aged nineteen to ninety.

Exhilaration filled her when her presentation was finished. The original drawings she'd shown Grace had been full-color, elaborate, designed to impress. They'd been good. These sketches were rough, but they were better— more original and yet simultaneously more commercial. She looked at Gabe, her expression challenging. ''That's it,'' she said, taking down the last of the sketches.

''What were the terms Grace offered?'' Gabe asked, his voice crisp, businesslike.

She told him.

His mouth finally relaxed into a small but genuine smile. "You're hired," he said. "Same terms and conditions. I'll get the contract drawn up. Congratulations, Lianne. Welcome to DeWilde's."

CHAPTER THREE

FOR THE SIXTH TIME since he got home, Gabe tried to phone his sister in San Francisco. "Kate, if you're there, will you pick up the phone, for God's sake? Don't you ever check the messages on your damn answering machine?"

A human voice, thick and groggy with sleep, finally answered him. "This had better be good, Gabe. I just came off an eighteen-hour double shift and I have to be back at the clinic in five hours. So if you're calling to chat about the weather, hang up now."

"I'm calling about Mother."

"Mother?" Kate's voice was instantly alert. "Is something wrong?"

"Obviously she hasn't called you. Damn! Didn't you get her letter, Kate?"

"Gabe, in the past thirty-six hours, I estimate I've had four hours' sleep and approximately three minutes of free time. Possibly less. I've no idea if I got a letter from Mother. I haven't checked my mail in days. What's up?"

"She's in San Francisco, I think. I'm not sure." Gabe steeled himself to deliver the bad news. "She's left Dad and handed in her resignation at DeWilde's. She and Dad are talking about getting a divorce."

"What?" Kate's disbelief echoed over five thousand or so miles of fiber optic cable. "A divorce? Our parents? Don't be silly, Gabe, that's not possible."

Gabe drew some comfort from his sister's reaction. At least he wasn't the only one to be caught totally unaware. When he'd spoken with Megan, his twin, earlier this evening, she'd astonished him by saying that she'd known something was bothering Grace and had even wondered a couple of months back if their father could be having an affair. Gabe would have been less startled if his sister had accused the Archbishop of Canterbury of seducing the choir mistress and had told Megan as much. Ever the peacemaker, she'd backtracked at once, but Gabe had been left with the unsettling conviction that Megan, in Paris, had seen more of what was going on in their parents' lives than he had, living in the same town.

"Unfortunately, Kate, it's not only possible, it appears to be true. Ramsbotham sent us each a godawful official announcement, and Mother followed with a letter of her own, which doesn't actually explain much of anything except that she's leaving. But Dad told me she'd taken a flight for San Francisco on Sunday. I thought she might have called you when she landed."

"Hold on and I'll check the answering machine." Kate came back on the line several minutes later. "No, there's nothing. If she's really here, I can't believe she didn't call me."

She sounded hurt, which wasn't surprising. Of the three DeWilde siblings, Gabe had always considered Kate to be the one most like their father in personality. She'd not only inherited Jeffrey's formidable analytical intelligence, she also shared his exceptional sensitivity and his difficulty in expressing his emotions. Gabe sometimes worried about his sister's choice of medicine as a career. He didn't doubt her technical competence for an instant. What he worried about was her too-generous heart, her willingness to shoulder other people's problems and her inability to ask for help when she needed it. She was the type of doctor who would keep taking on other people's pain until she collapsed under the weight of it.

The last thing he wanted to do was add to Kate's burdens. So, in an effort to ease his sister's mind, he made excuses for Grace, at the same time resenting the need to do so. "Mother probably called and decided not to leave a message when she realized you weren't home. She knows how busy you are with your work at the clinic. And you're bound to find the letters once you check your mail. Let me fill you in on what I know so far."

Kate listened in silence to his account of the day's events. He could visualize her sitting cross-legged on the bed, her wiry body taut with energy, her auburn hair a bright contrast to her pale skin. Unfortunately, he could also picture her mouth tightening and her fists clenching as she struggled to orient herself to the dramatic change in their parents' lives.

When Gabe finished talking, a small silence ensued. "It's odd to think of them as a couple in an intense personal relationship, isn't it?" she said finally, her voice not quite steady. "Until this moment I'd never really moved beyond the point of seeing them as Mother and Dad, providers of bedtime hugs when we were small and stern lectures about the dangers of alcohol, drugs and casual sex when we were teenagers. I don't think it ever crossed my mind that they knew anything personally about the temptations of drugs or alcohol, much less sex. Which was amazingly juvenile of me, I suppose."

"We've never had any reason to analyze their relationship," Gabe said. "At least until now."

"I suppose not, but I feel foolish all the same. Your situation's different, because you work with them, so you probably have a much more realistic mental image of them as people in their own right, not just as parents. I still have the selfish view of a child—they aren't Jeffrey and Grace, they're Mother and Dad, appendages to us kids.''

Kate was giving him far too much credit, Gabe thought with wry insight. He carried two separate images of Jeffrey and Grace: one as his parents, and the other as powerful, accomplished mentors in the world of retailing. He'd never really fused the two visions into one coherent whole, and he'd certainly never attempted anything as sophisticated as integrating their personal relationship into his mental picture of them. Like Kate, his image of Grace had a lot more to do with biscuits and milk at bedtime than the fact that she was a vibrant and exceptionally attractive woman. He wondered if she had a lover waiting for her in San Francisco, then clamped down on the impossible thought. He simply wasn't ready yet to deal with the full implications of his parents' separation.

"I know how busy you are, Kate, but if you can spare a few minutes tomorrow, try to track Grace down, will you? Even if she isn't willing to discuss her reasons for leaving Dad, there are a dozen important business issues on which her input is absolutely vital. Try Uncle Leland or Mallory. They're both in San Francisco. They might know something."

"Why would Mother call them and not me?" Kate asked, her voice threaded with hurt. "I'm her daughter, for heaven's sake. I know Mother sometimes wonders how she managed to produce a daughter without an artistic bone in her body—"

"Kate, I'm clutching at straws," Gabe said, mentally kicking himself for being so tactless. God, if he weren't close to exhaustion, he would never have been so clumsy as to suggest Grace might be in touch with her brother and her favorite niece rather than her own daughter. He might even have remembered how sensitive Kate was about her occasionally tense relationship with their mother. "I'm sure you'll hear from her within the next couple of days. And when you do, please tell her to call me. She has responsibilities to the company, even if she has gone off in some midlife temper tantrum—"

"That's not fair, Gabe. We have no idea what happened between Mother and Dad. For all we know, Dad may have asked her to leave."

"I'm sure he didn't. I've seen him, remember, and he's devastated."

"Just don't rush to make judgments, Gabe. Marriage is a strange relationship. I'm not sure outsiders can ever really understand the true dynamics."

"Maybe not. But that's no excuse for Mother to abandon DeWilde's without a thought to the consequences. We have five thousand employees worldwide. She can get mad at Dad if she must, but she has no right to hold the company and its employees hostage."

"You're right," Kate said wearily. "But you know how Mother is. She has these explosive fits of creative energy, then the practical side of her kicks in and she works like a supercharged beaver to catch up on the details. She'll come around."

"I wouldn't describe running out on Dad and the store as a burst of creative energy," Gabe said.

"I meant that when she calms down, she'll remember her responsibilities and run to put things right." Kate yawned. "Gabe, I'm falling asleep sitting up. I have a hell of a day scheduled tomorrow, and if I don't get some sleep, I'm not going to get through it. I'll be in touch the second I hear anything from Mother, you can count on it. Okay?"

"Okay, and thanks. Schedule a few extra hours of sleep for yourself, and that's an order, squirt."

"God how I hated that nickname! As if it wasn't bad enough to be three years younger than you and Megan, I had to grow up to be the shortest, too!" He was relieved to hear that a note of soft laughter had crept into her voice. She yawned again. "Good night, Gabe. I'll talk to you soon."

He'd barely disconnected his call to Kate when the phone rang again. He snatched it up. "Hello."

"Gabe, it's Monica. I hope I didn't wake you? I realize it's almost midnight."

"No, I'm still awake." He only realized how much he'd been hoping to hear from Grace when he recognized the voice of his father's secretary. "What can I do for you, Monica?"

"Nothing," she said. "I just wanted to let you know that I've heard from Jeffrey. He asked me to tell you that he'll be in the office at eight o'clock tomorrow morning. He said to reassure you that he will be up to speed and absolutely ready to take hold of the reins again."

Gabe ignored a slight pang that his father had chosen to contact his secretary rather than his son. "Did he say where he was calling from?" he asked.

He wondered if he imagined the infinitesimal pause before Monica answered. "I don't know exactly where he is at the moment, Gabe. But he sounded much more his usual self, and I'm sure you'll find him at his desk tomorrow morning, just as he promised."

Gabe warned himself not to imagine undercurrents where none existed. He was so mad at himself for not seeing what had obviously been under his nose for the past several weeks that he was in danger of rushing to the opposite extreme. Monica wasn't withholding information, and he had no reason to feel aggrieved because his father had chosen to deliver a message to his personal secretary rather than to his son. Jeffrey had sent hundreds of messages via Monica in the past, and he would probably send a hundred more in the future. He had no reason to suspect that his father was avoiding him. Or that Monica knew something he didn't.

He drew in a deep breath. "Thanks for passing on the information. It should certainly make things a lot easier at the office tomorrow if my father's available."

"Yes, I'm sure everything will seem easier tomorrow," Monica agreed. "Good night, Gabe, and try not to worry too much. DeWilde's has weathered greater storms than this one. Everything will work out in the end, you'll see."

MONICA'S WORDS CAME BACK to Gabe on Wednesday evening as he searched for a parking space in the crowded streets near Julia's flat. It was probably true that in the end everything would work out splendidly, he reflected. In the end, if you looked at the big picture, everyone would be dead, and the planets would disintegrate into atoms of hydrogen and helium. In the meantime, however, life had to be lived in the here and now, not in some nebulous future. The fact that he and Julia Dutton would one day be subatomic particles floating through the universe did not make it one bit easier to decide what he should do about their relationship now. He liked her a lot. She was pretty, friendly, and he enjoyed her company. He admired her hard work as a teacher, and her talent for domesticity. She was so sweet-natured he couldn't imagine having a real, honest-to-God fight with her. The trouble was, despite this impressive list of virtues, he couldn't seem to fall even the tiniest bit in love with her. The best that could be said about their sexual relationship was that

he found making love to Julia mildly pleasant and that he
sincerely hoped she did, too.

Three days ago he'd been quite certain that, since he
didn't love Julia, he ought not to marry her. Tonight, he
wasn't sure what he felt about their relationship anymore. His parents had built their marriage on love and
passion. They'd played together, worked together and
fought together, all with the fierce intensity of two people who were vitally important to each other. Their re-
conciliations had been as spectacular as their occasional
blazing rows. Not that Jeffrey ever raised his voice, of
course. He left all the shouting and storming around the
house to Grace. But Gabe had always known that his
father's emotions were just as fully engaged as his
mother's, even if less visible. Not to mention less audible.

And look what had happened to them, Gabe thought.
Maybe, in the long run, marriages worked out better if the
two people involved were friends rather than lovers.
Maybe passionate love between the sexes was a chimera
that would always betray you. And if romantic love was
an illusion, maybe that meant Julia was the ideal wife for
him: a partner who was more a friend than a lover; a
warm, caring mother for the children he hoped to have
one day. As for the sex—hell, he was thirty years old.
Surely he was getting a bit old to expect volcanoes to erupt
every time he went to bed with a woman?

He spotted a parking space and quickly backed his Jag
into it. The rain had finally stopped after two days of un-
remitting downpour, and the branches of the horse chestnut trees lining the street sagged under the weight of damp
buds and fresh green leaves. Behind the iron railings that
separated the houses from the streets, boxes of tulips and
a few late-blooming daffodils made bright splashes of

color against the gray flagstone of the courtyards. Julia's flat had been converted from the second floor of a house built in the late Victorian era, which had the shabby-genteel aura of an elderly lady living on a reduced income. The exterior was nothing special, but inside, Julia had converted the flat into an attractive haven from the noise and fumes of the city. When Gabe first saw her place, he'd been surprised to learn that Julia had decorated it entirely herself, and that she'd had no formal training as an interior designer. Much as he admired her dedication to teaching, he couldn't help thinking her natural talents were being wasted. She had a real eye for line and color.

He let himself into the lobby with the key Julia had given him and made his way upstairs. His pulse beat a little faster at the prospect of seeing Lianne Beecham, but he realized that a meeting was unlikely. Apart from one extraordinary night two months ago, he'd never encountered her at the flat, and Julia had mentioned that Lianne led such an active social life that she was rarely at home in the evening. He didn't doubt it. Unlike Julia, who was calm domesticity personified, Lianne was quicksilver, constantly moving, her emotions barely contained, her energy almost palpable.

Although she obviously had a tough inner core of discipline buried beneath the layers of effervescence, Gabe reflected. When she'd made her presentation to him at DeWilde's on Monday, the intensity with which she focused her creative energy had been awesome. Having worked with artists and craftspeople for the past seven years, he recognized that Lianne was the sort of designer who would go far—she not only possessed an inspiring artistic vision, she had a solid grasp of how to turn that vision into a commercially viable reality. He rang the

doorbell, bringing his thoughts back to Julia. He'd
stopped by the flat on an impulse after putting in a fourteen-hour day at the office, even though he and Julia
rarely got together during the week. There was no guar-
antee she'd be free to spend time with him, or even that
she'd be home.

The door opened almost at once, but Gabe's smile
faded when he realized that it wasn't Julia who had answered the door, it was Lianne Beecham.

"I came to see Julia—"

"Julia's still at school—"

He and Lianne both spoke at once. Then they both fell
silent. Gabe recovered first. "I'm sorry to have disturbed
you," he said with excessive courtesy.

Lianne's gaze wandered past him and focused somewhere to the left of his ear. "You haven't disturbed me,"
she said. "I wasn't doing anything important."

She was wearing jeans and a man's shirt, the sleeves
rolled up to her elbows but the shirttails flapping loosely
around her thighs. Her hair was piled haphazardly on top
of her head, with curls tumbling out of the tortoiseshell
clasp that was supposed to hold it in place. She looked
untidy, rumpled and almost unbearably sexy. Still avoiding his gaze, she pushed distractedly at a curl that had
fallen over her forehead. "Julia didn't say anything about
seeing you tonight."

"She's not expecting me. I stopped by just on the off
chance that she'd be home." He wondered, even as he
gave the explanation, why he was bothering to lie to himself. He'd come here despite the knowledge buried in the
back of his mind that Julia was helping her sixth-form
French class with the dress rehearsal for their production
of *Le Bourgeois Gentilhomme*. He'd come not to see

Julia, he realized, but because he wanted—quite badly—to see Lianne.

"Julia won't be home for another couple of hours at least." Not surprisingly in view of their last encounter in this place, Lianne didn't invite him in. Her voice and expression were equally wooden. "There's not much point in waiting for her, Gabriel. She warned me it could be close to midnight before she got back."

"Then I won't keep you. Tell her I look forward to our date on Friday evening, won't you? Seven o'clock."

"Yes. Of course. Goodbye, Gabriel."

He turned to walk away, expecting at any second to hear the sound of Lianne closing the door behind him. For some reason, the sound never came. When he reached the head of the stairs, he stopped and looked back. Lianne was standing just as he'd left her, her hand still on the doorknob, her body strangely rigid. As soon as he turned around, her gaze slid away again.

Gabe spoke to her quietly. "Do you have plans for tonight?" he asked. "Are you going out?"

There was a long pause. "No."

"Come and have a drink with me," he said quickly, the invitation made before he had a chance to question the wisdom of it. "I saw a friendly-looking pub just down the road and I'm not in the mood to go home just yet."

She finally turned around. "What sort of a mood are you in, Gabe?"

He looked straight into her dark blue eyes, forcing her to hold his gaze. "I'm not sure. You could help me find out."

Color flooded her cheeks. She looked down, staring at her bare feet, as if surprised to discover she had ten toes, all painted shocking pink. "All right," she said at last. "Wait one minute and I'll get a sweater or something."

He discovered that he had been holding his breath, waiting for her answer. He leaned against the wall of the hallway, twisting the gold chain of his key ring, aware of a hot pulse of anticipation pounding in his gut.

Lianne didn't keep him waiting long. She returned, a pair of scuffed brown leather loafers on her bare feet and her jeans topped by a Chinese-style jacket of padded silk in a brilliant shade of green, embroidered with blue and purple flowers at the neck and cuffs of the long sleeves. The ornate style should have looked all wrong with frayed jeans, but he'd noticed before that she had the knack of making whatever she wore look just right for the occasion.

They walked downstairs in silence, taking great care not to touch each other. Gabe tried hard to think of something witty and insightful to say, but the only thoughts that came to mind involved naked bodies and wild sex. He gave up on witty and decided to settle for coherent, or even polite.

His mind remained a cavernous blank into which jumbled and distracting images of Lianne intruded. The chestnut gleam of her hair in the light of the street lamp. The supple ripple of her silk jacket as she walked. The hint of her perfume on the night breeze. He'd noticed her scent at the office, on Monday. Elusive, barely there, it had been hovering on the periphery of his awareness for two solid days. It was driving him goddamn crazy.

Work, he thought, grasping at the conversational straw. They could talk about work.

"How were your first couple of days at DeWilde's?" he asked. "I'm sorry I didn't have a chance to check with you personally before you left today." As always when he was on edge, his voice became stiffer, his words more clipped. To put it bluntly, he sounded like a pompous ass.

"Everyone's been very cooperative," Lianne said, smiling as she jumped across a puddle. "And you don't need to worry about me, Gabe. Fortunately, Grace had already finalized her decisions on which bridal gowns DeWilde's would be carrying the season after next, so I know exactly what my design parameters are. Right now I'm studying the pictures and the design specs so that I can coordinate my headdresses to the gowns. I'm conferring with Adam to make sure that I keep the production costs within budget. Once I have the designs finalized, I'll organize a presentation for you. But I don't expect you to stand over me and hold my hand just because I'm new. I'm used to working alone, and I understand how frantically busy you must be with Grace gone."

"Do you?" He smiled without mirth. "These past three days I've felt that I've been running like hell just to keep from falling further behind than I was the day before."

"Well, Grace contributed so much to DeWilde's, it would be odd if nobody noticed she was gone, wouldn't it? You miss her even more than most people, I expect. You reported directly to her, after all—and she *is* your mother."

He was surprised to feel a surge of relief at hearing Lianne speak his mother's name in such a normal tone of voice. At work for the past few days people had acted almost as if she'd died. And she still hadn't called him. The worry about her safety and his concerns for the store were beginning to coil into a tight, hard knot of fury at the irresponsibility of her behavior.

Still, he didn't want to think about his mother for a while. That was one of the reasons he'd sought out Lianne, who barely knew her. They'd reached the corner of the road, and he pushed open the heavy door leading into the pub and ushered her to a small corner table.

The lounge was full, and the barmaid looked harassed. "What would you like to drink?" he asked. "I'll get it from the bar. That'll be quicker than waiting for the waitress to take our order."

"A brandy would be nice," she said, sliding along the padded leather seat. "I feel in the mood for something old and smooth and mellow."

Gabe returned to their corner table carrying two V.S.O.P. cognacs. Lianne had taken off her jacket while he was gone and hung it over the chair behind her, and he realized she was still wearing the oversize man's shirt underneath. She'd simply tied the ends in a knot under her breasts so that they wouldn't hang down under the hem of her jacket. She looked up as he approached and smiled at him, her first smile of the evening. Gabe stopped dead in his tracks, feeling the impact of her smile as a physical blow to his gut.

"Your cognac," he said stiffly, sliding into his seat next to her. He stopped a crucial six inches away from her.

"Thanks." She raised her glass to his, still smiling. "Here's to my new collection and the success of De-Wilde's first boutique." He wanted to take the glass from her hand, lean across the table and kiss her. Hard. He closed his eyes and took a slug of brandy. He opened his eyes. "Here's to you," he said. "I'm looking forward to seeing your first set of designs, Lianne."

The barmaid walked by carrying a tray laden with tall glasses of beer. Lianne pulled her feet out of the barmaid's path, and her knee collided under the table with Gabe's. They sprang away from each other as if they'd been scalded by boiling water, the reaction so swift and so obvious neither of them could pretend it hadn't happened.

Lianne put her brandy snifter down on her cardboard coaster and folded her paper napkin into a neat triangle. "Julia's my best friend," she said with seeming inconsequence.

Gabe's mouth twisted into an ironic smile. "Mine, too," he said.

Lianne's head jerked up, her eyes flashing. "Don't mock her," she said. "Julia loves you, damn it!"

Gabe's stomach muscles tensed at this confirmation of his worst fears.

"You know nothing about my relationship with Julia," he said. *Stupid pompous ass,* he berated himself.

She laughed angrily. "More than you do, it seems. She thinks you're going to ask her to marry you, Gabe. She's waiting for you to turn up some night soon with one of those nifty DeWilde ring boxes tucked into your pocket."

"How do you know that I don't intend to do just that?"

"And what are you going to promise her when you hand over the ring, Gabe? That you'll love and cherish her—and stay faithful until the next time your wandering eye happens to land on one of her friends?"

He shoved his brandy to one side and leaned across the table, his temper barely under control. "What's making you so angry, Lianne? The fact that I made love to you the first time we met? Or the fact that you were helping me to rip off your clothes so I could do it quicker?"

She jumped up from her seat, ignoring the brandy that spilled all over the table. She grabbed her jacket and walked to the door, shoving her arms into the sleeves as she walked. Gabe caught up with her outside. He gripped her arm and swung her around to face him. "What's the problem, Lianne? Don't you like hearing the truth? Or were you hoping I'd follow you home so that we could try a repeat performance?''

For a moment, he thought she was going to hit him. Not a ladylike slap across the cheek, but a hard, swinging punch to the jaw. Surprisingly, the rage went out of her as swiftly as it had come. She looked up at him, her eyes no longer blue but gray and stormy as the Atlantic. "I wanted you to follow me home," she admitted, her voice low and harsh.

He wished like hell that she'd punched him. It would have been easier to deal with than her honesty. He shoved his hands into his pockets so that he'd be able to keep them from touching her. "We can't pretend we like each other," he said, trading truth for truth. "We barely know each other. What we feel is nothing but sex. Sheer animal lust."

She wrapped her arms around her waist. "Embarrassing, isn't it?"

"Julia is exactly the sort of woman I've always planned to marry."

Her eyes narrowed. "And what am I? The sort of woman you always planned to keep as your mistress?"

He quelled an intense desire to throttle her. Or perhaps it was an intense desire to put his hands around her throat and hold her immobilized while he kissed her. "When I'm married, I don't plan to keep a mistress, Lianne."

"I'm sure Julia will be pleased to hear that."

How could he possibly pretend that he was going to marry Julia when he couldn't even trust himself to walk into Lianne's office for fear of what he might do once he got there? "Come out to dinner with me on Saturday," he said. "Let's get to know each other. As people instead of sexual partners."

"I can't." She turned away and started to walk down the street.

He followed. "I'm seeing Julia on Friday night."

She stopped but she didn't look at him. "What are you hoping to arrange for, Gabe? Conversation and friendship on Fridays, followed by hot sex on Saturdays? A well-rounded weekend of entertainment?"

"Getting mad at me doesn't change the fact that we both want to see each other again. I'm honest enough to admit it, and to say that I'd like to know more about you than the fact that you're stunning in bed."

"Gee, I'm just a bundle of accomplishments, Gabe. You've barely even scratched the surface of my potential as a bedmate."

"How many different ways can I say it, Lianne? I want to find out more about you as a person, not just as a bedmate."

Her voice was like the line of her mouth. Hard and flat. "Are you going to tell Julia that you invited me out to dinner on Saturday night?"

"If you accept my invitation, I'll tell her."

"And if I don't accept your invitation?"

"Julia should hear this first, but whether you say yes or no, either way I'm going to stop seeing her. It's not fair to either of us, especially Julia."

Lianne stopped at the iron gate leading into the courtyard in front of her flat. She made a small sound of acute distress. "If you stop dating Julia, she's going to be really hurt, Gabe."

"I hope that's not true," he said quietly. "But I'm not in love with her, and if I married her, she'd be hurt a lot more in the end."

Lianne pulled a leaf from the privet hedge and shredded it. "I don't know, Gabe—"

"Yes, you do," he said. "We both know." He crooked his finger beneath her chin and tipped her head back until they were looking straight at each other. He didn't put his arms around her or pull her toward him. Except for his finger, he didn't touch her. Slowly enough to leave no doubt about his intentions, he bent his head toward her. She didn't move away. She stood silently, her face drained of color in the streetlight, her hands clenched into fists. In the last second before his mouth claimed hers, she reached up and linked her hands at the nape of his neck, pressing her lips to his in a kiss that ached and trembled with the force of their passion.

When they finally drew apart, Gabe felt disoriented, as if he'd been swimming underwater and had hit his head on a rock when he surfaced. Lianne leaned against the gate but she didn't say a word. Her gaze locked with his for a long, weighted moment, then she turned and ran up the stone steps to her front door.

Gabe watched until she disappeared into the hallway. Her absence left him feeling hollow. He wondered how in the world he was supposed to wait until Saturday before he talked her into his bed.

CHAPTER FOUR

IT WAS DEPRESSING to discover that you had all the moral backbone of an earthworm, Lianne reflected, then wondered if she was insulting the integrity of worms. She wanted to go out with Gabe but couldn't bear to tell that to Julia, or to witness how her friend would handle the news of Gabe's defection. Julia Dutton wasn't the sort of person who talked a lot about her deepest feelings, but Lianne was quite sure her friend was in love with Gabriel DeWilde, and she had a sickening suspicion Julia would be desolated when she heard that he didn't feel anything for her beyond friendship.

Coward that she was, Lianne decided to avoid the issue by going to a party on Friday night and staying out until she was sure her flat mate would be in bed. What a great friend she was turning out to be, Lianne taunted herself grimly.

Weeks before she met Gabe in person, Lianne had known how Julia felt about him. Her idea of creating a line of bridal headdresses had been developed after she and Julia cheered up a dreary Sunday afternoon by sitting in front of the fake-log electric fire and designing a bridal outfit, complete with a floating silk net veil scattered with seed pearls, topped by a coronet of satin rosebuds—the perfect complement to Julia's fresh features and sweet smile. Julia hadn't admitted in so many words that Gabe was the unnamed groom at this fantasy wedding, but they'd both known quite well that he was the one.

Lianne didn't meet Gabriel DeWilde until a Friday night at the end of March when he'd already been dating Julia for nearly three months. Julia's mother had been rushed to hospital for emergency surgery to remove a ruptured appendix, and nobody had been able to reach Gabe to explain what had happened. When he arrived to pick up Julia for their date, Lianne invited him in and offered him a drink while they waited for news from the hospital.

Her attraction to Gabe had been instant and overwhelming. The two of them had talked for hours, the pot of coffee growing cold, their brandy forgotten. Even after Julia phoned to say her mother was safely recuperating but she wouldn't be home because she planned to spend the night with her father, Gabe hadn't made any move to leave. Worse, Lianne hadn't tried to send him away.

They continued talking and laughing, but the phone call had destroyed the illusion of casual friendliness they had both been clinging to. Their laughter faded and their conversation gradually died away until nothing was left except silence and the desire pulsing between them. A desire that was all the more potent because they'd spent the previous five hours pretending not to notice it.

Lianne had been curled up in her favorite position on the sofa, bare feet tucked under her, sipping her neglected glass of brandy, not because she wanted a drink but because, for the first time that night, she hadn't known what to say to Gabe. Without warning, he leaned toward her, prying her fingers from the snifter and setting it on the table.

"I want you, Lianne," he'd said, his voice hoarse, his hazel eyes no longer dancing with laughter but blazing with fierce passion. "God, I want you."

His words had slammed into her, giving instant shape and focus to her own unspoken desire. Instead of rejecting him, instead of reminding him about Julia, Lianne had moved eagerly into his arms, returning fevered kiss for fevered kiss, hot caress for hot caress. When he'd fumbled with the buttons on her shirt, she'd ripped it off, reaching for him, pulling his head to her breasts, writhing ecstatically in his arms as he suckled her. They'd stood up to take off their jeans and somehow never made it back onto the sofa. Within moments, she'd been a naked and willing captive beneath him on the rug in front of the fire. Within minutes, she'd been making gasping, greedy, passionate love to her best friend's lover.

The experience had been so intense, their lovemaking so explosive, that Lianne still wasn't comfortable thinking about it, especially her own role in what had happened. All she knew was that in the clear light of morning, the magnitude of her betrayal had been painfully apparent. Appalled by her behavior, Lianne had banished Gabe from her thoughts and dreams as well as from her life. He tried to call her only once, and she refused to speak to him. He'd never tried to contact her again, and he'd continued to see Julia on a regular basis.

He often came to the flat to pick Julia up for their frequent dates, but Lianne had turned the task of avoiding him into a minor art form. Julia was a homemaker, ready for marriage, longing to have children. Lianne was consumed by career ambition, with no plans to marry. Clearly, she had no right to disrupt Julia's promising relationship because she'd had an attack of the hots for Gabriel DeWilde. She'd even managed to convince her-

self that she was delighted Julia's relationship with him
seemed to be going well. Her meeting with Gabe at work
had blown that little fiction right out of the water. Their
encounter on Wednesday night had blasted through the
last tendrils of the myth.

Lianne despised herself for putting lust above friendship, but she had discovered over the past few days that
she could no longer ignore the intensity of her response to
Gabriel DeWilde. Working with him on a daily basis
made it impossible for her to pretend that she felt nothing for him. When he'd come to the flat on Wednesday
night, she'd been paralyzed, clutching the doorjamb for
support, terrified that if she moved she'd invite him in.
Not just into the living room, but into her bed. And she'd
known with a shocking, unsettling certainty that if she'd
made the offer, Gabe would have accepted it. Neither of
them would have given another thought to the fact that
Julia could return at any minute, much less to the ethics
of the situation.

She had no idea why Gabe made her feel this way.
Lianne had never considered herself Playmate of the
Month material. It was mind-blowing to find herself
tumbling head over heels into a relationship based on
nothing except sexual attraction.

Lianne believed that men and women needed to like
each other if they wanted to develop worthwhile, lasting
relationships. Did she like Gabe? The honest answer was
that she had no idea. When she was with him, she was too
busy controlling her lust to have time to analyze anything
else she might feel. All she knew was that she wanted very
badly indeed to go out with him.

Go out with him. Now, there was a great euphemism if
she'd ever heard one. But it sounded so much better than

admitting she wanted Gabe to take her to bed and spend the entire night having hot, fierce, passionate sex with her.

Creeping into the flat at two o'clock in the morning, Lianne was rewarded for her cowardly attempts at evasion by the sight of Julia sitting on the sofa in the living room, very much awake. Why was she surprised? Lianne thought resignedly. She should have known that dear, honest, open-hearted Julia wouldn't chicken out and go to bed before the subject of Gabriel DeWilde had been settled between them. Unlike Lianne, the earthworm, Julia respected friendship and all it stood for.

Other than giving her a splitting headache, the wine she'd consumed at the party was doing nothing for her, Lianne realized. Her betrayal felt every bit as sharp and bitter as it had before she slugged down four glasses of cheap burgundy. Although she and Julia had been complete strangers when Lianne responded to Julia's ad for a flat mate, the two of them had quickly become the best of friends. And now Julia was much more than a friend, she was the sister Lianne had never had and always wanted. If Gabe had hurt her... If she'd hurt her...

Yes? Lianne asked herself cynically. *If you and Gabe have hurt your best friend, what will you do—refuse to go out with him when your entire body throbs with anticipation at the mere thought of being in his company?*

"Julia, I didn't expect to find you still up," she exclaimed, her voice bursting with false cheer. She stumbled into the living room, feeling such a fraud that her natural coordination deserted her, making it difficult to walk without falling over her own feet.

Julia got up and put out a hand to steady her. "Fun party?" she asked with wry good humor. "It looks as if they had plenty of liquid refreshments on hand."

Lianne gave an exaggerated grimace. Better to pretend that she'd had too much to drink than to admit she was clumsy with guilt and nerves. "The party was thrown by some old friends from art school. There was too much booze, too much smoke, not all of it from tobacco, and way too many people trying to convince themselves they were having a decadent time. You know what that's like."

Julia chuckled. "Unfortunately not. I wish I did, but I ran with a very sedate crowd when I was at university. If they'd had their way, my brothers would have demanded two written references and a typed résumé before I was allowed out on a date." She sat down again and started to gather up colored skeins of embroidery wool, tucking them neatly into their special box, which was decorated with a trompe l'oeil pattern she'd painted herself.

Lianne sprawled in the armchair to the right of the fireplace. Unbuttoning her jacket, she sneaked a covert glance at her friend. As far as she could tell, Julia looked her usual pretty, pink-cheeked, brunette self, but Lianne didn't make the mistake of assuming that Julia's failure to show emotion meant that she had no feelings. Julia hadn't switched on the overhead lights, and she'd angled the table lamp so that its beam was directed at her embroidery, leaving her face in shadow so that it was hard to see her features clearly. Intentionally? Trying not to be too obvious, Lianne searched her friend's face, but she couldn't see any sign that Julia had been indulging in floods of heartbroken tears.

"How did your date go tonight with Gabe?" she asked, doing her best to sound relaxed and unconcerned.

Julia smiled slightly as she folded her needlepoint canvas. "Lianne, love, if that was meant to be a casual question, I feel compelled to tell you that you'll never make your living as an actress."

"Okay, so it wasn't casual. What happened tonight, Jules? I need to know."

"Yes, I suppose you do." Julia's voice caught for a moment, but she sounded just fine when she continued. "Gabriel and I enjoyed a very pleasant dinner at the Mirabel. Sometime between the quail eggs and the poached pears, he told me that he liked me more than any other woman he'd ever met. He also said that he was very sorry, but he wasn't in love with me."

"Oh, Jules, I'm so sorry!" Lianne ached with sympathy.

"Sorry, but not surprised, I'm sure. We've both known for weeks that my relationship with Gabe wasn't going anywhere." Julia got up rather abruptly and rummaged between the cushions on the sofa. "Bother! I've lost my embroidery scissors. I have to find them or someone will sit down and impale themselves."

Lianne walked over to the sofa. She reached out and took her friend's hand, abandoning any lingering pretense that this was a casual conversation. She drew in a deep breath. "Did Gabe tell you that he invited me to go out with him tomorrow night?"

"Yes, he told me." Julia straightened, a pair of tiny silver scissors dangling from her forefinger. "Ah, success! Here they are."

Lianne refused to be diverted. "If you want, I'll tell Gabe I can't go out with him. That I don't want to date him. Not tomorrow night. Not ever."

"But that would be a lie, wouldn't it?" Julia said quietly. "You and Gabriel are very attracted to each other, aren't you?"

Attraction seemed a laughably mild word to describe what she felt for Gabriel DeWilde. But how could she tell Julia that she'd spent the past two nights sweating through dreams so erotic that she'd woken up gasping for air, her skin so sensitized that Gabe could have brought her to climax with a single kiss and a few swift caresses?

Lianne gave the only answer she could. "Yes, Gabe and I are attracted to each other."

Julia bent over, tucking the scissors into her embroidery work box. "That's what I thought. And I certainly don't want to stand in the way of true love."

"But that's the whole point, Jules. We're not talking true love here. We're talking plain old lust. There's nothing between me and Gabriel DeWilde that's worth destroying our friendship over."

"How do you know that something worthwhile and lasting won't develop between you and Gabriel?" Julia asked. "You haven't spent much time with him, so you can't tell how your relationship might develop. Besides, how can you separate lust and love?"

Lianne was surprised into a stiff little laugh. "Well, I guess I'd always assumed that was pretty easy."

Julia shook her head. "I thought I knew the difference, but I'm not sure anymore. If a man and a woman don't feel any lust for each other, then they're just friends, aren't they?"

Lianne wasn't quite certain what that remark meant, but it didn't sound good. "Tell me the truth, Jules. Has Gabe hurt you? You're trying to make it sound as if this split doesn't mean all that much to you, but I know you too well. I don't believe you'd have dated a man for more than five months unless your feelings were pretty deeply involved."

"Yes, he's hurt me," Julia admitted. "But you needn't look so worried, Lianne. I've been sitting here for the last few hours thinking about it, and I've decided it's my pride that's wounded rather than anything else. I like Gabriel a lot. I enjoy spending time in his company and I know he enjoys being with me. But that's all there is between us. There's no spark of passion, and there really never has been. We've been friends more than anything for the past few months. I hope we can be friends again in the future.''

Lianne wanted to be convinced. God, she wanted to be convinced! Julia looked and sounded as if she were telling the truth, but some nagging inner voice wouldn't let her take her friend's words at face value. "Jules, two months ago you had me sketching wedding dresses and bridal headdresses. Two months ago you must have thought there was a spark between you and Gabe."

Julia walked over to the window, rearranging the folds of the rose chintz curtains, curtains she'd sewn herself. She didn't turn around when she spoke. "I'm twenty-nine, Lianne, and I'm tired of teaching French to other people's children. I want to get married and have children of my own. Gabe is good-looking, intelligent, and he has a fascinating job. When I met him, he seemed the answer to any woman's prayer, and especially to mine. Obviously, he's a very eligible bachelor and a kind man. I suppose we could have married and even been reasonably content together. But he wants more than contentment from marriage, and tonight I realized I want more, too." Her voice became husky. "I want passion and lust and unbridled hot sex along with the companionship and the children."

"Hot sex? Jules, I'm shocked!" Lianne was only half joking.

"Are you? You shouldn't be, you know. Why do you suppose I want any less from my marriage than you do?" Julia snapped the lock on the sash window, closing it. "To get back to the subject of Gabe, if you want to go out with him, don't think you have to ask permission from me, Lianne. You don't. Anything there might have been between the two of us is over. Finished. Nothing you do or don't do is going to change what happens between Gabe and me.''

If anybody else in the world had been this friendly and rational when their lover had just dumped them, Lianne would have been instantly suspicious. With anybody other than Julia, she would have been sure that all this superficial sweetness and light was covering up some dark and murky feelings. How was it possible that Julia still described him as a kind man? Gabe had been dating Julia for more than five months. Surely the situation called for a little more rage on her part at being unceremoniously ditched because he now wanted to jump into the sack with another woman—a woman who happened to be your best friend?

Of course, Gabe wouldn't have told Julia the whole story, Lianne reminded herself. Presumably Julia didn't know that she'd already been betrayed, not only by Gabe but by Lianne, as well. She wished she could tell Julia the truth. The trouble was, for Lianne to clear her conscience, she needed to make a confession that would hurt Julia, so she was just going to have to carry the burden of her deception awhile longer. Once you left childhood behind, you began to realize that confessing your sins often made you feel a lot better than the person who was forced to hear your confession.

"I think you and I have opposite problems where Gabe is concerned," Lianne said carefully. "Gabe and I seem to generate lots of heat when we're together, but I'm not sure if we actually like each other all that much."

Julia smiled, albeit somewhat wryly. "I wish Gabriel and I could have generated at least a bit of your heat," she said. "But since we didn't, I'm sure it won't be long before I'll be feeling truly grateful that he called a halt before we allowed ourselves to drift into getting married."

"Julia, honest to Pete, you're too good to be true! Why aren't you yelling and screaming at me? Why aren't you stomping around the flat, sticking pins in pictures of Gabe and telling the world that all men are scum?"

"I can't."

"What do you mean, you can't? Sure you can. Look, here's how. Stamp your foot. Shake your fist. Yell. Go on, do it."

"I can't." Julia drew in a quick, hard breath. "You don't understand, Lianne. You find it so easy to express your emotions. I'm afraid to."

"This might be a good time to learn," Lianne suggested. "Start small and work up. Couldn't you try just a quick, ladylike yell? Smash the photo you have of Gabe in your bedroom, maybe?"

"You don't understand, Lianne. I'm afraid once I started, I wouldn't be able to stop."

Lianne's stomach knotted. "Darn it, Jules, I knew it! Gabe's hurt you, hasn't he. We've hurt you way more than you're willing to admit."

Julia's voice was too calm. "At the moment, I'm still feeling sorry for myself, but I told you that already."

She flicked her neat plait of dark brown hair over her shoulder, then shrugged. "I really fancied myself in a couple of those headdresses you designed. I'm not quite ready to abandon my dream of an autumn wedding, with you as my chief bridesmaid, looking elegant in bronze satin. But that should tell me something, shouldn't it? My desire to float down the aisle in a long white dress is a silly reason to get married. It's an even sillier reason for you to refuse to date Gabriel. He isn't going to fall in love with me, Lianne, and wishing isn't going to change that.''

''One day there'll be a wonderful man to fit into your fantasy of the perfect wedding,'' Lianne said, the cheap wine churning sickly in her stomach. ''You'll find him, Jules, I know you will.'' She wished as soon as she'd spoken that she hadn't offered such false comfort. They were both too old and too wise to buy into the myth that Mr. Right was always lurking somewhere in the wings, just waiting to be greeted and brought onstage. Divorce statistics proved each year that for a lot of women, there was no Mr. Right, and that women routinely settled for something that turned out to be a lot less than the best.

Julia was too polite to point out that Lianne was talking rubbish. She smiled a bit wanly. ''If I ever meet him, you'll be the first to know. I'm tired, Lianne, I'm going to bed. Good night. I expect I'll see you tomorrow morning?''

''Probably not,'' Lianne said. ''I have to go into work for a couple of hours first thing. With Grace gone, everyone's so busy I have to grab the people I need whenever I can.''

Normally Julia would have asked a dozen eager questions about Lianne's new job. Not tonight. Looking suddenly weary, she simply nodded. ''See you on Sunday, then. Good night, Lianne.''

Deeply troubled, Lianne watched her friend go. Julia was lying about her feelings, she realized with unwelcome and painful insight. She was devastated by Gabe's rejection, just as Lianne had feared she would be. Their whole conversation tonight had been a charade, a ploy on Julia's part to ensure that Lianne wouldn't feel guilty. Very cleverly, Julia had expressed just enough regret to briefly lull Lianne into believing she'd heard all of it.

But despite the fact that Julia was suffering a lot more than she was willing to admit, some of what had been said tonight was true. Julia would only be courting unhappiness if she continued to date Gabe, knowing that he didn't love her. Drifting into marriage with him would have been a terrible mistake, guaranteed to make both of them miserable in the long run. However great Julia's misery now, it would be far worse if the breakup had come later, perhaps when there were children in the picture.

Lianne spent the few hours left before her alarm went off lying on a bed that felt as if it were made out of prickly pear spikes, wondering how she was going to look Julia in the eye ever again. Wondering how she was going to get through the fourteen hours remaining before she would see Gabe. Wondering what she would say if he invited her back to his flat. And knowing that where the last question was concerned, she wasn't really wondering at all.

GABE WAS DRINKING his fourth cup of black coffee and slugging through some of his mother's files when he was interrupted by the persistent ring of the doorbell. Irritated at the interruption—his mother's cross-referencing systems were idiosyncratic, to put it politely, and he needed all the concentration he could muster—he strode into the hall and yanked open the door.

A tall, slender woman stood in the hallway, her finger poised over the bell. "Megan!" He stared at his twin sister blankly for a second or two, then swept her inside and gave her a warm hug. "Meg, this is wonderful. Come on inside. When did you arrive?"

"I flew over from Paris this morning." Megan made her way to the living room, tossing her coat over a chair and kicking off her shoes. She didn't sit down but paced restlessly in front of the empty fireplace, her body radiating energy. "Mmm . . . that coffee smells good. Do you have any left? The stuff they were serving on the plane was even more disgusting than usual."

Gabe shook the pot, testing. "Only dregs. Come into the kitchen and I'll brew us some fresh." He gave his sister another quick hug as they walked into the kitchen, worried by her drawn appearance and almost febrile restlessness. Ever since that bastard Edward Whitney left her at the altar last summer, she'd thrown herself into her work with an obsessive, workaholic tenacity that was great for DeWilde's Paris store but not so good for Megan. "You're looking very dashing, Megan. I think brown hair suits you better than the bleached straw look you seemed to be aiming for last time I saw you."

She grinned. "It's not brown, Gabe, it's luxurious sable, and it's all part of my new businesslike image. Note the pearl stud earrings, crisp tailored skirt and neat yellow twin set."

"Businesslike is great," he said. "So long as you remember to take the occasional hour off to play."

She wrinkled her nose in a gesture familiar since childhood. "Play? What does that mean?" She turned away quickly, opening cupboard doors with a lot more noise than was necessary. "Where do you keep your cups, for heaven's sake? Why do men never store anything in a logical place?"

He opened a cupboard and pointed to the row of mugs and cups. "Stored with typical masculine illogic right above the place where I unload them from the dishwasher."

She laughed and took a mug, cradling it between her hands. "It's a good thing you're so damned handsome, Gabe, otherwise no woman would put up with you for five minutes."

He felt the hot color steal across his cheekbones and heard the startled intake of her breath. "My God, you're blushing! My sophisticated, jet-setting, ultimate man-of-the-world brother is actually blushing! Does this mean Julia Dutton's finally decided to make an honest man out of you?"

"No, of course not." He spoke sharply because he was so embarrassed. Good Lord, things had come to a sorry pass when an inconsequential remark from his sister could provoke images of Lianne so erotic that his cheeks turned visibly red. "As a matter of fact, Julia and I aren't seeing each other anymore."

"I'm sorry to hear that. She seemed to be a really nice person."

"She is. But she isn't the woman I want to spend the rest of my life with."

"How can you tell, Gabe?" Megan's smile faded. "It's so difficult to understand a relationship when you're in the middle of it, if you know what I mean?"

"Sure I do. But it seems safe to assume that if you can see problems even before you're married, then you'll see hundreds more afterward."

"I've been thinking about that recently," Megan said. She poured herself a cup of the freshly brewed coffee and sniffed appreciatively. "I was so upset and humiliated when Edward left me at the altar. My spirits were wilting faster than my bouquet. But you know what frightens me the most? I realize now that he was right to leave me—"

"Not that way, he wasn't. Not with such a brutally public rejection."

"No, the way he left was wrong, but at least he had enough sense to realize we shouldn't get married. I just got carried along on the tidal wave. You know, once you start planning a wedding, the event turns into this monster with a life of its own. You stop being a couple hoping to spend the rest of your lives together and instead become an entity, the Bride and Groom. I was so busy deciding what music to play when the bridesmaids walked down the aisle, and what color table napkins to have at the reception, that I lost track of the fact I'd have to live with Edward once the guests had packed up and gone home.''

"Do you think that's what happened to Mother and Dad?" Gabe asked. "Their wedding was one of the biggest social events of 1964. Do you think they just got swept away by the social juggernaut?''

"And took thirty-two years to notice they'd made a mistake?" Megan asked. "It doesn't seem likely, does it?''

"No. But nothing about their separation makes any sense. We agreed on that the last time we talked.''

Megan leaned against the counter, running the tip of her finger around her coffee mug. "I got another letter from Mother yesterday. Did you?''

Gabe muttered an expletive beneath his breath. Not that it made him feel any better to swear. Nothing about his parents' separation made him feel better. "Yes, I got a letter from Mother," he said tightly. "International express mail, delivered by courier, no less. I wouldn't say it exactly shed any more light on the situation. She's sorry she left so suddenly, but living with Jeffrey had become so painful she simply couldn't bear it anymore. She loves me very much and hopes to talk to me soon. There were a few fancy flourishes, but that's about the gist of it.''

"Mine was along the same lines." Megan's hazel eyes, so like Gabe's, were troubled. "That's why I flew over today, actually. Gabe, I have some news that I almost can't believe is true. Kate called me last night. She tried to reach you as well, but you weren't answering your phone.''

"I was out until past midnight. What's happened?"

Megan poured herself another cup of coffee. "Mother didn't send Kate a letter, like she did to you and me. She phoned her instead, and suggested that they should meet for lunch. You know how busy Kate always is at the clinic, but of course she realized how important this meeting was, since nobody from the family had spoken to Mother since she left, but she couldn't make lunch, so she called to try to arrange another time. But Mother didn't answer the phone—"

"Meg, stop! My God, you're scaring the hell out of me." Megan was never rambling or incoherent. One of her major skills as a businessperson was her ability to deliver precise, pithy presentations. "The short version, please. How was Mother? Did she look okay? And what did she and Kate talk about?"

"They didn't actually meet, but they had a long phone conversation. Mother sounded more or less okay, according to Kate, although she never once mentioned Dad or their split."

"So what did they talk about?"

"They talked about Mother's plans for the future."

"Which are?"

Megan put down her mug with a slight thump. "Gabe, you're not going to like this one bit, and Dad's going to be so angry I don't even know how we're going to tell him, but as far as I can gather, Mother's planning to open a store in the San Francisco area."

Gabe frowned. "She can't do that," he said. "It's a crazy idea. Quite apart from the fact that it would be very awkward to have a major new venture opening up when she and Dad are barely speaking to each other, De-Wilde's is a public company, and any expansion in the number of stores has to be approved by the board of directors—"

"You don't understand," Megan said. "Mother isn't planning to open a branch of DeWilde's. She's planning to open up a store of her own. In competition with DeWilde's."

The idea was so preposterous—so treacherous—that for a moment Gabe's mind went blank. "That's not possible," he said finally. "Kate's misunderstood. She must have. Mother would never open a rival store."

"Kate has an IQ somewhere around 160," Megan said wryly. "She spent three hours listening to Mother outline her plans. I think we can rely on Kate's information. Which is that Mother intends to open a bridal store somewhere in the Bay Area, modeled on the concepts that have made DeWilde's famous in five countries. When they finally said goodbye, Mother left to meet with a real estate agent. They were going to spend the afternoon looking at prospective sites for Mother's new store."

For the past several days, Gabe's feelings toward his mother had been in turmoil. Bewilderment and childish hurt had mixed inextricably with sympathy for his father and a more adult regret that his mother had felt unable to turn to her son for advice or comfort. Megan's news changed everything. Gabe could accept that his parents' marriage had run into trouble. He could even accept that marital problems might drive his mother back to San Francisco for a period of adjustment and reflection. He couldn't think of a single reason, other than spite, that would motivate her to launch a rival store in San Francisco.

His already turbulent feelings boiled over and coalesced into hard, icy rage. "Then we'll have to make sure she doesn't succeed, won't we," he said. "There isn't room in this world for more than one chain of DeWilde bridal stores, and Grace knows that better than anyone."

Megan put out her hand, resting it on his forearm. "She's hurting, Gabe, can't you see that? She's opening a store because it's the only thing she knows how to do. Losing herself in plans for a major new project is the only way she can find to ease the pain of being separated from Dad."

"She should consider coming home and discussing these matters with Dad like a mature adult," Gabe said coldly. "If you speak to her, you might point out that confronting the situation rather than running off would be a much more effective way of easing this pain you insist she's feeling."

"You could tell her yourself," Megan said. "Gabe, right now I really think she needs to hear from us. Pick up the phone and give her a call. The right words from you might persuade her to put her plans for a San Francisco store on hold."

"If she'd wanted to speak with me, she knew exactly where I could be found," Gabe said. "Which is more than I can say about her. I still don't have a phone number for her."

"I have one. Kate gave it to me. Mother's been staying at a hotel and has only just found an apartment-hotel, so she didn't have a permanent phone number to give us. Let me get my handbag and I'll give you—"

"Give it to Dad," Gabe said. "He's the managing director of the DeWilde Corporation. He's the one who should deal with this situation. Along with the lawyers, of course."

"But you're her son," Megan protested.

"Yes," Gabe said icily. "I wonder if Grace is going to remember that at any time in the near future?"

CHAPTER FIVE

LIANNE WASN'T LATE for her date with Gabe, but he was already seated at the table when she arrived at Bruges, the restaurant where they'd agreed to meet. He stood up to greet her, his manner courteous enough, but the tension radiating from him so powerful that she could feel it pricking her skin, setting off little minishocks like malfunctioning electrical wiring. Oddly enough, for the first time since she'd met him she had the impression that the tension was only partly sexual, and only partly caused by her.

On the point of asking what was bothering him, she realized that she had no right to probe for such personal information. This was the first time they'd been out on a date together, and for all that she knew his body so intimately, the two of them weren't friends. In some ways, they were barely acquaintances. Aside from those few magic hours in her flat when they'd seemed to talk about everything in the universe, the only intimacy they'd shared was sex. And tonight Gabe didn't seem to want to share even sex with her. The barriers he'd erected against her were as visible to Lianne as the dark, tailored elegance of his Savile Row suit or the subtle, abstract design of his Grieves and Hawke tie.

She sat down opposite Gabe, answering his polite questions with mechanical fluency and quelling a bitter disappointment that was out of all proportion to the reality of what was happening. She'd expected Gabe to be a fascinating, sophisticated companion, and he didn't let her down. Lianne herself was no slouch in the social chit-chat department. That was one thing you could say for growing up on military bases around the world. It sure taught you how to spend an evening jabbering eloquently about nothing in particular.

The restaurant Gabe had chosen was a new one, tucked away in an unlikely side street near Piccadilly. The chef was Belgian, the food scrumptious and the service impeccable. All this and Gabriel DeWilde sitting across the candle-lit table being charming. Any sensible woman would have been in heaven. Lianne was in hell.

Aching with misery, she talked about nothing with worldly aplomb. Gabe talked right back. No embarrassing moments of silence were allowed to develop. When all else failed, they discussed the wine and the details of the menu. She discovered that they both preferred artichokes to asparagus, and that they both considered the Grand Cru Montrachet that Gabe had ordered to be one of France's finest wines. She refused dessert with a smile. She refused coffee with another, even bigger smile. Gabe barely managed to conceal his relief. He paid a very large bill and they walked outside, only to discover that it had started raining.

What else, Lianne thought wryly. The perfect finish to a disastrous night.

"I'll drive you home," Gabe said. He sounded as if he would more willingly have volunteered to sit in a torture chamber and have rats gnaw on his toes.

She wasn't sure how much longer she was going to be able to hold on to her bright and cheerful smile. "Please don't bother, Gabe. I can easily get a cab."

But of course she couldn't. It was eleven o'clock on a Saturday night and it was raining, which meant she could almost as easily have found a camel padding through the streets as a cabdriver looking for a fare. "We could ask the restaurant to call for a minicab," she suggested, when ten excruciatingly long minutes had passed by without success.

"No, this is ridiculous." He grabbed her hand. "Come on. My car's parked just around the corner. And the rain seems to be letting up for a few minutes. Let's make a dash for it."

They ran, dodging puddles, with Gabe holding her hand so that she'd know which way to run. They reached his car slightly damp and slightly breathless. "I'll get the door for you as soon as I find my keys," Gabe said, sounding more natural than he had all night. "Watch out for the traffic. That red car on the other side of the road is parked illegally. There isn't much room left for anyone else to get by."

He'd just retrieved his keys from the inside pocket of his jacket when a van drove past, sending a spume of chilly water shooting toward them. Lianne instinctively jumped back in an effort to avoid the mud spray, bumping against Gabe because there was nowhere else to go. Her hair bounced against his cheek. Her hands splayed out against his chest. Her hip nudged his thigh. His arms shot around her, steadying her. They both froze, chest to chest, knee to knee, hearts beating in unison.

Oh, my God, Lianne thought. Oh, my God.

Gabe stared down at her, his eyes darkened by awareness and a kind of desolate resignation. His mouth twisted into a grim smile. "We almost made it, didn't we?"

She didn't—couldn't—answer. Her heart was racing so fast her lungs couldn't seem to keep pace. With slow deliberation, Gabe bent his head until his mouth covered hers. He kissed her with a ferocious passion that paid not the slightest heed to the fact that they were in a public place, on a street where cars were whizzing by, inundating them with dirty water. Lianne kissed him back, mouth open, body welded to his. A part of her stood to one side, shamed by her mindless passion, recognizing the bleak truth that tonight's dinner had proved conclusively—if proof were needed—that she and Gabe shared absolutely nothing except some strange body chemistry that triggered instant mutual desire.

He was fully aroused and she was shaking when he broke off the kiss. His gaze locked with hers. "Spend the night with me, Lianne."

No softening lies, no beguiling promises, just the curt offer of a night of sex. She closed her eyes, shutting out temptation. She had never expected to feel this sort of relentless drive for sexual fulfillment, so she had no mechanisms in place for coping with it. "No." The one-word denial was all she could manage to articulate.

His grip on her arms tightened as if he might refuse to accept her answer. Shockingly, she wished for a split second that he would ignore her rejection and simply bundle her into the car and drive her straight to his flat, refusing to take no for an answer. All the pleasures of mindless sex, with none of the responsibility. For a couple of seconds he neither moved nor spoke. Then he released her, turning abruptly to open the door on the passenger side of his Jag. "I'll drive you home," he said, his voice hard and flat. "Get in."

The traffic was heavy, and the rain started again as an annoying drizzle that distorted depth perception and made driving difficult, but Lianne didn't fool herself that the silence inside the car was caused by the driving conditions. The air around them crackled and sparked with their thwarted desire. Her body was still on fire. Why didn't Gabe say something? she thought, feeling aggrieved.

Perhaps because he was finding it as difficult as she was to think of something appropriate to say. He was thirty years old, long past the stage of needing to bed a woman just so that he could record another sexual conquest in his little black book. He'd spent five months dating Julia, which suggested he was a man who valued friendship as an element in his relationships with women. Since he didn't seem to like her very much, he was probably as embarrassed as she was by the stupid, inexplicable intensity of their sexual response to each other.

"Maybe we should just set aside a weekend to have wild, uninterrupted sex," she said, thinking aloud. "Maybe that way we'd get whatever it is we feel for each other out of our systems and be able to move on with the rest of our lives."

His mouth quirked into a rueful smile. "Isn't that supposed to be my line?"

"Why? Because you're the man? Are you sexist enough to believe that women don't have sexual urges? I'm just as aware of what's going on between us as you are, Gabe. Am I supposed to pretend I haven't noticed that we practically ignite whenever we touch? And that we have nothing much in common except mutual lust—and a good friend we betrayed?"

His hands tightened on the steering wheel. "Julia and I hadn't made each other any promises," he said quietly. "And I think she understands we didn't mean to hurt her."

"She's a much more generous person than I am. And the fact is, we have hurt her." Lianne laced her fingers in her lap and stared at them fiercely, aware that tears were gathering ominously at the corners of her eyes. Damn, she hated it when she went into emotional overload like this! If only she had some of Julia's wonderful British reserve. But all she had was a flaming Irish-American temper, mixed with a liberal dollop of Czech passion, and a British name passed on by a solitary English great-grandfather without any of his stiff upper lip to go with it. She brushed impatiently at the mud splotches drying in hard gray patches on the short skirt of her evening suit. None of them budged. Her expensive new outfit was ruined, she realized, stained and discolored beyond repair. Blinking back tears, she turned to stare out of the car window. Her suit seemed the perfect metaphor for her relationship with Gabe. Destroyed on the first outing.

Gabe turned the Jag into Kensington High Street. Another couple of minutes and they'd be home, thank heavens. Home, where she would spend the night alone. Lianne swallowed hard over the lump in her throat, not even sure why she still felt so depressingly close to tears. Surely the fact that she had resisted a night of meaningless sex was cause for celebration? By tomorrow morning she'd be delighted that virtue had triumphed over hormones and that Gabe hadn't taken her up on that silly offer of a weekend of wild sex.

She wished it would hurry up and be tomorrow morning.

For once, there was room to draw up to the curb right in front of her flat. Gabe parked swiftly and cut the engine.

"There's no need to see me to the door," Lianne said, already half out of the car. "I'll be fine. The entrance is well lit. Thanks for dinner, Gabe. You chose a wonderful restaurant—"

He got out of the door, slamming it behind him. He intercepted her as she stepped onto the pavement. "I behaved like a major pain in the ass tonight," he said. "I'm sorry, Lianne. Will you accept my apologies?"

She had her bright smile back in full working order. "Of course. Apology accepted. Thanks again for a delicious meal, Gabe. I'll see you at the office on Monday."

He put out a hand, restraining her. "It's no real excuse for my miserable behavior, but for what it's worth, I had bad news about my mother this afternoon," he said.

Lianne swung around in midstep. "Oh, no! I'm so sorry. She isn't sick, is she?"

"No." Gabe rubbed the back of his neck, the gesture weary enough to make Lianne ache to comfort him. "No, she's not ill. Apparently, she's planning to open a bridal department store in San Francisco."

Lianne frowned, puzzled. "A branch of DeWilde's, you mean? Why is that such bad news?"

Gabe laughed without the slightest trace of mirth. "Not a branch of DeWilde's," he said. "If you can believe it, I heard this afternoon that my mother intends to set up a rival store based on the concepts she's perfected over the past thirty years with DeWilde's."

Lianne was shocked. "She can't. Surely she can't do that. She'll never get backers or start-up financing. There must be noncompete clauses in her contract."

"What contract?" Gabe asked bitterly. "When my mother started working for DeWilde's it was a family-owned company, and she'd just married the son of the managing director. I hope I'm wrong, but I don't suppose the thought of a contract crossed anyone's mind."

Lianne shook her head in disbelief. "What does your father say about the situation?" she asked.

"Nothing." Gabe frowned, as if impatient with his own failure to act. "Actually, I haven't told Dad yet. There wasn't time to go and see him unless I canceled our date."

Lianne knew that their date had been the excuse, not the reason, for Gabe's failure to inform his father of Grace's plans. She moved closer, taking Gabe's hand. "You have to tell your father," she said. "Tonight, Gabe, or first thing tomorrow morning. It's going to be much worse if he hears rumors or finds out via the international gossip mill."

"You're right, but I don't know how to tell him. I've been wrestling with the problem for the past several hours since my sister gave me the news. How the hell am I supposed to explain to my father that his former wife is planning to do something that is the equivalent of holding a dagger to his chest and shoving it into his heart slowly, without benefit of anesthetic?"

Lianne winced at the image. "Well, for a start, I'd recommend that you work on finding some less inflammatory language to let him know what's happening," she suggested dryly.

"Whatever words I use, nothing is going to change the basic truth. Which is that my mother plans to open a store that will be in direct competition with DeWilde's."

"That's not quite true, is it, Gabe? If Grace had wanted to be in direct competition with your father, presumably she'd have chosen to open her store in one of the cities where DeWilde's is already operating. There's no DeWilde store in San Francisco. The only American branch is in New York. DeWilde's may be very famous and prestigious, but I doubt if many San Francisco brides travel three thousand miles across the country to shop in New York."

Gabe drew in a sharp breath. "I hadn't looked at it that way. But I should have. I know our customer base in New York is largely drawn from the East Coast."

"Put it that way to your father. Maybe it'll help to take the edge off Grace's plans just a little."

He looked down at her hand, stroking his thumb across the top of her knuckles. "Why is she doing this, Lianne?" The question seemed to come almost against his will, as if he hesitated to admit an outsider into the intimacy of his conflicting feelings. "My parents have been married for so damn long, and they seemed perfectly content with each other. Astonishingly content, in fact. What happened to them? What went wrong?"

Lianne thought of her own parents, now in their midfifties. Their marriage had always been happy, despite the tensions generated by her father's frequent career moves to air force bases often located in obscure parts of the world. She knew other military couples who'd seemed just as much in love as her parents, and yet their marriages hadn't survived the strain of constant separations and transfers, not to mention the looming threat of battles and death. Unlike Grace, Lianne's mother had never pursued a career outside the home, but Lianne refused to believe that it was Grace's career that had caused the breakup of her marriage. Disagreements over jobs and work schedules might be a symptom of a failed marriage, but they weren't likely to be the sole cause. So why were her parents happier than ever as they moved into their fifties, whereas Jeffrey's marriage to Grace was falling apart?

"I can't give you any good answers, Gabe," she said. "I guess if I could I'd be winning either the Nobel Peace Prize or making a fortune selling leather-bound volumes of my secret tips for a happy marriage."

He gave her a reluctant grin. "Some things just seem to get more complicated as we get older, don't they? When I was eight, I knew exactly what love was. It was my father buying me an ice-cream cone at the beach, and my mother sitting on the bed reading *Willy Wonka and the Chocolate Factory.*"

"Seems like a great definition of love to me," Lianne said.

"It was great. Unfortunately, each year since then I seem to understand a little less about what it means to love someone. It's depressing to think I reached my most profound insights on the subject of human relationships at age eight."

Lianne laughed softly. "Don't give up hope, Gabe. Deciding that you know absolutely nothing is probably the first sign of wisdom where love's concerned."

He glanced down at their hands, which were still linked. "Thanks for listening, Lianne. Talking to you has helped put things in perspective. I'll arrange a meeting with my father for first thing tomorrow morning."

"I'm sure that's a good decision."

He carried her hand to his lips, kissing the tips of her fingers with a touch that felt almost tender. "Have lunch with me tomorrow," he said quietly.

She wanted to say yes, but she didn't think she could bear sitting across a restaurant table, eating another expensive meal and exchanging brittle, meaningless conversation. She stared at the back of the hand holding hers. His skin was tanned, and she wondered where he'd been to get so brown at this time of year. There were so many things she didn't know about Gabriel DeWilde, and she realized suddenly that she was hungry to find out more about him. Not just as a sexual partner but as a man, and a potential friend.

"Where were you thinking we should meet?" she asked, her voice constricted, her thoughts flying in every direction.

He paused for a moment. "We could drive into the country and find somewhere by the river...."

"That seems like a lot of driving just to eat lunch."

"Where would you suggest, then?"

She looked up at him, the blood pounding in her ears. "How about your flat?"

He went very still. "I don't cook."

She held his gaze. "I rarely eat in the middle of the day, so lunch isn't a big deal for me."

A smile glinted briefly in his eyes. "You don't eat and I don't cook. It sounds like a date made in heaven, doesn't it? What time shall I expect you?"

Her fingers twisted in the strap of her beaded evening bag. "One o'clock?"

"I'll be waiting."

He gave her directions and she turned to go, scared by the confusing tumult of her feelings, but Gabe pulled her back. He cupped his hands around her face, kissing her long and hard. "Until tomorrow."

"Until tomorrow," Lianne repeated, and ran up the stone steps leading to her front door before she could change her mind. Whether to cancel tomorrow's date or to beg him to take her home with him tonight, she wasn't sure.

CHAPTER SIX

IT HAD BEEN TWO HOURS since Gabe told him about Grace's plans for a new store, but Jeffrey's anger seemed to have increased rather than diminished with the passage of time. Carrying his glass of whiskey, he strode through the elegantly furnished rooms of his flat, trying to find somewhere to sit, somewhere to put himself where the raw ache of his fury might be soothed. The down-filled cushions of the sofas, even the soft, worn leather of the chair in his study, seemed about as inviting as a bed of nails. The rooms echoed with emptiness, mocking him with reminders of Grace's absence, tantalizing him with memories. The elusive hint of her scent was everywhere, too strong to escape, too faint to satisfy.

Last night he'd slept in one of the guest rooms rather than breach the cavernous horror of their silent bedroom. Now he opened the door again, peering into the room as if he expected to be greeted by a tiger who'd missed out on breakfast. There was no tiger, of course, but the sight of the bed he'd shared with Grace was almost as frightening. Its puffy chintz bedspread was immaculately arranged, devoid of rumples and indentations, just as he liked it—the way Grace never managed to keep it, because the bed was her favorite place to sit. Each morning, she would roost cross-legged in the center of a pile of pillows, reading glasses perched on the end of her nose, mug of black coffee in hand, skimming through the

newspaper and driving him to distraction when she discarded unwanted pages in a haphazard pile on the floor.
Each night, she'd sit in the same spot at the center of the
bed, wearing one of those crazy T-shirts that belonged in
a college dorm, or one of her hand-embroidered satin
nightgowns that belonged in a courtesan's boudoir. Then
she'd slowly pull the pins from her trim French braid until her hair tumbled down onto her shoulders in a heavy
silk curtain.

God, even now, after all these years, she could still ex-
cite him just by taking the pins from her hair and looking
at him with a certain teasing light in her eyes. He could
remember with bittersweet accuracy how long it had been
since they last made love: one month, two weeks and six
days. With a pang of regret so sharp it was physically
painful, Jeffrey realized he would be willing to give up five
years of his life to see his wife again, this very minute,
sitting in the middle of the bed and messing up the spread
as she brushed the tangles out of her long blond hair. Or
even scrawling incorrect answers to the crossword puzzle
clues, and laughing when he pointed out her mistakes.

Jeffrey turned away from the too-neat bed, swallowing
a hefty swig of whiskey. It burned all the way down into
his stomach. Why had he never realized how much he
loved watching Grace do a crossword puzzle until it
seemed possible that he'd never watch her again?

He closed the bedroom door with a bang and marched
back down the hallway. Funny, he'd never noticed until
these past few days how damned depressing all that dark
walnut paneling could be. He gulped the last of his drink
and poured himself another, not bothering to add water
or ice. His third whiskey of the day and it wasn't even
noon. With a muttered oath, he set the full glass on the
trolley and strode impatiently through the drawing room.

He'd tried drowning himself in a bottle last week, when Grace finally left him, and he'd already discovered that getting drunk was no solution to his problems. Although, God knew, at the moment there didn't seem to be any solutions.

He pushed open the French doors leading out onto the balcony. He ignored the planter boxes full of bright tulips and budding geraniums and stared across the river to the south bank of the Thames without really seeing it. The rain had stopped sometime in the hours before dawn, and the sun was warm on his face. The roar of buses and cars was muted in this isolated cul-de-sac, the air clear of petrol fumes. A breeze blew in from the distant salt marshes of the Thames estuary, carrying with it the faint tang of the sea.

Grace wasn't even on the other side of the Atlantic Ocean, Jeffrey thought with maudlin self-pity. She was almost three thousand miles farther away, on the shores of the Pacific, closer to Asia than she was to England. And the gap between them emotionally was at least as wide as the physical distance that separated them. He closed his eyes, letting the sun sink into his skin, searching for peace, striving for acceptance. Grace was gone. She wasn't likely to come back. He'd destroyed everything—

No! The howl of pain and regret started so deep inside him that his body shook when he finally bellowed out his denial. Startling the sea gulls flying overhead, he banged his fist on the iron balustrade of the balcony and stormed back into the flat. He grabbed the phone, fumbling for his reading glasses when he couldn't decipher the number written neatly in his Rolodex. Damn, he hated the subtle signs of encroaching middle age. Especially today when he felt so cast adrift, so rootless. Ah, here it was: Grace—San Francisco.

The mere sight of that alien notation was enough to feed several more twigs to the flames of his anger.

He punched in the numbers, aware that it was still early in San Francisco, too impatient to work out the precise time difference. Grace answered on the third ring, her voice thick and husky with sleep. "Hello?"

The sound of her voice made him hot with longing. Though he had no reason to believe she'd flown to meet a lover, he irrationally wondered if she was alone. His hand, suddenly sweaty, slipped around the receiver. Jealousy clawed at his gut, burning and corrosive. He wanted to scream, and so he kept his voice cool, low and utterly controlled—his only defense against total breakdown. "This is Jeffrey," he said. "We need to talk, Grace."

"At three-thirty in the morning? I have nothing to say to you, Jeffrey. We've said it all, many times."

She sounded clipped, cold, indifferent. Grace never sounded that way. She always yelled and stormed and cried when she was upset, forcing him to confront the emotions that he kept buried so deep inside. But today, it seemed, she wasn't going to shout. Apparently she no longer deemed Jeffrey worthy of raised voices or floods of her tears.

He hurt so much that he couldn't bear it, so he let his anger explode. Not in a healing outburst, but in a deadly, ice-cold listing of her sins. "Well, my dear estranged wife, I have a great deal to say to you. According to Megan, you've been very busy in the week since you arrived in San Francisco. Tell me, Grace, just when did you decide that you hadn't punished me enough? When did you decide you needed to turn the screws one more time, just for good measure?"

"I don't know what you're talking about, Jeffrey."

He was too angry to wonder about the faint note of uncertainty in Grace's voice. "I'm talking about the store you plan to open," he said. "The luxury store you plan to start in San Francisco for the Bay area's lucky brides." The rage was welling up inside him, threatening to spill over, so he clamped down, making his voice colder, more punishing than ever. "I understand you intend it to be the ultimate bridal emporium, a supreme rival to DeWilde's. Is there any reason at all for this venture, Grace, other than to irritate me?"

"Oh, the store, that's what you're talking about." She hesitated a moment. "I have to do something with the rest of my life, Jeffrey."

You could come home where you belong. You could come home and be my wife again. His heart cried out the words, but his voice didn't speak them. The temptation to grovel was overwhelming, so he fought it by stoking his anger. Anger that bored more deeply inward with each passing second.

"Let me state my position, Grace, which is also that of the DeWilde Corporation and its board of directors. Any skills you may possess in management, merchandising and retailing were acquired while you were an employee of the DeWilde Corporation. If you attempt to open a store that capitalizes in any way on the expertise you gained while working for our company, or infringes on our trademarks, or utilizes our corporate logo, I shall personally see to it that you are served with enough lawsuits to keep you and your potential financial backers fighting in court for the next several hundred years."

"You can try," she said, and now—finally—she sounded angry. "Good luck, Jeffrey. Have one of your fancy lawyers look up the State of California's laws concerning restraint of trade. I think you'll find that De-

Wilde's won't have a legal leg to stand on. The fact that you're quoted on the London stock exchange won't help. From the American point of view, DeWilde's is a foreign company."

Jeffrey unclenched his jaw just enough to allow him to speak. "I would remind you that when the DeWilde family took this company public, we signed agreements with strongly worded noncompete clauses in order to protect nonfamily shareholders. You signed that agreement and I intend to see that you honor it. I trust that I have made my intentions, and those of the DeWilde board, crystal clear?"

"Crystal clear, Jeffrey." Her voice was husky, ridiculously sexy, considering what they were saying to each other. "You have many problems when it comes to communication, but lack of clarity isn't one of them. Let me try to be as crisp and succinct as you. Here's my answer. I plan to open a store, and you haven't a hope in hell of stopping me. See you in court, Jeffrey."

He heard her slam the receiver back into its cradle. The sound of silence, of the absence of Grace, echoed in his ear. He realized that he'd handled the situation about as badly as he possibly could have done. He'd killed any hope for negotiation, compromise or explanation. If Grace's plans for a new store hadn't been entirely serious before, they would be now. The phone began to buzz a warning beep into his ear. He hung it up with exaggerated care and walked over to the trolley and his abandoned glass of whiskey.

There were no answers in the bottom of a bottle, Jeffrey reminded himself, his hand curling around the neck of the decanter. True. But there were no answers anywhere else, either. He held the glass to his mouth, tipped it up and swallowed. The throbbing ache of his loss eased just slightly as the single malt trickled with warm comfort down his throat. He tucked the Edinburgh crystal decanter under his arm and weaved a path into the study. The newspaper lay, pristine and unread, on the floor by his chair. The way he'd always told Grace he longed to see it. He kicked it to one side and sank into his favorite chair, squinting at the upside-down headline.

He had, unfortunately, an extremely hard head for liquor, so it looked as if it were going to be a long, unpleasant afternoon. A fitting end to a long and unpleasant week. A rotten end to a marriage that had once seemed uniquely and gloriously happy.

GABE HADN'T REALIZED how much he was looking forward to seeing Lianne until he opened the front door and saw her waiting in the hallway. She managed by some odd alchemy to look both spring fresh and enchantingly rumpled all at the same time. She was wearing jeans, paired with a silk blouse in a soft shade of leaf green. An oversized jacket slid off her shoulders, and her chestnut hair was already beginning to tumble out of the clip that was supposed to hold it in a loose ponytail. He felt a surge of desire, tinged by some other sensation that was warmer, more subtle and harder to identify. Surprisingly, though, the tension that had been tightening in his gut ever since he spoke with his father that morning suddenly loosened.

He smiled at her, glad that she was there and that they had the rest of the day ahead of them. To do what, he wasn't quite sure. He'd been fantasizing about having sex with her ever since he interviewed her at the store, and last night's fiasco had merely sharpened his need. He'd intended to conduct her into his living room, stage a swift, expert seduction and have her in his bed within the hour.

Now the plan seemed shallow, the prospect of instant sex not very satisfying.

Confused by his own muddled feelings, he found that his usual repertoire of sophisticated one-liners had deserted him. Since he couldn't think of anything witty to say, he simply smiled and told her the truth. "Hello, Lianne. It's good to see you."

"Hello." She smiled back at him, holding up a small paper bag. "I brought us a present. Two Bath buns, still warm from the oven."

"You baked them yourself?"

She chuckled, her laughter light and happy. "I wish, but my culinary talents don't extend that far. It's such a beautiful day I decided to walk, and I found this wonderful bakery open. So if you can brew coffee, or make a decent pot of tea, I guess we can have lunch, after all."

"Coffee's my specialty," he said, stepping back. "And I love Bath buns. Come on in. If you've walked all the way here from your flat, you must be thirsty."

"It's less than five miles," she said, following him into the kitchen. "And it was perfect weather for walking. The parks and squares look so beautiful at this time of year it seemed a shame to take the tube and miss the views."

Gabe poured beans into the grinder and nodded to a cupboard behind her. "You'll find plates in there."

She set the sweet rolls on the plates and watched in companionable silence while he ground beans for the coffee and set it to brew. "You have an impressive kitchen for a guy who doesn't cook, Gabe."

He smiled ruefully. "When I bought this flat three years ago, I hoped the kitchen would inspire me into becoming an instant gourmet chef. After a couple of disasters, I realized there was more to being a great chef than buying a cookbook and reading the recipes. I signed up for a couple of courses in basic cooking, but I never got beyond the introductory lecture. Some crisis would erupt at work, and I'd be putting in fourteen-hour days again. And the truth is, I eat out so much these days that when I do have a meal at home, a bowl of cereal suits me just fine.''

''The pace at DeWilde's seems very fast,'' Lianne said. ''I'm getting used to the crisis-of-the-day approach already. DeWilde's is such a famous store, almost an institution, I'd expected the management to be a bit more conservative.''

''According to legend, the organization was very staid until the late seventies. Changes came rapidly then, mostly because of my mother's input. After the company went public in 1986, a lot of the old-timers took early retirement and left. The new hires and the staff who stayed appreciate the loose management structure and the creative freedom we're given to try new ideas. And when you try new ideas, you inevitably get the occasional screwup. Personally, I would never trade the satisfaction I get working for DeWilde's for the leisure time I'd get from a regular nine-to-five job. And I know my parents wouldn't, either, even though they both put in killer hours.''

''You miss her a lot, don't you, Gabe? Your mother, I mean.''

For a second, while he'd been talking about the store, he'd forgotten that his mother no longer worked at DeWilde's. He was disconcerted by the rush of regret he felt at the reminder of her defection, not only a personal regret but a professional one that he would no longer be working for a woman who was both talented and supremely knowledgeable about the world of fashion retailing.

"I'm sure that Adam will manage very competently once he gets the hang of things," Gabe said, not managing to inject much conviction into his voice.

"Yes, I'm sure he will. How long have you worked at DeWilde's?" Lianne asked, tactfully changing the subject.

"Three years. I was promoted to merchandising manager for the London store five months ago. And why are you looking so surprised?"

"I guess I'd sort of assumed that since you were the DeWilde son and heir that you'd been working there since the day you graduated from college."

He grimaced. "Lianne, you're treading on my ego. Hard. I like to tell myself that I got hired on my merits, not because I'm the boss's only son." He sighed. "Sometimes it feels as if the DeWilde name is this bloody great albatross hanging round my neck, insisting that I carry it everywhere."

"It must be difficult. Have you ever considered working for a rival store?"

"Not only considered it, I've done it. I worked for Bloomingdale's and Tiffany in New York. But in the end, nobody in either of those organizations wanted to promote me to a position with real responsibility, since they all assumed that one day I'd simply go back to DeWilde's, taking all their trade secrets with me. In the end, I swallowed my pride, gave up beating my head against a concrete wall and applied for a job at DeWilde's."

"Why did you have to swallow your pride?" she asked, taking the cup of coffee he handed her and sipping appreciatively.

"Well, I'd left home at seventeen assuring everyone that I was never going to work in the family business. I finally agreed to go to university instead of joining the marines, generously allowing my parents to support me, of course. But once I finished college, I plunged headlong into another attack of rebellion.''

''I expect you were wriggling every which way to escape the albatross,'' she said.

He was surprised at her immediate understanding. ''Yes, you're right. I wanted to be around people who'd never heard of DeWilde's, who just accepted me as Gabe, a useful bloke to have near you if you were in a tight corner.''

''How did you rebel?'' she asked.

''All the usual stupid ways. No illicit drugs, though. I had just enough sense in my testosterone-filled brain to avoid that. But except for the drugs, I tried everything. I made myself so unpleasant to my sisters that they stopped talking to me for the best part of a year. I drank too much, made friends with dangerous men, got involved with all the wrong women. I worked on an oil rig in Texas and on the gas pipeline in Alaska. You could say that I generally wasted an enormous amount of energy proving that my parents couldn't force me to join DeWilde's if I didn't want to. Which, of course, everyone except me already knew.''

Lianne took a luxurious bite of her sweet roll and sighed in sympathy. ''Lord, I wouldn't want to be twenty again. The world's such a terrifying place at that age, and of course you can't tell anyone just how darn scared you are. Most of all, you can't admit it to yourself. How did your parents react while all this rebelling was going on?''

He grinned. ''From my point of view, they didn't really cooperate as well as they should have done. On the rare occasions when I called to tell them I was still alive, they invariably told me that they were thrilled to hear from me, but if I really enjoyed digging ditches in the

Arctic tundra or baking my hide climbing rigs in the Gulf of Mexico, then that was absolutely what I should do. Go for it, son, with our blessings. After nine months in Alaska, I got tired of freezing my ass off and having nobody to talk to except the moose, so I decided that business school and an MBA looked like a much better option."

She laughed. "God, growing up is a painful experience, isn't it? I ran away to join an artists' colony in Maine when I was eighteen. But I guess I'm not as stubborn as you. Once winter set in, which was right around the first week in September, I decided that my creative talents were in grave danger of freezing to death along with the rest of me. So I called home and said that maybe I'd consider applying to college, after all. When I told the commune leader I was leaving to catch the next bus home, she shook her head sadly and said that I would regret selling out my artistry to vulgar commercialism. I didn't have the heart to tell her my departure had nothing to do with art. It was the thought of hot water in the shower and a pizza place close enough to make deliveries that lured me away."

Lianne's eyes danced as she talked, and her mouth seemed to quiver on the brink of a smile. Gabe felt his stomach twist with a tug of awareness that wasn't exactly sexual. Much as he wanted to take her to his bed, he realized that what he felt for her had become something more complex than simple lust, a realization that left an oddly discordant note twanging inside his head.

The domestic intimacy of the kitchen suddenly seemed threatening and he wanted to escape. "Come through to the sitting room," he said. "I have a balcony that's about the size of a bathtub, but it's such a lovely day, if I open the doors we'll get a fresh breeze even if we sit inside. We might even smell a whiff of lilac blossoms."

"Sounds perfect." She smiled outright this time, her pleasure sparkling around her like an oversized halo. "On a day like today, it's easy to remember why I decided to live and work in London."

He absolutely was not going to kiss her. He wasn't so besotted that he needed to kiss her just because she smiled. And where had that word *besotted* sprung from, anyway? "Why did you choose London as the place you finally settled?" he asked, his voice carefully cool. "If you wanted the challenge of making it in a European city, why not Paris, or Rome, or Vienna?"

"I guess part of the reason is that in London I more or less speak the same language as everyone else." She set her empty coffee mug in the sink, washing the sugar glaze from her sticky fingers. "But mostly it's because London has always struck me as one of the most beautiful and interesting cities in the world. Of all the places our family lived while I was growing up, I don't think we saw another city that has quite so many magnificent trees and flowers and public gardens. Then there are all the wonderful theaters." Her smile deepened. "And now that I'm an employed person, I can even afford the ticket prices at some of them."

Gabe handed her a towel, taking care to avoid touching her. "I like the theater, too. We should go together sometime. Is there anything special that you like to see?"

"I guess I like straight drama best of all. The more dazzling they make the special effects in movies, the more I realize how much I appreciate a straightforward play, where all the fireworks come from the talent and technical skill of the actors."

"I agree. Did you see *Silent River* at the Barbican last autumn? I found the emotional impact of that stunning."

"Yes, it was." Her cheeks became washed with color. "I cried through most of the last two scenes. I'm a sucker for neglected kids and lonely old folks. The combination of the two did me in."

Gabe found himself wishing that he'd seen the play with Lianne, rather than the elegant journalist he'd escorted, who'd later treated him to a brandy in her flat, accompanied by twenty minutes of rather boring sex and a thirty-minute analysis of the technical flaws in the performance of the male lead. Gabe had wondered if she would subject his performance in bed to the same critical analysis and had decided he didn't much care if she did.

He opened the door to the sitting room, and Lianne looked around appreciatively. "This is lovely, Gabe. Did you decorate it yourself?"

"With the help of some friends in the furniture trade. The antique pieces in here are all recovered, repainted and refinished castoffs from Kemberly."

"Kemberly?" she asked.

"My parents' home in Hampshire," he explained. "My great-grandparents bought it in the thirties, when they first arrived in England."

Lianne was surprised. "I didn't realize your family had arrived here so recently."

"By British standards, we're fresh off the boat. My father was the first DeWilde to be born here. My ancestors were diamond merchants in Amsterdam and my great-grandparents founded the first DeWilde bridal store in Paris right after World War I. Then, when Hitler came to power in Germany, they decided it was time to protect the family fortune by spreading the risk and opening a branch of DeWilde's in London. That was in 1934."

"And the London store was an immediate, outstanding success," Lianne said.

"Yes, fortunately. So my great-grandfather celebrated his first year's profits by buying Kemberly from a profligate baron who immediately took off to slaughter helpless wildlife in Africa. It's one of those rambling places with its very own secret staircase, and so much storage space in the attics that nobody ever throws anything away. The furniture in this room was probably declared too shabby to use sometime during the last century and got stashed away in the attics until I went up there and found it."

She sighed wistfully. "Now you're making me acutely jealous, Gabe. I always fantasized about having an unknown great-uncle who'd die and leave me a house that had been in the family for generations, one my parents had forgotten existed. Which is probably a reflection of the fact that I never lived anywhere longer than three years when I was a child."

"It must have been hard to move around so much, especially since you had no control over where you'd go and when you'd leave."

She shrugged. "But children never have any real say in where they live, do they? Besides, I was proud of what my father was doing, so I guess that made it easier for me to accept the demands of his career. The hardest part was losing friends. In the end, you learn to protect yourself by not making any friends, and that's the worst of all."

Gabe thought about his stint at boarding school and the security of living, studying and playing with the same group of people for five years. Boarding school might seem like a harsh environment, but in comparison to uprooting yourself every eighteen months or so, he suspected it was a piece of cake. "Were there any places that you really disliked living?" he asked, watching her as she examined a Victorian writing case with almost sensuous pleasure. "Surely there must have been at least a couple that you disliked?"

"There are several places I wouldn't choose to go back to," Lianne said. "But in the end, you can find something positive about almost anywhere if you look hard enough. And I was fortunate that my mother made sure we took advantage of everything the locality offered, whether it was Colorado Springs or the Arabian desert. What I find really surprising is how well my parents have settled down to suburban life in Michigan after all those years of exotic foreign travel."

"Is that where they're living now? In Michigan?"

"Yes, in a cottage right on the shores of Lake Michigan in a town called Benton's Inlet. They've settled in so well you'd think they'd lived there for thirty years at least. Mom's teaching a couple of classes in photography at the local community college, and Dad's opened up a small insurance agency. They seem as happy as clams."

Gabe wasn't sure that he wanted to hear about middle-aged parents who were blissfully happy. He pushed back the curtains and unbolted the French doors that led to his tiny balcony. He hadn't realized that Lianne had followed him to admire the view and was standing behind him. When he stepped back to swing the doors inward, he bumped into her. Their bodies collided, precipitating them into each other's arms.

He never made a conscious decision to kiss her. One moment they were looking at each other, gazes locked, bodies tense. The next moment his mouth was crushing down on hers, his tongue thrusting against her teeth, desire pulsing hot and heavy in his veins. Her lips opened instantly and she returned his kiss with an eager passion that simply fed his hunger for more. He couldn't seem to get close enough to her, and his hands threaded through

her hair, her soft curls winding around his fingers in a
silky, teasing caress.

He was awash in the touch and feel of her, drowning in
the scent and taste of her. With the tiny part of his brain
that still functioned at a rational level, Gabe ordered
himself to step back before they ended up making love on
the floor for the second time in their brief acquaintance.
Even as he was forming the thought, he grabbed her hips
and ground himself against the flat, welcoming softness
of her belly. Far from being repulsed by the blatant evidence of his arousal, she gave a low, husky murmur deep
in her throat, pressing herself even closer to his body. Her
blouse slid to the floor. The satin and lace camisole that
she wore underneath revealed the enticing swell of her
breasts and the creamy smoothness of her skin. He lowered his head, tracing the curve of her breasts with a trail
of hot, openmouthed kisses.

Her pleasure shivered through him, churning in his
veins, intoxicating him. Through the shattering boundaries of his self-control, he managed to latch onto the solid
fact that there was a sofa only a few feet behind them.
They didn't have to end up making love on the floor, he
realized with relief. Fumbling with the buttons of his shirt,
he propelled Lianne backward toward the sofa, tumbling
with her into the deep down cushions.

Her face was flushed, her eyes brilliant. Even in passion, she didn't appear drowsy or languid, but alive and
vibrant and infinitely desirable. Her gaze locking with his,
she shrugged her shoulders, twisting with slow deliberation until the straps of her camisole slipped down her
arms, revealing her perfect breasts and the hard peaks of
her nipples.

Gabe struggled to draw breath. He reached out and
touched her swollen lips with fingers that weren't entirely

steady. "You're so beautiful, Lianne. God, I want you so damn badly."

She framed his face with her hands, pulling his head down toward her mouth. "I want you, too, Gabe." Her voice was husky, faintly breathless. He wondered why her voice—why everything about her—seemed sexier than in any other woman. Then he kissed her again, and he no longer cared about his reasons for wanting her, only that he did. The world narrowed into a space that held nothing except Lianne, her body cradled beneath his own, warm and curved and inviting.

The sound of his mother speaking was such a shocking intrusion that for a couple of seconds Gabe didn't register that he was listening to the Answerphone and that Grace wasn't actually present in the sitting room, talking to him. Galvanized, he tore himself out of Lianne's embrace and sat bolt upright, realizing belatedly that he'd turned off the ringer on the phone, which was why he hadn't heard any warning sounds before the answering machine clicked in.

His mind was still foggy with desire, and his thought processes seemed slow and cumbersome. There wasn't another human being on the face of the earth who could have caused him to pick up the phone at this precise moment, but his need to speak to Grace was strong enough to cool the heat of his passion, allowing him to reach out and grab the phone before she hung up.

"Hello," he growled, not intending to sound deliberately aggressive, but his body was jangling with need and he didn't have full control over his reflexes. "What do you want?"

Not surprisingly, his mother seemed disconcerted by his roughness. "I'm sorry, Gabe. If I've called at a bad time, I can try you again later."

He wasn't thinking clearly enough to respond to the nervousness in his mother's voice or to consider how she might be feeling. He spoke brusquely, the frustrations of the past few days mingling with his unfulfilled lust. "No, this is fine. Lord knows, if we don't speak now you may decide to take off for the Caribbean and it'll be six months before anyone hears from you again."

Several seconds passed before she answered him. "Gabe, I'm sorry, really I am. I never intended to leave London so abruptly without speaking to you. I did try to phone from the airport, but you weren't home." She hesitated, seeming to search for the right words. "I hope you weren't too shocked when you heard the news, Gabe."

"Shocked? Why should I be shocked?" He didn't even try to control the bitter sarcasm that honed his words to lethal sharpness. "You and Dad have only been married for thirty-two years, so why should I be surprised because you suddenly woke up one morning and decided to leave him?"

"It wasn't quite that sudden," she said. "Things have been—difficult—between us for quite a while."

His father had said the same thing. Gabe's anger faded into puzzlement. "How have they been difficult?" he asked. From the corner of his eye, he saw that Lianne had finished pulling on her clothes. With a tactfulness he appreciated, she went out onto the balcony, closing the glass doors behind her so as to afford him some privacy. "Mother, what happened between the two of you?"

Once again she seemed to choose her words with excruciating care. "I said some things to your father a while ago that he didn't understand . . . that he misinterpreted."

"What kind of things?"

"Personal stuff. Ancient history, really." Grace's hesitation was longer this time. "Jeffrey was badly hurt. One thing led to another and... Well, the situation just became untenable. We were inflicting so much pain on each other, it was unbearable. That's all I can say, Gabe."

"And is your current situation any better?" Gabe asked incredulously. "Are you happy over there in San Francisco? Have you any idea what you're doing to Dad? He looks like hell, and he's drinking himself to sleep most nights as far as I can tell—"

"If Jeffrey's drinking, that's his own choice."

"You're forcing him into making that choice."

"No, I'm not," Grace said, her voice diamond hard. "I'm not responsible for Jeffrey's actions."

"He loves you, Mother. He needs you." Gabe swallowed hard. "We both need you. Come home."

"Gabe... don't ask that, please."

He refused to hear the note of desperation in her voice. "You don't have to come back to live with Dad, but you need to come back to work, Mother. You have responsibilities to the store and to all the people who work for DeWilde's. However bad things are between you and Dad, I don't understand how you can run away from your professional obligations like this."

"I can't work with Jeffrey," Grace said flatly. "Gabe, you don't know what you're asking."

"Then explain to me. Make me understand, for God's sake."

"I can't," Grace said again. "Try to see things from my point of view. This is a rough time for me, and I guess I'm asking for your understanding. I need to know that you're willing to accept that I had good reasons for what I did, even though I can't necessarily explain those reasons. I need your support right now, Gabe. I really need it."

Hurt and bewilderment made him cruel. "Support for what?" he asked. "Support for your insane decision to open a rival store in San Francisco? If that's what you're hoping to get from me, then I can tell you here and now that you're not going to get it."

He could almost hear her flinch. She drew in an audible breath. "Sometimes, you know, you sound frighteningly like your father."

"I take that as a compliment."

Grace's voice was harsh with sudden weariness. "Let's not argue, Gabe. I've found an apartment overlooking the Bay, and I want to give you my new address and phone number. I'll be moving in next weekend."

Gabe wrote down the information that his mother gave him. "Thanks for the number," he said. "Although I'm not sure what we have to say to each other at this point."

"You're my son, and I love you," Grace said. "I can think of lots of reasons why I'd like to talk to you. I hope very much that you'll soon find just as many reasons to call me. I'm still your mother, Gabe, even if Jeffrey and I aren't living together anymore."

"It seems to me that conversation might be a little difficult," Gabe said dryly. "You don't want to talk about Dad, and I sure as hell don't plan to talk to you about DeWilde's. Not when you're threatening to open a rival store."

"A bridal store in San Francisco is hardly a threat to the DeWilde retail empire," Grace said. "Be reasonable, Gabe. What am I supposed to do with myself for the next thirty years? Sit at home and knit socks?"

He wanted her to spend the next thirty years in the same way that she'd spent the last thirty—with her husband. But he was too much his father's son to tell her that she was the heart and soul of their family and that he didn't know if he would ever be able to visit Kemberly again if she wasn't there to welcome him. Much as Gabe admired and loved his father, he had always known that Grace was the anchor of their family's relationships. Without her at the center, all of them would be adrift.

"You've chosen to leave DeWilde's," he said coolly, but what he wanted to say was, *You've chosen to leave me.* "I suppose since you've decided to take early retirement, you'll have to find a hobby, just like any other retiree. I don't see why your hobby needs to be a department store, however."

"I'm not sure why you feel the need to be deliberately rude, Gabe."

He wanted to apologize, but the words stuck in his throat—sharp, jagged lumps of resentment. "Thanks for giving me your new address, Mother. I'll be in touch with you sometime."

He hung up the phone, seething with anger that had no place to go. The concept of his mother as a retiree was not only insulting, it was laughable. Grace was the most dynamic, vital fifty-two-year-old he'd ever encountered, a woman constantly on the move, bursting with creative ideas, laughter never very far from her eyes.

For no apparent reason, an image of Lianne flashed into Gabe's mind, juxtaposed with his image of his mother. Lianne was laughing up at one of her co-workers, sketching improvements to the design of a bridal headdress with deft, nimble fingers. It was a scene he'd observed three or four times in the past few days since Lianne had started work at DeWilde's.

Gabe was suddenly able to identify the subtle discomfort that had been nagging at him whenever he was with Lianne. She and his mother were very much alike, he realized, strikingly so, in fact. Not in looks, of course, but in personality.

If Grace could break her husband's heart after thirty-two years of marriage, it seemed to Gabe that he would be every kind of a fool to embark on any sort of permanent relationship with Lianne—a woman who was endowed with all the same fatal charm as his mother.

And the same unreliability?

CHAPTER SEVEN

AFTER THE DEBACLE of their Sunday date, which ended with Gabe once again freezing her out with polite conversation, Lianne decided never to accept another invitation from him. She simply didn't need the grief in her busy life. It had been difficult enough trying to cope with her too-vivid memories of the night they'd made love, but it was well-nigh impossible to deal with the capriciously changing emotions and unsatisfied desire that the recent dates with Gabe had seemed to produce.

Her overwhelming urge to go to bed with him was disconcerting, to say the least. Looking back over the years at her tepid interest in sex, Lianne wasn't sure whether to bemoan her previous ignorance or curse the fact that her body was now well and truly aware of what all the fuss was about. Rather than analyze her own confused feelings, it seemed easier simply to feel angry with Gabriel DeWilde, who was, after all, the source of that confusion.

After Sunday, the only positive traits she could find about the wretched man were his great body and handsome profile, and the fact that he was darn good at his job. The great body and handsome profile she could train herself not to notice. At least she assumed that one day, when she was well into the bifocal years, she would eventually succeed in watching him walk by without an involuntary clenching of her stomach muscles and an immediate acceleration in her pulse rate.

Gabe's professional expertise was harder to overlook, since she was reporting directly to him, and final approval of the *Lianne for DeWilde* designs had to come from him. Seated across the desk from him on Thursday morning, Lianne watched him work through the cost sheets she'd prepared, aligning her estimates and procurement data with the finished sketches for each headdress, veil and jeweled comb. Every question he asked was insightful. Every comment or suggestion he made was valid. She wasn't sure whether to be struck dumb with admiration, or to be furious that he was always so damned right. She decided that, in the circumstances, fury was much the better way to go. She seethed silently, answering him in monosyllables, delighted to have an excuse to let her resentment build.

"I think that takes care of everything." Gabe pushed back his chair and gave her one of the polite, impersonal smiles he'd been lavishing on her for the past several days.

She returned his smile with a scowl, stacking her drawings and estimates into their appropriate folders in dour silence.

"Is something wrong?" Gabe asked mildly. "Lianne, if you don't agree with any of my suggestions, you must speak up. You're the designer. It's your name that's going on the label of the finished products, and it's important for you to feel happy with the way your designs are developed—"

"Your suggestions were all excellent," she snapped. "I'll have the revised estimates on your desk by the end of business hours tomorrow afternoon. Is that satisfactory?"

"We have until Monday," Gabe said quietly. "Don't work overtime on this, Lianne. You need to take it a bit easier for a couple of days. You're here when I arrive in the morning and you don't leave until seven or eight at night. Nobody can keep up that sort of pace indefinitely."

"Thank you for your concern," she said woodenly. "But I'll have the revised estimates on your desk by tomorrow afternoon."

"Damn it, Lianne, would you stop trying to prove you're Superwoman?" Gabe strode around his desk. "The estimates are due on Monday. Go home tonight at five o'clock. That's a direct order, okay?"

"Yes, sir." She touched her hand to her forehead in a mock salute. "You're the boss, sir."

The next thing she knew, her back was flat against the wall and Gabe's hands were splayed on either side of her head, his body fused with hers from shoulder to thigh. "You're driving me crazy," he said, grinding the words out between clenched teeth. "Totally damn crazy."

"Don't give me too much credit," she snapped.

He didn't bother to answer, just slammed his mouth over hers, his kiss hard, demanding, almost brutal. His hands were hot against the bare skin of her rib cage. It was a moment before Lianne realized that he'd tugged her blouse out of her skirt and thrust his hands underneath her camisole. Another moment before she realized that the shock of reaction she felt was pleasure, not outrage. She closed her eyes, letting the impact of his touch explode into every cell and fiber of her being.

He finally lifted his head, but he didn't move away. His breath came swiftly. His eyes glittered. Color darkened his cheekbones. She wondered if she looked as thoroughly and completely aroused as he did.

"Come back to my flat," he said. "Now."

She braced her hands against the wall to prevent her knees from buckling. "No."

"You want me."

"Yes." She kept her gaze locked with his. "I wanted you on Sunday, too, and look what that got me."

A grim smile flickered across his face. "Trust me, Lianne, this time I won't send you away."

She stiffened. "You're right about that, Gabe. You won't send me away, because I'm not going anywhere with you. Especially not into your bed. You've blown your last chance with me."

"I screwed up," he said. "Lianne, I'm really sorry. There's not much I can do except apologize for the way I behaved on Sunday. I let problems within my own family interfere with our relationship."

"And how about on Wednesday?" she asked. "Are you apologizing for that, too? And then there was that delightful little outing on Saturday, since we're reminiscing about past encounters. I'm not a masochist, Gabe. I like to have fun on my dates. So far, fun has been spectacularly missing from our relationship."

Jeffrey DeWilde's voice carried from the doorway. "Gabe, if you could spare me a moment out of your busy schedule, I need you in my office. Immediately, please."

"Yes, sir. I'll be with you in a moment." Gabe moved away slowly, giving Lianne a couple of seconds to straighten her clothes. He turned around to face his father. "I was just inviting Lianne to join us at the theater tonight. She's been kind enough to agree to come with us."

Jeffrey's patrician gaze flicked briefly toward Lianne, and she resisted the urge to run her fingers up and down the buttons on her blouse to make sure they were all closed.

"How very good of you to fill in at such short notice," Jeffrey said with cool irony. "But I gather the invitation my son extended was quite—enthusiastic. I'm delighted you'll be joining us." He stepped back into the corridor without waiting for her to reply. "Gabe, in my office. Now."

"Give me two minutes, please." Gabe closed the door behind his father and swung around, leaning against it. Lianne didn't give him the chance to speak. She exploded.

"Of all the despicable, lowdown, dirty tricks, that has to be the worst! What was all that garbage you fed me the other day about how oppressed you felt by the DeWilde name, and how you hated people to think you'd take advantage of it? I can't believe you actually stooped to using your father's position in the company to coerce me into accepting an invitation from you. Well, it won't work, Gabe. I'm not coming."

"You've every right to be angry—"

"Don't you dare patronize me! Damn right I'm angry—"

"Let me explain. It's the opening night at the Royal Shakespeare for their new production of *Richard II*. It's a gala performance in aid of the new pediatric cancer unit at the Great Ormond Street Children's Hospital. My mother was chairwoman for the benefit and my father's filling in for her at the last minute. Even if you don't want to spend time with me, the fact is you'd be doing my father a real favor if you'd come. I think it will help him to get through a difficult few hours if he has people around that he's forced to entertain. He needs to think about something other than the fact that Grace organized all of this and she isn't here to enjoy the success of her hard work."

Some of Lianne's anger faded, but she wasn't about to let him off the hook that easily. "I don't respond well to intimidation, Gabe, however much sugar coating you slap over the top."

"If it makes you feel any better, there'll be half a dozen other people in our party. You don't have to speak to me all night if you'd prefer not to."

"Is that a promise?"

"It's a promise."

"On those terms, it seems a shame to miss out on a great opportunity. Thank you. *Richard II* is probably my favorite of Shakespeare's historical plays."

"Then I'll pick you up at six-thirty," Gabe said quickly. "It's a black-tie affair, by the way." He left the room before she had time to point out that it would be a great deal easier to avoid speaking to him if she took a cab.

"Ah, Gabriel, I'm glad that you finally found yourself free to join us." His father's greeting carried a sardonic note that Gabe found oddly comforting, perhaps because Jeffrey's habitual irony had been so conspicuously absent since his wife's departure.

"Sorry to have kept you waiting, sir."

"Yes, you appeared to be working with quite remarkable intensity. I trust your—project—was brought to a successful conclusion?"

"More successful than might have been expected," Gabe said wryly, his gaze flicking to the other occupant of the room—a tall, dark, powerfully built man who stood silently by the window.

"Good. Well, now that you're here, I'd like to introduce you to Nick Santos. He just arrived on this morning's flight from New York." Jeffrey gestured to the man by the window, who stepped forward, right hand outstretched, left hand holding his briefcase. "Gabriel."

An impressive man, Gabe thought, shaking Nick Santos's hand and wondering who he was and what he was doing in Jeffrey's office. "Welcome to London," he said. "Did you have a good flight?"

"Uneventful." Nick's voice was deep, his accent hard to pinpoint. "In the circumstances, uneventful was about the best I could hope for."

"That sounds ominous. Is there a problem?" Gabe asked, looking from Nick to his father.

"You could say that." Jeffrey's voice was dry. "Nick brought me something from New York that I want you to see." He got up, depressing the intercom button as he walked around his desk. "Hold my calls, Monica, please. I don't want to be interrupted for the next half hour."

He crossed to the door of his office and turned the key in the lock. Then he drew the drapes and switched on the overhead lights. Gabe frowned, puzzled and a little alarmed by such strange behavior. His father had seemed more at peace with himself and the world for the past day or two. Gabe hoped that peace hadn't been illusory or the first signs of an impending breakdown.

His office arranged to his satisfaction, Jeffrey sat back down behind his desk. "All right, Nick, I believe we're now ready to relieve you of your baggage."

Nick walked silently to Jeffrey's desk. The briefcase he held in his left hand was one of the aluminum styles advertised as indestructible by the manufacturer. Gabe's eyes widened when Nick pulled up the sleeve of his conservative business suit and revealed a set of workmanlike steel handcuffs that attached the case to his wrist.

For the first time a faint smile flickered in Nick's dark eyes. "I sincerely hope you have the keys to unlock these cuffs, Mr. DeWilde. Otherwise we're going to need a blow torch.''

Jeffrey opened his desk drawer and took out a small key on a heavy chain. ''I have it here.'' He leaned across the desk and unlocked the cuffs. Nick caught them expertly, as if he'd worked that maneuver many times before. Then he gently set the aluminum case in the space Jeffrey had cleared in the center of his desk. ''Do you want to open it, Mr. DeWilde?''

Jeffrey shook his head. ''No, go ahead. You brought it here, you do the honors.''

The briefcase was closed by two numerical combination locks. Nick took thirty seconds or so to align the tumblers. Then he pressed the latches and lifted the lid of the case.

Jeffrey gave a small murmur of satisfaction, but Gabe was stunned into silence. He stared in blank astonishment at the glittering tiara nestled on a custom-designed bed of padded blue satin. Braided rows of sparkling diamonds refracted the glow of the overhead lights, creating a rainbow of fiery color. At the front of the tiara, six teardrop pearls—famous for the exquisite symmetry of their shape—shimmered in opalescent splendor, each suspended from a four-carat diamond of superlative brilliance and clarity.

Since he'd walked past the real Empress Eugénie tiara when he came into the store that morning, Gabe realized he must be looking at a copy. But what a magnificent copy! He picked the tiara up and examined it more closely, wishing he had his loupe with him. He'd been around gems and jewelry all his life, and he'd never seen a fake of this caliber. Frowning, he set the tiara back in the case and looked at his father.

"Is it paste?" he asked. "Or were there two tiaras made for Empress Eugénie?"

"No, there's only one Empress Eugénie tiara," Jeffrey said.

Gabe held the tiara closer to the light. "The workmanship is extraordinary. If I didn't know better, I'd swear these pearls were genuine. It must have cost a small fortune to make an imitation this good, even using zircons instead of diamonds. Why would anyone bother?"

"It isn't paste," Jeffrey said, reaching inside his drawer and handing Gabe a loupe. "Look for yourself and you'll see. Not only are the stones real, this is the original Empress Eugénie tiara. The one and only genuine article. I authenticated it myself four weeks ago."

"My God!" Gabe screwed the loupe to his eye and stared at approximately three-and-a-half million pounds' worth of gems and history perched on his father's desk. "How did it get up here?"

"I brought it with me from New York," Nick Santos said. "It made for a wakeful night, knowing that I had nearly six million dollars' worth of famous jewels manacled to my wrist."

Gabe set the loupe down. "You brought it from New York?" He stared at Nick, hardly able to believe his ears. "Bloody hell, Dad, the executives at the insurance company would have a collective heart attack if they knew we'd taken the tiara out of the display case. Lord alone knows what they'd do if they heard it had made a trip to New York and back again!"

"The insurance executives wouldn't give a damn if they knew we had it sitting here on my desk," Jeffrey said. "And they wouldn't care if Nick had dropped it into the middle of the Atlantic." He gave a wintry smile. "The tiara isn't insured."

The niggling fear that his father was teetering toward a breakdown returned to haunt Gabe. He spoke with careful calm. "Of course it's insured, Dad. Your father put the entire DeWilde jewelry collection into a family trust sometime way back in the fifties, and we use two companies to insure the collection—Global Associates and Commonwealth International, remember? I'm not sure which company has this particular piece on their books—"

"Commonwealth International thinks the tiara is insured by Global, and Global thinks it's insured by Commonwealth," Jeffrey said. "Actually, it's insured by neither company for the simple reason that until six weeks ago I had no idea the tiara still existed. I assumed it had been broken down into its component parts decades ago."

His father sounded in full command of his faculties. In fact, Gabe thought that he looked rather more cheerful than he had at any time since the devastating announcement of Grace's departure. "Dad, we have fifteen thousand pounds' worth of electronic surveillance equipment sitting downstairs in the middle of the store, guarding the Empress Eugénie tiara. We had that equipment installed because the insurance company demanded it."

"Well, that's what I told people when we arranged for a new storewide security system. But actually, I spent all that money on elaborate electronic security devices for the tiara because it made the setup downstairs look more authentic, as if we really had something to protect. In this day and age, nobody would believe we had a three million pound tiara on display unless we also had some very visible security."

Gabe went cold. He was beginning to understand—and wished he wasn't. "Dad, you can't possibly be telling me that the tiara we have on display downstairs is a fake?"

"That's exactly what I'm telling you," Jeffrey said, confirming Gabe's fear. "The tiara we have on display in the store is an expensive, well-made fake, with a 22-karat-gold setting, but not a genuine gemstone anywhere in the entire piece."

Gabe sat down abruptly. "Let's start this story from the beginning, shall we? All of a sudden I feel as if we're speaking a different language."

"This may take a while," Jeffrey said. "Do you have any meetings you need to reschedule?"

"Nothing until this afternoon."

"Then the first thing to make clear is that everything we say here this morning is to remain strictly confidential for reasons I'm sure will soon become apparent. I plan to fill Megan in on what's happening at lunch tomorrow, since she'll be here for the gala tonight."

Gabe would have sworn that he didn't so much as glance toward Nick, but the American picked up instantly on Gabe's unspoken question. The man obviously had great instincts. "I'm a private investigator," he said. "Your father approached me last month and asked me to make some inquiries for him regarding the provenance of the tiara you see sitting on his desk."

"Nick came to me with the highest possible recommendations," Jeffrey said. "He was a lieutenant with the San Francisco Police Department until a couple of years ago, and he's been very successful in solving some high profile cases since then. Anyway, apart from you, Megan and Nick, I see no reason to involve anyone else in the situation, at least for the moment."

"Shouldn't we alert the board of directors—"

"No." Jeffrey shook his head. "The jewels are owned personally by the DeWilde trust, so this is strictly a family matter, although—unfortunately—I think it's a family matter that might have an unfavorable impact on the reputation of the company, not to mention the share price. Nick has been hired by me personally, not by the De-Wilde Corporation."

The DeWilde organization recently seemed to be suffering from more than its share of "family matters" that threatened to impact the share price, Gabe thought ruefully. "If it's strictly a family matter, shouldn't we tell Kate?" he said.

Jeffrey steepled his fingers. "There's absolutely nothing she could do about the situation, and she's under so much pressure with her studies right now that there seems no reason to burden her with extraneous problems she can't hope to resolve."

"All right," Gabe agreed. He glanced at his father, and Grace's name flashed silently between them. Neither of them spoke the name out loud, but it reverberated between them nonetheless. Was Grace the reason why his father didn't want to bring Kate into these discussions? Because she was in San Francisco and might say something to her mother? Did his father's mistrust of Grace now extend that far? Gabe wondered bleakly.

"We're going to have to hash over a fair bit of family history, so let's get started," Jeffrey said, glossing over the tense moment. "Do you ever remember hearing anyone mention my uncle Dirk DeWilde?"

"Yes, but I can't remember much about him," Gabe said. "Wait, wasn't he Grandfather's older brother? He founded the DeWilde store in New York, but he died in the Second World War, or something like that. There are several pictures of him at Kemberly. He was very good-looking, if I'm remembering the right person."

"That's the one," Jeffrey agreed. "As you said, he was my father's elder brother, and the major heir to the various DeWilde enterprises. But he didn't die in the war. He disappeared a couple of years later, sometime early in 1948, I believe."

"You believe?" Gabe said. "Don't you know? I mean, it's rather difficult to mislay an uncle."

"You would think so, wouldn't you?" Jeffrey said ruefully. "But deciding exactly what happened nearly fifty years ago isn't as easy as it sounds, especially since Dirk's disappearance was always treated as a family secret of the highest order."

"Had he done something horribly scandalous?"

"Possibly. Or possibly not." Jeffrey sounded resigned. "Nowadays, what with the gossip journals, tabloids and TV talk shows, it's almost impossible to put ourselves back into the mind-set of people who believed that there was no family scandal too small to cause social ruin, or too huge to be swept under the rug. Incredible as it may seem, I can't find out precisely when Dirk disappeared, or even if he had a good reason for disappearing. I don't know if he ran away because of strictly personal reasons, or if he was fleeing two steps ahead of the law after committing some terrible crime. All I know is what my father chose to tell me when I became managing director of the London store, which was astonishingly little."

"And what did your father tell you?" Gabe asked, intrigued by this introduction to a family mystery.

"Basically my father explained that Dirk had always been a man with a restless spirit, and that he seemed to find it exceptionally hard to settle down into the routine of running the New York store after four years of working as a battle-hardened Marine Corps intelligence officer, with hundreds of lives hanging on the outcome of his missions. According to my father, Dirk struggled along for a couple of years after the war, but he allowed a lot of important business to slide. Then, in April of 1948, he handed in his resignation as president of the American branch of DeWilde's and sent a notarized letter to my father saying that he was relinquishing all rights to the DeWilde family property, including the inheritance due to him under his parents' will. Then he disappeared."

"What do you mean, he disappeared? Presumably we're not talking *pouf,* in a cloud of colored smoke."

"I don't know what I mean precisely." Jeffrey sounded frustrated at giving the same unsatisfactory answer he'd given before. "Transatlantic phone calls in those days cost an absolute fortune, so my father sent a few cables asking his brother to clarify what was going on and where he could be reached. Dirk didn't respond, but as far as I can tell, nobody paid much attention at the time. They knew he had a restless spirit and assumed he'd taken off on an extended vacation and would eventually return."

"Somebody must have worried about the business aspects of his disappearance," Gabe pointed out. "What about DeWilde's, New York? When Dirk left, who was minding the store?"

"That's when your great-uncle Henry was sent to take charge," Jeffrey explained. "But right from the start, Henry seems to have been overwhelmed by the day-to-day tasks associated with running the store. He'd stepped into a crisis situation, and he certainly didn't spend any time searching for his missing brother." Jeffrey looked disapproving, as he usually did when the New York store was mentioned. "With Henry supposedly in charge, De-Wilde's Fifth Avenue location quickly went from being the most profitable of our stores to being the least profitable."

Having worked at both Tiffany and Bloomingdale's in Manhattan, Gabe was well aware of the problems De-Wilde's still faced in the competitive New York retail market, and the antics of Henry's large brood of children didn't help to improve the situation. Sloan De-Wilde, Henry's son, was nominally in charge of running the store, although he'd never shown much interest in the place. He had plenty of talent and an incisive, clever mind. But so far, nobody had been able to find the key that would unlock Sloan's talents and persuade him to apply himself to the demanding task of making the New York store profitable.

Still, this wasn't the time to deal with the problems of DeWilde's Fifth Avenue store. "What happened when Dirk didn't come back from his supposed vacation?" Gabe asked.

"From what my father told me, it seems that serious efforts to find out where Dirk had run off to weren't started until the family received a letter from him saying that he was well and happy, but he had no intention of returning to the stranglehold of the DeWilde family business ever again."

Gabe felt a moment of empathy with his long-vanished uncle. He could certainly understand why Dirk might have felt the need to distance himself from the oppressive weight of family duties and obligations. "Where was the letter posted from?" he asked. "Surely that would have been a good place to start looking for him?"

"It was posted in Hong Kong, and naturally, that was the first place the family searched for him. My father hired a Pinkerton's detective early in 1949, and he spent almost two years looking for Dirk. They never found a trace of him, and in the end, my father gave up and called off the search."

"How old were you in 1948?" Gabe asked his father. "Seven? Eight? Don't you remember hearing anything about your uncle's disappearance at the time it happened?"

"Unfortunately not. I'm sure it was discussed, but perhaps not in my presence. Or else anything I may have heard must have passed in one ear and out the other. I don't even remember being curious about the fact that he'd disappeared. You have to realize that he'd been living in New York, so I'd never met him personally. Uncle Dirk was simply a name to me."

"And I suppose you were still very young to understand the ramifications of his sudden disappearance."

"Yes, but quite apart from that, the war created a lot of very strange circumstances, and Dirk's disappearance just seemed part and parcel of the general madness. The situation in our family was especially strange because we had so many different nationalities within the same generation. In fact, to give you an example of the oddities of our family heritage, my father and my two uncles all fought in World War II, but they each fought for a different country."

"I remember Grandfather Charles talking about that," Gabe said. "Henry was in the Royal Air Force, wasn't he? Dirk was in the U.S. Marine Corps, and Grandfather Charles joined the French army. I'd never really stopped to think how bizarre that was. How in the world did it happen that way?"

"The day after Britain declared war against Nazi Germany in 1939, my father was packed off to Brazil by his parents, specifically so that he wouldn't be called up to active duty. He had a history of rheumatic fever, and my grandparents decided his heart would never stand the strain of military service. That didn't sit too well with him, since Uncle Henry was already training to fly fighter planes for the RAF and my father didn't intend to be outdone by his little brother. So after the fall of France in 1940, he defied my grandfather's orders to stay in Brazil, sneaked back to England with my mother, and signed on to fight with the Free French Army, which was being organized by General de Gaulle.''

"Why the French army, though?"

"You have to remember that he'd been born in France, and he was trilingual in French, English and Dutch. And the medical exam probably wasn't as stringent as it would have been for the British army because General de Gaulle was desperate for volunteers. He needed all the men he could recruit."

"What about you?" Gabe asked. "Had you already been born when Grandfather Charles joined the army?"

"No, I was born three or four months after he'd shipped out on some secret mission to North Africa, so for the first five years of my life, I grew up not sure whether I actually had a father. When he did finally return from the war, from my childish perspective, it was as if he'd just arbitrarily popped up out of nowhere, and for a couple of years I was always waiting for him to vanish again, just as inexplicably as he'd appeared."

Gabe shook his head. "Good Lord, Dad, I bet all the child psychologists would have a field day hearing about that setup. The war must have played havoc with an entire generation of children's psyches."

"I'm sure it did. That may be why the disappearance of Uncle Dirk aroused so little interest on my part. It was simply part of the pattern I considered normal. I expected people in my family to vanish and reappear with no apparent rhyme nor reason. Just as I expected houses to be standing one day and destroyed by a bomb the next."

Gabe's grandfather, Jeffrey's father, had been dead for several years. But his grandmother was still alive, an active eighty-year-old with a keen wit and the energy of many women half her age. No wonder Grandmother Mary had always struck him as a woman of endless courage, Gabe thought. She would have needed an indomitable spirit to raise her son with bombs raining down nightly and no idea whether her husband would survive to see the child he'd fathered.

"I can't even begin to imagine how families learned to carry on for weeks or months at a stretch with no idea if the people they loved were alive or dead," Gabe said.

"And as if six years of wartime uncertainty weren't bad enough, you have to remember that conditions didn't normalize in 1945 just because the fighting finally stopped," Jeffrey said. "All across Europe there were thousands of prisoners to be repatriated, millions of soldiers to be returned to civilian life, whole cities to be rebuilt that had been wiped off the map, factories to be converted from producing weapons to producing consumer products. There was such a profound sense of relief that the bombs had stopped falling and the guns weren't firing anymore that we tend to gloss over the fact that there was absolute chaos over most of Europe for at least another three years."

Nick looked thoughtful. "I hadn't considered that," he said. "Once Dirk decided to disappear, it would have been a lot easier to succeed in 1948 than it would be nowadays, especially with his international background."

"That's very true," Jeffrey agreed. "Virtually every country in Europe had missing records, and officials in countries that had been under Nazi rule often deliberately falsified their records. Not to mention all the confusion caused by people fleeing in front of the advancing

Soviet armies of occupation. Hundreds of thousands of people couldn't prove their citizenship, and the authorities more or less had to take their word as to who they were and where they'd come from. If Dirk went back to Europe, he could easily have claimed that his birth certificate was destroyed. With only a little finagling, he could have acquired a new passport and documentation in almost any name he pleased.''

"It's possible that he changed his name,'' Gabe conceded. ''But surely there's also the possibility that he disappeared because he died. Aren't you discounting that rather too casually?''

"He's almost certainly dead by now,'' Jeffrey said. ''Either that, or he's an old man well into his nineties. But my father and Uncle Henry were both convinced that he voluntarily chose to disappear in 1948. To his dying day, my father never expressed any doubt at all that Dirk was alive and well somewhere. He just didn't know where.''

"I've run some checks of my own,'' Nick Santos said. ''And I haven't turned up any evidence of foul play. Working with some old documents your father found at Kemberly, I managed to discover that Dirk maintained checking accounts with two banks in New York. Both accounts were closed within hours of each other on April 24, 1948, giving Dirk a combined payout of $2,700. Which was a lot more money in 1948 than it is today, of course. His bank account in London was closed a month later, on May 20. The last check drawn on his London account was for £1,352, payable through a corresponding bank branch in Hong Kong.''

"Hong Kong again!'' Gabe exclaimed. ''That's where Dirk's final letter came from, isn't it? And, Dad, didn't you just say he fought in the Far East during the war?'' Gabe's imagination took flight. ''Maybe he fell in love with a Chinese woman during the war and went back to marry her. God knows, it wouldn't have been easy to make an interracial marriage in those days, so perhaps he decided to cut his ties and live with her in peaceful obscurity."

"My father considered that possibility," Jeffrey said. "But if Dirk set up residence in Hong Kong, with or without a wife, he covered his tracks well. As I told you, Pinkerton's sent one of their Far Eastern specialists out there in 1949, and they couldn't turn up a trace of him."

"All this is very interesting," Gabe said. "But I can't imagine why we need to keep his disappearance a secret now, fifty years later. These days it would be considered a definite social plus if we announced that Uncle Dirk had had the courage of his convictions and defied cultural and racial prejudice for the sake of love. And I certainly don't see the connection between Uncle Dirk's disappearance and the fact that we have fifteen thousand pounds' worth of surveillance equipment downstairs guarding a fake tiara that's worth less than the equipment beaming down on it."

"There's a very direct connection," Nick Santos said grimly. "There seems to be a strong likelihood that Dirk DeWilde stole some of the family jewels before he fled to places unknown. Six pieces, in fact, including the Empress Eugénie tiara, the most famous and valuable piece in the entire collection."

Gabe whistled softly. "Good Lord, I should have realized. Of course! He gave up his share of the DeWilde inheritance and helped himself to the family jewels in exchange."

"Unfortunately, it's not quite that simple," Jeffrey said. "We don't know for certain if Dirk stole the missing jewels."

"What?" Gabe stared at his father in disbelief. "And nobody took steps to find out for sure?"

Jeffrey smiled. "It's incredible, isn't it? But fear of scandal seemed to override every other concern in those days, and finding out the truth would have been so messy, requiring people to open a lot of cupboard doors where there were very bony skeletons. Dirk had already been gone for almost three months when several pieces in the London collection were scheduled for a routine inspection and cleaning. In those days, the cleaning was done by an old family friend, an elderly jeweler who'd worked with my grandparents in Amsterdam and had emigrated to London just before the start of the Second World War. He came to my father with the stunning news that the tiara he'd been given for cleaning was a copy—a first-rate fake, superlatively well crafted, but a fake nonetheless. You can imagine the consternation that ensued. The jeweler was sworn to secrecy—he's dead now, of course—and my father personally made an inspection of every piece in the collection, including the items normally kept in New York and Paris. He discovered that there were five other pieces, in addition to the tiara, that were copies."

"There doesn't seem to be much of a mystery about what happened," Gabe said. "Doesn't it seem logical that Uncle Dirk decided to supplement his retirement benefits by helping himself to the family jewels?"

Jeffrey smiled wryly. "I don't know," he said. "My father estimated that during the three months between Dirk's disappearance and the discovery of the missing jewels, thirteen people had access to at least one of the missing pieces. Four people had access to all six of them— my father and his brother Henry in London, his sister, Marie-Claire du Plessis, in Paris, and his brother Dirk in New York."

"Even so, surely Dirk is the logical suspect," Gabe said. "Your father knew he hadn't stolen the jewels. There was no reason for Henry or Marie-Claire to steal them. Which leaves good old Uncle Dirk as the guilty party."

"You're leaping to conclusions," Nick said. "Your Uncle Henry enjoyed a very expensive life-style, and his income was tied directly to the profits of the store he ran. Which, as your father has pointed out, wasn't very profitable. He could obviously have benefited from the extra income the jewels provided."

"But Uncle Henry married money," Gabe objected. "Aunt Maura comes from the Connecticut Kellys, and her family has oodles of money. They aren't quite on a level with the Gettys or the Rockefellers, but Henry didn't need to steal jewelry in order to keep a private plane, drink French champagne every night and smoke Havana cigars after dinner."

"Henry didn't marry Maura until 1956, years after the thefts," Jeffrey said. "And my father always suspected that Henry knew more about Dirk's disappearance than he let on. In fact, I think my father was more suspicious of Henry than he was of Dirk."

"That would explain some of the hostility I always felt simmering between Grandfather and Uncle Henry even as a little kid," Gabe said. "And I certainly never understood why he was so hostile toward our cousins."

"Possibly it was because they are, by and large, as lazy and hedonistic as Henry himself," Jeffrey said austerely.

Gabe captured a gleam of laughter in Nick's dark eyes that vanished almost as soon as it came. He bit back a smile of his own. On the subject of hard work, knuckling down to business and treating life seriously, his father had a tendency to be somewhat pompous.

"It's also possible that two or more people were working together on the thefts," Nick pointed out. "There are four people who each had access to more than one of the missing pieces. By joining forces, it turns out that any combination of them could have stolen them all. And, surprisingly, your great-aunt Marie-Claire might have had a motive. She was once very much in love with a man called Armand de Villeneuve, who chose to leave Paris almost at the same time as Dirk disappeared from New York. As you may know, Armand de Villeneuve eventually turned up again as the founder of a very successful textile company in Hong Kong. And your father tells me that nobody knows where his start-up capital came from."

He did indeed know of Armand de Villeneuve, Gabe thought grimly. And Philippe de Villeneuve, Armand's son, who seemed to bear a determined grudge against the DeWilde family. "I think it's ridiculous to ignore all these links to Hong Kong and pretend they're just coincidences," he said. "But no matter who stole the missing jewels, I still don't understand why we have a fake tiara enshrined in bullet-proof glass downstairs, and why Nick just brought the genuine, long-lost Empress Eugénie tiara across the Atlantic from New York. What was it doing there? And, Dad, if you dare say 'I don't know' one more time, I think I may do you a mortal injury."

Jeffrey smiled, the first genuinely amused smile Gabe had seen in ten days. He felt a surge of relief. If puzzling over a fifty-year-old mystery could keep his father from obsessing about Grace, Gabe hoped the mystery would take another fifty years to solve. "I'll answer the first part of your question," Jeffrey said. "We have a fake tiara on display downstairs because your grandfather had no idea how he could announce that the real one had been stolen without immediately casting suspicion of theft on all three of his siblings."

"At least if he'd spoken up, there'd have been more chance of unearthing the real thief," Gabe said, unconvinced by his grandfather's rationale. "And there's a strong probability we wouldn't be scrambling around wondering what happened to Uncle Dirk fifty years after the fact."

"True, but there was another, more profound, reason for my father's reluctance to reveal the theft. All through the war, even during the height of the blitz, DeWilde's prided itself on keeping the Empress Eugénie tiara on display, just as it had been ever since the day the London store first opened. That gesture of defiance generated tremendous amounts of favorable publicity for the store. And what was more important, Londoners came to regard the tiara as a symbol of hope and beauty in a world that was singularly short of both. With those memories fresh in everyone's mind, can you imagine how upsetting it would have been if my father had announced in 1948 that he was sorry, but he'd just realized the tiara was a fake?"

"That might have been a reasonable decision in 1948," Gabe said. "But we've had almost half a century since then to break the sad news."

"Once my father initiated the deception, the whole embarrassing situation just snowballed," Jeffrey said. "I didn't hear the true story until fourteen years ago, when I became managing director. At that point, we were beginning negotiations to take the company public, and it certainly didn't seem appropriate to announce to the world that DeWilde senior management had practiced a thirty-four-year-old fraud on the general public. The fact is, Gabe, the longer the deception went on, the more impossible it became to rectify it. Hence the god-awful mess we found ourselves in when a jeweler called me from New York three weeks ago and said that, as far as he could tell, he'd just been offered the chance to buy the Empress Eugénie tiara.''

''Is that why you flew to New York with such urgency that you had to miss Mother's birthday?'' Gabe asked.

''Yes, and she thought that I was going to mee—'' Jeffrey broke off in midword, bleakness returning to his eyes. ''The jeweler agreed to keep our negotiations secret for forty-eight hours but no longer. I had no choice but to go.''

His mother had obviously been deeply hurt by Jeffrey's absence on her birthday. Gabe wondered why in the world his father hadn't simply explained the truth of the situation to Grace, but with Nick in the room he didn't like to ask such a personal question. ''You were able to confirm on that visit that it was the genuine Empress Eugénie tiara?'' he asked, hoping to bring his father's attention back to the mystery and away from Grace.

''Yes,'' Jeffrey said. ''We have the original descriptions of the major stones. We also have technically enhanced insurance photographs dating back to 1926, when your great-grandfather Max bought the tiara as an anniversary gift for his wife. There's no doubt that the tiara sitting on my desk is the tiara that Max bought from Eugénie's heirs.''

Gabe frowned. ''If the tiara has survived almost fifty years, then it seems as if whoever stole it didn't take it for the money, after all. Otherwise, surely it would have been broken up and sold years ago.''

''You would think so,'' Jeffrey agreed. ''Nick, you told me on the phone that you'd made some headway in discovering how the tiara ended up being offered for sale at Blackstone's in New York?''

"Yes, sir, and I think you're going to be surprised," Nick said. "Apparently the tiara was on prominent display in the window of a well-known Australian jewelry store, where it was spotted by a visiting American who'd just won six million dollars in the Florida state lottery. He bought it for his wife, who decided when she got back to the States that she didn't have all that many occasions to wear a diamond tiara and would rather have a yacht instead. Her husband sold it to Blackstone's Miami branch, where it was finally recognized as so nearly identical to the Empress Eugénie tiara, famously kept on display in DeWilde's London store, that Mr. Blackstone, Sr., called you to find out if he was dealing in stolen property."

"What did you tell him, Dad?"

"I told him very little," Jeffrey said dryly, "and Mr. Blackstone, a jeweler of infinite tact, was kind enough to ask only sufficient questions to make sure that he was not involved in a crime. Then he sold me back my own property, at a price that would have bought the English Crown Jewels in 1948. Now that I'd acquired the tiara, the next problem was what to do with it. I couldn't just pack it in my suitcase and bring it home with me. The damn fake we have on display downstairs precluded that option. How was I supposed to explain to Customs that I was bringing home a tiara that officially was already safely installed behind plate-glass security on the ground floor of De-Wilde's?"

"So you hired Nick."

"Yes." A trace of color momentarily darkened Jeffrey's cheeks. "As I told you earlier, he came very highly recommended."

"I'm a good friend of Allison Ames," Nick said. "We once worked together on a case that involved breaches of security at an American electronics company with a major telecommunications branch in France."

"Who is Allison Ames?" Gabe asked blankly.

"She owns the security firm of Alliance de Securité Internationale," Jeffrey said smoothly. Too smoothly, Gabe thought, scrutinizing his father with suddenly heightened intensity. Jeffrey was looking at Nick and seemed unaware of his son's searching gaze. Or was he deliberately avoiding Gabe's eyes? Some sixth sense told Gabe that he had stumbled onto a name that his father would have preferred to remain unmentioned.

Jeffrey turned to the detective, not giving Gabe a chance to ask any more questions. "Nick, you say the tiara was on prominent display in an Australian jewelry store with an international reputation. Now, that's a mystery in itself. I can't imagine how any jeweler of repute ever bought the tiara in the first place. I wouldn't have thought there was an experienced jeweler anywhere in the world who isn't familiar with the piece. What's the name of the store?"

"H. Morgenstern and Sons," Nick said. "I understand that Harry Morgenstern, the original founder of the store, is still active in the business despite the fact that he's in his eighties."

"Morgenstern...Harry Morgenstern..." Jeffrey stared unseeingly into the distance. "Hmm, that name's vaguely familiar, and Mr. Morgenstern's reputation used to be excellent, if I'm remembering the right man. We've even done business with his store, before Ryder opened a branch of DeWilde's in Sydney. Mr. Morgenstern emigrated from Germany to Australia in the thirties, getting his family to safety two steps ahead of the Nazi storm troopers. Have you managed to find out how he acquired the piece, Nick? If we knew that, we could decide whether or not to trust him with the information that five other pieces are still missing.''

''I can't get him to talk to me,'' Nick said. ''I've written, faxed and phoned. So far, although I've spoken to three different assistants, I've never yet managed to speak to Harry Morgenstern himself. In fact, I decided it would be much better if I went out to Sydney and dealt with him in person, if I have your permission to authorize the expense, Mr. DeWilde. That way, I'll be on the spot if he suggests any leads that need to be tracked down in a hurry.''

''Excellent idea. How soon can you go?''

''Tomorrow?'' Nick suggested ''Provided there's room on the London to Sydney flight, that is.''

''Ask Monica to book your ticket. She has friends at all the airline reservation desks. And she'll find you a quiet room in a comfortable hotel for tonight, too.''

''In the meantime, what are we going to do with the tiara?'' Gabe asked.

Jeffrey pointed to his wall safe, hidden rather obviously behind a portrait of Maximilien and Anne Marie DeWilde, the matriarch and patriarch who had founded the DeWilde family fortune in Amsterdam during the previous century. ''That's the safest place I can think of—at least without causing a great deal of speculation.''

Nick walked across the room and examined the safe. ''Any serious jewel thief would be able to crack this in less than five minutes,'' he said.

''But first the jewel thief would have to know there's something in there that's worth stealing,'' Jeffrey pointed out. ''Besides, I don't see that I have any alternative until

I can work out a plan for switching this tiara with the fake downstairs."

Nick grinned. "You should hire Allison Ames. She's a whiz at that sort of thing. Better than any cat burglar I've ever encountered."

"I'd prefer not to bring another outsider into this," Jeffrey said austerely. "Fortunately, I have access to all the security codes protecting the display case downstairs. It shouldn't be too difficult a task to switch tiaras one night soon. In the meantime, this safe will have to do." He closed the tiara into its carrying case and walked quickly over to the safe, putting the case inside and locking the safe door.

"There, it's done." He turned around, permitting himself a small smile. "That felt very good," he said. "After almost fifty years of wandering in the wilderness, Empress Eugénie's tiara is back where it belongs."

CHAPTER EIGHT

BY THE TIME she'd changed her outfit four times, Lianne was willing to concede that she wasn't behaving like a woman who planned to ignore her escort for the entire evening. Tossing aside her bra, she discarded the ivory stockings she'd worn with the last dress she'd tried on and wriggled into a pair of iridescent black panty hose. Scowling into the mirror, she stepped back into the plain black silk crepe sheath that was the first dress she'd put on thirty minutes ago. She zipped it closed before she could change her mind yet again.

She turned sideways and squinted at herself from the new angle. Now that she'd taken off her bra and panties, at least the lines of the darn dress were smooth, and the couple of pounds she'd lost over the past ten days had resulted in a satisfyingly flat stomach. But wasn't the dress too short and too lacking in glitter for a black-tie affair, even with the fancy stockings? And there seemed to be a heck of a lot of bare skin in the space between her chin and her breasts. Sighing—she knew that tonight, nothing was going to look quite perfect enough to meet her impossible standards—she sprayed herself with a light cloud of perfume and slipped into her high-heeled black evening shoes. This was it. She was not going to humiliate herself by changing yet again.

At least her hair, by some miracle, was deciding to cooperate. For once, the unruly mass of curls had allowed

itself to be tamed into a semblance of upswept sophisti-
cation, and she rather liked the effect of the few wisps that
had already tumbled down to coil haphazardly against her
neck. She clipped on a pair of outsize crystal earrings that
she'd designed and made herself. They were long enough
to touch her bare shoulders, and she decided not to wear
any other jewelry, not even a watch, so that their impact
would be all the more powerful.

She picked up her black evening purse from the bed and
walked into the sitting room. Julia was correcting student papers, and she looked up with a smile when Lianne
walked into the room. She gave a gasp of heartfelt approval. "Wow, Lianne, you're going to knock 'em dead.
That dress looks stunning." She grinned. "Of course, the
great body inside doesn't hurt the effect."

"Thank you." Lianne couldn't think of anything else
to say. If her date had been with anyone other than Gabriel DeWilde, she knew quite well that she and Julia
would have spent the past hour together, examining the
joint contents of their wardrobes, pooling the resources
of their cosmetic and jewelry drawers, laughing and joking as they made their final choices. She twisted her purse
awkwardly, with hands that weren't quite steady.

"Gabe's late," she said, then flushed as she always did
whenever she had to say his name to Julia. Her friend was
as sweet-tempered and pleasant to be around as ever, but
Lianne could never set aside her conviction that Julia was
suffering from the breakup a great deal more than she let
on.

"Traffic's horrible at this time of night," Julia said
with apparent tranquillity, putting down her pen and
pushing aside the pile of student essays. "Gabe's very
polite, so he wouldn't keep you waiting unless it was un-
avoidable."

Gabe certainly had elegant and sophisticated manners, Lianne thought, and perhaps with Julia his behavior had always been scrupulously polite. However, polite was about the last word she would have used to describe his attitude toward her. For about the thousandth time, Lianne wondered what in the world she was doing, pursuing a relationship with a man for whom she seemed to feel nothing but an urgent desire to tear off his clothes and tumble into the nearest bed. This from the woman who had always sworn that it was more important to like the men you dated than to lust after their bodies.

The buzz of the outer doorbell sounded loud in the silence of the sitting room. "That'll be Gabe," Julia said. "Shall I let him in?"

"Thanks. I'll get my coat."

When she came back from the bedroom, Gabe was already at their front door. He was talking softly to Julia, and Lianne didn't even try to hear what he was saying. But she couldn't help noticing the warmth in his eyes and the gentleness of the smile he was giving Julia. He took her hand and cradled it briefly within his clasp. Lianne's throat tightened with misery. Oh, God, if only Gabe would look at her like that just once, instead of with his usual heated mixture of passion and contempt.

She didn't say anything. As far as she knew, she made no sound. But Gabe sensed her presence, and his head jerked up, the tenderness in his gaze vanishing instantly. She'd never seen him in evening dress before, and the impact of his presence quite literally took her breath away.

For a second, the room was heavy with silence. Then he spoke. "I'm sorry I'm late," he said, his voice cool, the apology perfunctory. "Traffic's particularly grim tonight, so we'd better hurry."

She'd told him that she wasn't going to speak to him, and although she'd never intended to stick to such a ridiculous vow, his attitude didn't inspire her with any immediate desire to change that plan. She swept past him without another glance, only turning back to say goodbye to Julia.

"Enjoy the play, both of you." Julia smiled and waved cheerily. "David Weldon's supposed to be wonderful as Richard II. Hurry up now, or you're going to miss the opening curtain." She shut the door rather suddenly.

Lianne headed for the stairs, but Gabe stopped her. "Wait," he said. "Let me help you put your coat on. It's chilly out tonight."

Lianne stopped walking away, but she didn't answer or look at him. He took her coat and helped her put it on, his hands brushing with tantalizing softness across the nape of her neck as he adjusted the collar. He turned her around until she was facing him. His face was expressionless, his gaze agate hard. "You're beautiful," he said, his voice harsh. "So beautiful that when you came into the sitting room just now, it was as if somebody had slammed a fist straight into my gut."

Lianne started to shake. She felt the heat rise into her cheeks and she briefly closed her eyes. She didn't reply, not because of her stupid announcement that she'd only attend the play if she didn't have to speak to him, but for the simple reason that she couldn't find the breath to stumble through a coherent sentence.

Gabe sighed and brushed his thumb across her trembling lips. "I know. You're coming out with me under duress and you're not speaking to me." His eyes gleamed with sudden amusement. "Of course, a policy of stony silence does have its disadvantages from your point of view."

He bent his head and kissed her with ravaging thoroughness. When they broke apart, he was actually grinning. "That was delightful, thank you. I wonder how many more times I'll be able to kiss you tonight before you decide to break your vow of silence and tell me to go to hell?"

She stared at him, appalled and simultaneously fascinated by the idea that had just taken root in her pitiable, sex-starved brain. If she continued not to talk to him, would he continue to pursue her? She met his gaze head-on, then turned without saying another word and walked out to his waiting car.

THE PLAY HAD BEEN magnificent, the charity gala itself a smashing success. Mingling with the actors and guests of honor at the champagne reception following the performance, Gabe chatted up a dowager Dame of the British Empire and secretly watched Lianne. She had the sort of sparkling personality that made her the center of attention even when she wasn't doing anything more than standing around, looking ravishing. But tonight she wasn't just standing around. She was dazzling anyone who moved within her glittering orbit, tormenting him by engaging in witty, insightful conversation with every single member of their party except him. He'd been watching her most of the night, torn between longing and fury, which seemed to be pretty much his constant emotional state when she was anywhere near.

In many ways, Lianne had proved herself the perfect date, enthralled by the play and not at all intimidated by the high-powered gathering of guests in his father's box. She'd been charming to his father, knowing exactly where and how to draw the line between the social situation in which they found themselves tonight and the fact that tomorrow Jeffrey DeWilde would once again be the managing director of the company she worked for. During the two intermissions, she'd not only been charming, she'd been actively helpful, deflecting questions about Grace and—on at least one occasion that Gabe had witnessed—protecting Jeffrey from the curiosity of a wealthy donor with a great deal more money than tact.

She'd been equally charming to Megan, who'd flown over from Paris for the night to act as a stand-in for her mother. In fact, there was only one person who hadn't been the recipient of Lianne's bountiful dispensation of charm, and that was Gabe himself. He watched in a silence that was steaming rapidly toward the boil as one of his father's guests brought Lianne the glass of white wine she'd requested. She accepted it with a delightful smile and some teasing comment that set the guest, a prominent pediatrician not known for his good cheer, simultaneously chuckling and preening. The idiot was actually sucking in his stomach and smoothing his hair over his bald spot. Did she have to flirt so outrageously with every damn male in the entire theater? Gabe asked himself. Didn't she realize that the man had a wife and grandchildren, for God's sake? It seemed that she did, because within minutes she'd cleverly steered the doctor back to his wife and was talking animatedly to Megan. What could she possibly need to say to his sister that was so all-fired consuming that she had no time to spare him so much as a glance? Enough was enough, Gabe decided, glaring so fiercely at the dowager that she immediately doubled her promised donation.

He had just enough self-control left to thank the elderly Dame for her unexpected generosity and escape without giving offense.

With the expertise gained at a hundred charity balls and gala functions, he managed to make his way across the crowded room without getting waylaid again.

"Megan, I've barely managed to see you all evening," he said as he came up to his sister. Despite his best efforts, his gaze fixed hungrily on Lianne.

Megan gave him a faintly amused glance. "We did spend most of Saturday together, Gabe."

"But I'm sure you still have a lot to say to each other," Lianne interjected smoothly. "Twins are supposed to be inseparable, aren't they?" She smiled at Megan with genuine warmth. "I've so much enjoyed meeting you," she said. "If I may, I'd like to take you up on your offer of a tour of the Paris store next month. I'm hoping that my designs will be at the point that production can take over sometime within the next three weeks."

"I'll look forward to seeing you," Megan said. "I know several wonderful places to have lunch, a little bit off the beaten tourist track. By the way, have I mentioned how impressed I was by the preview you sent me of your designs for the *Lianne for DeWilde* collection?"

"You have now. Thank you." Lianne's smile was strictly for Megan. "Excuse me, please," she murmured, studiously avoiding Gabe's fulminating gaze. She slipped away to talk to the actor who'd played the role of Henry Bolingbroke—a handsome newcomer who looked a damned sight too interested in Lianne's cleavage, as far as Gabe was concerned.

Megan's hazel eyes were brimming with laughter. "Gabe, my pet, I think it might be a really good idea if you stopped staring at her as if you were a drowning man and she was the last lifeboat in the entire ocean."

"She?" he demanded, dragging his attention back to Megan with excruciating difficulty. "Who?"

"The same woman you've been glaring at all night long," Megan said, laughing outright this time. "The same woman who has been doing one of the most splendid jobs of driving a man crazy that I've seen in a long time."

He muttered something unrepeatable. Megan laid her hand consolingly on his arm. "Gabe, you're my twin, and I love you, so I'll betray the sisterhood and let you in on a secret. Lianne couldn't possibly have managed to avoid you so consistently all night long unless she'd been watching you as closely as you've been watching her."

He brightened, then sank back into gloom. "There's no reason for her to watch me except that she's determined to avoid me. She despises me."

Megan bit her lip to keep back the laughter. "I'm not totally convinced that you've assessed her feelings with complete accuracy, Gabe. I hate to betray yet another secret of the sisterhood, but I doubt Lianne chose that outfit because she wanted to make an impact on the chairman of the British Medical Society."

"What do you mean?"

"You can trust my judgment on this, brother dear. Lianne isn't wearing anything but skin under that dress."

"She's not wearing anything?" Gabe said, his voice hoarse.

Megan shook her head. "Nothing. Unless you count panty hose."

Gabe swallowed hard, fighting the urge to run to Lianne's side and throw his jacket over her shoulders before the idiot who was staring down her dress came to the same interesting conclusion as his sister. He started to storm across the foyer, but Megan restrained him.

"If you talk to her now, Gabe, one or the other of you is going to explode. Wait until you're somewhere more private before you confront her with how you feel."

"I don't know how I feel," he muttered, embarrassed when he realized that he sounded as immature and petulant as he felt. "I just know I can't stand to be around her, and it's worse when we're apart."

"I'm sure a few hours in bed together would help to clarify the situation for both of you." Once again, Megan sounded amused. "If you'd like to hear the opinion of a mere bystander, I'd say that both of you are in a near-terminal state of mutual lust. Get that out of the way and the pair of you might—just possibly—discover what else you have going as a couple."

Gabe glowered at her. "When did you get to be so damn smart?"

Megan sighed. "Where other people's feelings are concerned? Years ago. As far as my own feelings go, I still haven't a clue."

"That bastard Whitney really did a number on you, didn't he, Meg."

"I wish I could blame everything on my late, unlamented fiancé, but a lot of this is coming from me and has nothing to do with him. At this point, I'm not sure that I even want to get seriously involved with another man, ever again. Work can be just as all-consuming as a love affair, and the results are usually a heck of a lot more tangible and rewarding."

Gabe would have answered except that he noticed his father had crossed the room to speak to Lianne. The damn-fool idiot actor who'd been peering down her dress looked disappointed. Good. Whatever Lianne said to his father set both men to laughing. Seeing Jeffrey look reasonably relaxed, Gabe was almost willing to forgive

Lianne for her sins, which, to be fair, amounted chiefly to driving him crazy because she was too attractive to be ignored.

"Dad's asked me to stay over tomorrow until lunchtime," Megan said, interrupting Gabe's train of thought. "He says he has something important to discuss with me, family business that affects the company." She paused, her voice darkening with concern. "Is it about Mother, do you know?"

"No, I don't think so. I expect it's about the DeWilde jewelry collection."

"The jewels?" Megan sounded surprised. "Oh, Lord, I do hope Dad doesn't want to organize another one of those international exhibitions. The insurance company drives me insane with the precautions they force me to take whenever those darn jewels are moved out of the store."

"No, I don't think he's planning anything like that. Not for the moment, at least. But he should be the person to tell you what's going on. It's a long story and this isn't the place." Gabe frowned as a memory from the session with his father and Nick Santos tugged at his mind. "Meg, on a slightly different subject, have you ever heard of a security firm called Alliance de Sécurité Internationale?"

She thought for a moment. "No, I don't believe so. From the name it sounds as if they're headquartered in France. Why? Is Dad thinking of hiring them?"

"Not as far as I know, although the name came up because Dad's hired a private investigator who was recommended to him by the president of Alliance. Or at least I think that may be why he hired this particular man. Alliance itself is a small outfit, from what I gathered. The president, or the owner, is a woman called Allison Ames."

Megan suddenly went very still. "She's about our age? Blond, slim, striking dark blue eyes? Very athletic?"

Gabe turned and looked at his twin. "I don't know. To the best of my knowledge, I've never set eyes on the woman. Her name came up in conversation this morning."

"With Dad?"

"Sort of. Indirectly." Gabe glanced across at his father, who was still talking to Lianne. "Dad looked—uncomfortable—when her name was mentioned, as if he wished Nick Santos hadn't mentioned the connection."

Megan didn't answer for several moments. "No, I don't know her," she said finally.

Gabe shot her a quizzical look. "So who's the blond, blue-eyed woman you thought she might be?"

"I was confused," Megan said. "She's nobody."

Gabe might have pursued that slightly ridiculous answer further, but after an entire evening during which Lianne had kept herself permanently surrounded by people, she was finally alone. He hurriedly kissed his sister's cheek. "Gotta dash, Meg, love. Call me next time you're coming to town. Stay at my flat and we'll do one of our night-on-the-town specials."

"Sounds great. We haven't done that in ages, and we used to have fun, didn't we. You have a date, Gabe." Megan pulled him back as he started to walk away. "Since you're my favorite brother, here's a word of wisdom in your ear. Count to ten before you say anything to Lianne, okay?"

"I'm your only brother. But trust me, I'm going to be the soul of tact." Gabe strode purposefully across the room.

GABE WAS COMING, striding across the damned foyer as if he owned it. Having ignored her for the entire evening, he thought he could now claim her like a suitcase abandoned in Left Luggage. God, he had to be the best-looking, most magnetic man in the entire room, not excluding the actors.

Lianne drew herself away from the column she'd been leaning against and he stopped in front of her, glaring through the lock of light brown hair that had fallen forward into his eyes. "Are you wearing anything at all underneath that damn dress?" he demanded.

She spoke her first words of the night to him. "Go to hell, Gabe."

"I'm already there," he said tautly.

"Enjoy the fires." She turned and walked away, genuinely wanting to escape from him, and wanting equally for him to follow her. She closed her eyes and clutched the stair rail, aware of dizzying elation surging through her when she heard his footsteps follow in her wake. She'd spent the entire night trying to provoke him into precisely this mood of outraged male sexual aggression, but now that she'd achieved her goal she wondered if she was going to be able to handle the results of her success.

Silence, thick and dark with anticipation, blanketed them again as they walked downstairs. Her anticipation as well as his, Lianne admitted to herself. He retrieved her coat from the cloakroom attendant and tipped a parking valet to retrieve his car. He drew her into the shadows of the sheltered portico to await the arrival of his Jag and pulled her roughly into his arms, his mouth ravishing hers, his body pressed impossibly close.

"Lianne, come home with me." He murmured the words against her mouth, the stark statement more an order than a request.

The fiasco of their Sunday date was still painfully clear in her memory. Doubts returned, crowding in, cooling the fever of longing. Could she trust him enough to open herself to the possibility of yet another rejection? Worse yet, if they ended up in bed together, was she ready to cope with the emotional consequences of having sex with a man who didn't seem to like her? What if they indulged in another night of passionate lovemaking and he simply walked away from her as he had done once before? She was ready to admit that what she felt for him was more— much more—than simple sexual attraction. Gabe didn't seem ready to admit any such thing.

Everything in her that was rational said that she should protect herself and insist on being driven straight home. But when she looked up at Gabe, the yearning she saw in his normally controlled features made her heart skip a beat. Without speaking, he lowered his head just enough to close the tiny gap between their mouths. He kissed her again, this time with such aching, desperate hunger that her answer gradually became inevitable. With a sense of reaching a foregone conclusion, she surrendered—not to his passion, but to her own. She gave a small, incoherent murmur of assent, then clasped her hands behind his neck, holding his mouth tight against her own, returning his kiss with all the fierce longing she'd been struggling to suppress for the past several days.

They were both breathing hard when they broke apart. Lianne had consumed no more than two glasses of wine, but her surroundings refused to stay in focus. The parking attendant drove up, and she stumbled to the car in Gabe's wake, already so aroused that she barely registered their journey through the deserted streets of the City and into the West End. He parked the car right in front of his block of flats, beneath a large sign that warned this was a tow-away zone. She knew this ought to be cause for concern, but she couldn't concentrate long enough to remember why.

They blundered into the lift and he slammed her against the wall, ripping off his tie with one hand while he shoved her velvet evening coat open with the other. He caught her chin, tilting her head back, his face stark with the fierce concentration of sexual desire. His mouth came down on hers, hot and demanding, the thrust of his tongue almost savage. She locked her arms around him and felt his erection pulse against her belly. Her heart started to pound at twice its normal speed. Her nipples peaked, and the aching sensation in her womb made her knees go weak. She clung to him, the rock-hard solidity of his muscles the only firm points in a world that seemed ready to dissolve into a misty gray cloud.

A rush of air and the sound of doors gliding open made her blink. Before she could fully register the fact that the lift had arrived at the fifth floor, Gabe had swept her into his arms and carried her to the door of his flat. He put her down while he searched for his key, then picked her up again without saying a word, walking through the door and slamming it shut behind him with his foot.

Her coat and his jacket were shed somewhere in the hallway. Their shoes got lost at the entrance to his bedroom. Already his skillful hands were unfastening the zipper of her dress, caressing her skin, seeking her breasts. Without asking, he carried her to the bed, dropping her onto the mattress and following her straight down onto the pillows. He pushed aside the straps of her dress, shoving the top down below her waist so that her breasts sprang free.

His breath caught on a harsh sigh, and he set his mouth over her nipples, suckling and caressing her with a craving so intense that waves of answering need immediately surged through her. She wanted to touch him, she wanted to be naked beneath him, to hold him naked in her arms, but her hands couldn't move fast enough to satisfy the urgency she felt. Her fingers grappled with the onyx studs that closed his evening shirt, desire making her clumsy.

"Here, let me." Gabe tore at his shirt, ripping out the studs. Stripped to the waist, he braced himself over her, his eyes glittering, his face taut with sexual arousal. "I want to bury myself so deep inside you that you can't feel anything in the world but me." His voice was harsh with passion, dark with need.

"I want you, too," she said.

"Do you?" His mouth twisted into a self-mocking smile. "Do you know what wanting means, I wonder? I didn't hear a single word of the play tonight," he said. "I spent the entire evening trying to decide if you were really wearing as little underneath that damned dress of yours as it seemed."

"Now you know," Lianne murmured.

"Yes, now I know."

In a flash, Gabe had dispensed with their remaining clothes. Lianne's breath hissed out as he lowered the weight of his body onto her. Passion exploded deep inside her, a wild burst of energy that ate up reason and caution. There was only now: this moment, this man, and this all-consuming mutual need. Lianne locked her arms around him, her fingers tangling in his hair, her mouth opening beneath his. She writhed against him, the sensations he aroused so powerful that she wasn't sure whether she felt her pleasure or his, her need or his. His kisses were hot, fierce, elemental. Her body vibrated against his, ready for his possession even before his hand reached down and parted her thighs.

His touch was almost more than she could bear. Lianne moaned softly. Her skin felt unbearably sensitive, too fragile to survive the intensity of her pleasure. The drumroll of her heartbeat pounded in her ears, and she clutched his shoulders, needing to anchor herself against the buffeting storm. A pulse throbbed deep in her womb, beating to a rhythm she had felt only once before in her life, the night Gabe first made love to her.

Desire and need were building so quickly, spiraling together, demanding to be appeased. When it finally came, Gabe's penetration of her body was an exquisite relief. Lianne felt herself falling, tumbling headlong toward a climax that was utterly out of her control. Her entire body tensed, then imploded, and she crashed down into the blissful darkness of release.

GABE LAY WAKEFUL, watching the first pale fingers of dawn thread through the blackness of the night sky. Beside him, Lianne slept, exhausted from their hours of lovemaking. He turned onto his side so that he could see her. She slept with the same restless intensity that she did everything else, her hair tumbling over the pillow, one arm flung out, the other curved in toward her waist.

He let his fingers comb through the long, chestnut richness of her hair. A couple of her curls wrapped around his fingers and clung fast. Instead of shaking his hand free, he tightened his fingers around the soft strands, gripping them in his fist. He closed his eyes, shaken by the intensity of the feelings that rocked him. Before he could stop himself, he'd bent down and buried his face in the mass of curls spread out on the pillow.

Unbelievably, he felt desire stir within him. Despite all their hours of sex, there was an ache deep inside him that hadn't been assuaged. Lianne stirred, still sleeping, and the sheet slipped down to her waist. Unable to resist, he reached out and laid his hand over her breast. She made a tiny snuffling sound and rolled onto her side toward him, trapping his hand beneath her breast. The ache inside him intensified. He wanted to hold her close. He wanted to ravish her, protect her, care for her. He wasn't sure that he ever wanted to wake up again without finding her lying beside him.

And that thought scared the living hell out of him.

Very gently, he brushed his thumb across her nipple. She woke up, just as he'd known she would, her flesh sensitized to his touch. Her eyes flickered, drowsy with sleep, sated with sex. Sated with him. She took one look at his expression and her eyes widened, darkening to an impossibly vibrant blue in the feeble predawn light. She recognized what he wanted—needed—and she gave a sleepy groan.

"Gabe, you can't be serious!"

He said nothing. He wasn't at all sure he was capable of speaking without saying something he knew he'd live to regret. For answer, he grasped her wrists and held her hands over her head, leaving her entire body vulnerable to his gaze. And to his touch. Swiftly, silently, he lowered his head to her breasts.

The desperate, pounding urgency of their first coupling was gone, but Gabe felt impelled by a need that was both more subtle and more profound than anything he'd felt earlier in the night. He made love to her with all the expertise at his command, exploiting everything he'd learned during the previous few hours about giving her pleasure, summoning all his skill to take her to a pinnacle she'd never known before. When she climaxed, he held her shuddering body in his arms and poured himself into her, the intensity of his own release so violent that he collapsed for a few seconds on top of her, unable to move.

When he could think again, he realized the ache was still there, throbbing deep inside him, waiting to be soothed.

Lianne stroked her hands very gently down his spine, holding him to her, not protesting the burden of his weight. "I love you, Gabe," she said softly. "I thought maybe you should know that."

Her words were like arrows, winging their way straight to the ache inside him, piercing the wound, lodging inside the pain, intensifying it a hundred times over.

He stared down at her, silenced by the enormity of his vulnerability. Lianne touched her hand to his face in a caress that scraped across the rawness of the wound she'd inflicted. "It's all right, Gabe, you don't have to look so stricken. You're not required to say anything in return, you know."

He finally found his voice. "I don't know what love means," he said. "All I know is that I want you more than I've ever wanted any other woman."

Even as he spoke, he knew that he wasn't telling the truth. He did know what love meant—it was what he felt for Lianne.

And the thought that he loved her scared him half to death.

CHAPTER NINE

FOR SEVEN DAYS IN A ROW, the clouds and mist that so often veiled San Francisco had been burned away by the heat of the late spring sun. Grace stood at the magnificent picture window of her newly rented luxury apartment and wished stubbornly for rain. The sun seemed a cruel mockery of her mood, a taunting, in-your-face declaration that summer was fast approaching and life was busy renewing itself after the winter hibernation.

Except that she was still stuck in the depths of emotional winter. Her life had been shattered with no possibility of renewal, her grief so profound that some days it required almost superhuman effort to drag herself out of bed and into her clothes. She'd made it a little test for herself, to get dressed every day, put on makeup, do her hair in its usual neat style and go out somewhere. She forced herself to run some errand, no matter how meaningless, no matter how much she resented the intrusion of the outside world into her protective cocoon of grief.

Realizing that she was in danger of sinking into a state of clinical depression, she'd deliberately rented an unfurnished apartment just so that she'd be compelled to buy furniture and household goods. Which had been a good idea in theory, she thought, glancing ruefully around her almost bare living room, except that her sense of taste and style hadn't vanished along with her energy. Since she couldn't make herself buy something unless it really appealed to her, her total furnishings so far amounted to a bed, an antique dressing table and the sofa in the room where she was standing, plus such bare necessities as telephones and a few items for the kitchen.

Grace wandered aimlessly to the sofa, picked up one of the cushions and plumped it vigorously. Pillow clutched in her arms, she stared unseeingly at the spectacular view. Even now, when she'd taken the final step of putting more than five thousand miles between her and Jeffrey, she still couldn't quite accept the reality of their separation. It didn't seem possible that only last Christmas—five short months ago—they'd been content and happy. Ecstatically happy.

No, naively happy, Grace thought. We always got along so well together that we had no mechanisms in place for resolving problems. At the first major test, our marriage fell apart.

Most people who got divorced after years and years of marriage wouldn't be able to identify the precise set of circumstances that had caused the breakup. Usually it was some combination of too many rows, the boredom of overfamiliarity, the grating irritation of intimacy without love. But Grace could pinpoint the exact moment when her marriage began to self-destruct. It had been on New Year's Day, at two o'clock in the morning, when she and Jeffrey returned from a New Year's Eve party that they'd both found tedious in the extreme.

Jeffrey had yawned as he tugged off his black tie, returning it with his usual meticulous care to the special niche in his tallboy where it belonged. He slipped the studs out of his starched shirt, dropped them into their custom-designed walnut box, and fiddled with the heavy gold cuff links that had once belonged to his grandfather.

"Here, let me help you." Grace slid off the bed, where she'd been lying fully clothed, too sleepy and, perhaps, a tiny bit too full of champagne to get undressed. Jeffrey obligingly stuck out his wrist and she wrestled with the recalcitrant cuff link, which point blank refused to slide out through the designated slit in his shirt cuff.

She swore with unladylike vehemence, and Jeffrey grinned, tipping up her chin and dropping a kiss on the end of her nose. "Gracie, my love, you're drunk."

Nobody except Jeffrey was ever allowed to call her Gracie, but when he said it, her heart always gave a tiny little leap of love. "I am not drunk," she said, enunciating with care, mortally offended by the suggestion. "The hole in this sleeve is too small for the cuff links, that's all."

He chuckled. "If you say so. I wouldn't blame you if you were drunk, anyway. That was a hideous party, wasn't it?"

"Mmm." She gave up on removing his cuff link and decided to take off his shirt instead. When his top half was satisfactorily naked, she rested her cheek against his chest, sighing contentedly and letting his shirt dangle from her hand. "New Year's Eve parties always strike me as rather sad."

"Why is that, my love?"

"You know, a frantic attempt to pretend that time and fate aren't both marching on, dragging us with them, willy-nilly."

"Very profound," he said, absentmindedly stroking her hair. "However, I doubt if most of the guests tonight were devoting much energy to philosophical reflections on the meaning of life. They were simply trying rather too hard to have a good time and making themselves ridiculous in the process."

Grace was getting tired of holding Jeffrey's shirt. She tossed it vaguely in the direction of the bathroom and the laundry hamper, despite the fact that his cuff links were still attached to the sleeves. Jeffrey winced but didn't say anything.

She smiled to herself at the silent wince and ran her hands approvingly over his chest. "Did I ever tell you that you have just the right amount of hair on your chest, Jeffrey?"

He grinned. "No, I don't believe you ever did."

"Chest hair is very important in a man," she said with the earnestness of the mildly drunk. "I can't bear those men who look like gorillas, but I think male models who shave it all off look even sillier, don't you?"

"I can't say I've ever devoted a great deal of thought to the subject," Jeffrey said, retrieving his cuff links from the discarded shirt and tucking them into their box. "But I'm flattered that my chest hair meets with your approval, since I know your taste is impeccable."

He took off his trousers and hung them neatly over the clothes valet, despite the fact that the next day they would be going to the cleaners. No woman should be required to live with such a guy, Grace thought. She deserved a place in heaven for tolerating his persnickety ways. Lord, he was impossible! And she loved him just about to distraction.

Desire curled softly through her veins, as familiar and welcome as a favorite pair of slippers. She turned her back to Jeffrey, dipping her head forward, holding her hair up with her arm. "Would you undo me?" she said. "I can't reach the zipper."

A gleam appeared in Jeffrey's hazel eyes. He slid the zipper slowly downward, and her dress fell in a pool at her feet, revealing the interesting fact that at fifty-plus, she could still manage to wear a strapless evening gown without a bra underneath. Standing behind her, he bent his head and pressed a kiss to the nape of her neck, his arms coming around her to cup her breasts. "God in heaven, Gracie, but you're so beautiful I only have to look at you and I want to make love."

That was certainly great to hear. She twisted in his arms, smiling. "I guess we're allowed. Since we're married an' all."

His eyes darkened, and he slanted his mouth across hers with an urgency that was both gratifying and arousing. She kicked off her shoes and walked with him to the bed, their kisses becoming rapidly more impassioned. They tumbled onto the bed, their bodies adjusting instantly to the rhythms they'd made their own. Jeffrey made love to her with satisfying fervor, but also with a caring and tenderness that had become vitally important to her over the years. She supposed that one day the heat of their lovemaking would have to cool, but when they were lying together, locked in each other's arms, it seemed impossible to imagine a life that wasn't sweetened by the pleasures of their passionate sexual relationship.

Afterward, they didn't fall immediately asleep as they often did. Jeffrey stretched out his arm, and she lay nestled against his shoulder, blissfully and utterly happy. Perhaps because it was the first day of a new year, he seemed in a reminiscent mood. "Do you ever regret that we didn't have more children?" he asked, running his forefinger over the faint scar of her hysterectomy.

"I think it bothered me more when I was younger." She smiled into the darkness, her hand resting over his. To her, the scar was a reminder of the ups and downs they'd shared together, and come through safely. The growth in her uterus—barely caught in time—had been one of the very definite downs, the fears and the pain of the surgery made easier to bear by Jeffrey's unwavering love. "Now I just want grandchildren, lots of them, as soon as possible."

"It would be nice, wouldn't it? To see another generation coming into the world. And I'm sure all three of our children will make spectacular babies."

She laughed. "No bias in that remark, of course. Why did you suddenly ask me about having more children? Are you wishing we'd had another baby? If you are, my darling Jeffrey, you can't possibly be remembering what hell it was when they were teenagers."

"Trust me, I can remember every excruciating moment. No, for some reason, it just flashed into my mind that when we got married, you informed me you wanted at least six children."

"I said a lot of incredibly stupid things in those days, Jeffrey. Fortunately, I got smarter as I grew older." She laughed again, yawning as she felt sleep creep up on her again. "I guess there have to be some compensations for the pangs and aches of encroaching middle age."

"You're not middle-aged. The rest of us are getting there, perhaps, but not you." He rolled onto his side, gazing down at her, his expression so warm and tender that she felt an absurd impulse to cry. Jeffrey was such a reserved man. Grace cherished the knowledge that only with her did he ever manage to let down the incredible barriers of his self-control and just be himself. Even with the children, much as he loved them, he was rarely totally relaxed. He had never managed to give himself permission to let them see his flaws and his weaknesses, as well as his strengths.

He took her hand and carried it to his lips. "I love you, Gracie. I love you more than I ever dreamed it would be possible to love someone."

"I love you, too." She cupped his face between her hands, drawing his head down and kissing him softly. She found herself wondering why fate had been so kind to her, and so cruel to other, far more deserving people. "I can't believe how much I've grown to love you, Jeffrey."

For a second, she felt him tense. Then he relaxed and smiled. "Now, if I were an overly sensitive sort of fellow, I'd be getting worried. I might even think you sounded a bit surprised to realize you actually loved me."

She laughed. "Well, I wouldn't go that far." After thirty-two years of marriage, it seemed safe to confess the truth—a gift of honesty to show her husband how foolish she'd been when she was younger, and how deeply she cared for him now. "The truth is, Jeffrey, I didn't love you nearly as much as I should have done when we got married."

His hand stilled, resting on the curve of her thigh. "Well, I can understand that. You were incredibly young, years younger than Katie is now. All our emotions are fairly hormonal at that stage in our lives."

"No, that wasn't it." Suddenly it seemed important to make him understand the truth. "Looking back on it, I can barely recognize myself in the self-absorbed young woman I was in those days. I married you for all the wrong reasons, Jeffrey, and I don't deserve the good fortune that made everything turn out so wonderfully right."

"Why, exactly, did you marry me, Grace?"

She must have been more tipsy than she'd realized. In retrospect, that was the only reason Grace could come up with for her total and complete failure to hear the betraying chill that had edged Jeffrey's question.

"I married you because you were Jeffrey DeWilde," she said. "The most eligible bachelor in London and the catch of the season." She chuckled suggestively. "You

were also, of course, absolutely fabulous in bed. I'm sure
that must have had something to do with my instant decision not to let you wriggle away from me."

"And I'm sure the fact that I had money didn't hurt."

She heard the cynicism in his words. Fool that she was,
she'd interpreted it as cynicism that mocked the young,
twenty-year-old Grace, not cynicism that mocked her, his
wife, the woman who now loved him with every fibre of
her being.

"It sure didn't," she admitted, sharing his disdain for
the thoughtless, shallow woman she'd been. "To be honest, it was simply wonderful to find myself part of a family that actually had the funds to live up to their public
image."

"In contrast to your own, no doubt."

With destructive honesty, she agreed with him. "Absolutely. My brother's done such a fantastic job of re-
storing the Powell family fortunes that it's hard to
remember what it was like for us when we were growing
up. The Powell family name was a force to reckon with in
San Francisco society. The problem was, my parents
scarcely had two cents to rub together." She shuddered.
"I loathed all the scrimping and saving and getting into
debt, just so that we could turn up at the right functions,
with the right people, wearing the right clothes."

Grace had never wished her parents were richer. She
had simply wished they would drop out of the social circle
they could no longer afford. She assumed that Jeffrey
would understand. After all, he'd lived with her for thirty-
two years. He couldn't help but know that maintaining
her social position was slightly less important to her than
the color of underwear Scotsmen wore under their kilts.

"I can see that I must have been the ideal prospective
husband," Jeffrey said. "Rich, socially acceptable, and

so incredibly stupid that I didn't realize I was being married for my position and my money.''

Too late, Grace finally registered the appalling truth that Jeffrey hadn't really understood a word she'd been saying. Or at least, he might have understood the individual words, but he'd totally failed to grasp the meaning or significance of what she'd been trying to explain. Horrified at the misunderstanding, Grace had hurried to correct his mistaken impressions. Jeffrey had been polite and listened attentively. After an hour of frantic attempts to clarify everything she'd said, Grace realized that he was still mired in his original misconception. Jeffrey had heard that Grace married him for money and position. The thirty-two subsequent years of learning to love him—with a love that was deeper and more enduring than she could ever have imagined—counted for nothing. The more subtle truth, that even as a young woman she'd been looking for security rather than wealth and social acceptance, totally escaped him.

In the weeks that followed, Grace realized she'd dealt her marriage a mortal wound. But in the end it was Jeffrey who delivered the final blow.

The phone rang and she ran to grab it from its temporary perch on a built-in shelf. It might be Jeffrey calling to say... To say what? That the past three months were a hideous mistake? That he still loved her? Surely to God she was past that stage of wishful thinking and willful self-delusion. Grace wrapped her arms around her waist, tucking her hands against her body, forcibly keeping them away from the receiver.

The answering machine clicked in. ''Mother, this is Megan. I'm sorry to have missed you—''

''Hello, Meg.'' Grace picked up the phone, rather proud of the steadiness with which she managed to speak.

She gave a passable imitation of a carefree laugh. "I was rather busy, so I was hiding out behind the machine. You know how that is."

"I hope I didn't interrupt something important. I just called to chat." Megan sounded wary, unnaturally polite. All three of her children had sounded that way since she and Jeffrey split up, as if she'd suddenly turned into a person they didn't know and weren't sure how to handle. Except Gabe, who seemed to have decided that he'd handle the problem by not speaking to her at all.

She'd really messed up with those farewell letters, Grace thought, and Jeffrey, of course, had only made the situation worse by instructing the family solicitor to inform the children of her departure in yet another letter.

She should have stayed in London long enough to call Gabe, although God knows what she could have said to explain the inexplicable. Still, with the wonderfully clarifying vision of hindsight, she realized she should have phoned and made up some sort of a story, a rationale that justified her behavior without exposing her to the shattering humiliation of her children's pity. But at the time, it hadn't seemed to matter much whether she called Gabe from London or waited until later, when she hoped to be feeling calmer and marginally less wounded.

And, in truth, she hadn't been prepared for the swiftness of the final break with Jeffrey, despite the months of mounting anguish. After a week of stony, tension-filled silence, the prospect of spending another night in his bed had come to seem unbearable. She was worn out with too many nights of waiting and wondering if he would come home, dreading where he might have been and what he might have done during all those long hours of separation. Her fears, her heartache and her rage had all mingled in one giant explosion, and after their final hideous confrontation, she could think of nothing except escape. The need to find some bolt hole where she could run and nurse her wounds in private had overwhelmed any other considerations.

"Mother, are you still there? Shall I call back? I must be interrupting something important."

"No, you're not interrupting at all. I'm delighted you called." Having claimed to be hiding out behind the answering machine in order to work, Grace tried to think up some plausible task she might have been engaged in. What could she pretend to have been doing? "I was just working on a tentative floor plan for my new store, but I'd much rather talk to you." She injected a note of cheer into her voice, hoping Meg wouldn't notice its brittleness.

"Oh, Lord, Mother, I was hoping you'd forget about that idea of opening a store," Megan said. "I realize you have far too much creative energy to sit at home doing nothing, but are you sure you want to go ahead with this particular plan? You know how many problems we're having with DeWilde's in New York right now, and Dad and Gabe are both angry—"

"These days Jeffrey always seems to be furious about something," Grace said, not quite managing to filter the bitterness from her voice. "I may as well give him a genuine cause for complaint. Not that I can see any reason why a bridal store here in San Francisco would have the slightest impact on DeWilde's Fifth Avenue store, except in Jeffrey's overfertile imagination. Brides in France may travel to Paris to shop for their trousseaux and their wedding gowns, and the same for English brides traveling to London, but American women shop for their wedding gowns in their hometowns. My store here in San Francisco is going to open up a new market, not siphon off DeWilde's existing customers."

As Grace spoke, the idea of opening her own store, which had been nothing more than a weapon to use against Jeffrey, a wild caprice thrown out without any coherent plan or serious thought behind it, suddenly began to take shape. A tiny knot of excitement uncurled in the pit of her stomach as she contemplated the possibility of days crammed with enough activity and decision-making to fill the bleak emptiness of her life. She could take all those exciting ideas that the DeWilde board of directors had refused to approve and use them as the foundation for a store that would bear the exclusive stamp of her own personality. And by golly, she'd make it a success. Jeffrey might think that she was old and undesirable, but she'd show him she still had what it took to make a store zing.

"Dad's never going to accept that you're opening a store for any reason except to annoy him and undercut DeWilde's." Megan sounded subdued. "Mother, honestly, if you could see him . . . He's terribly unhappy, sort of all withdrawn into himself—"

"I really have no interest in hearing about your father's moods and behavior," Grace said, closing her eyes to shut out the tormenting images that Meg's words evoked. "To be brutally frank, I don't give a damn whether Jeffrey approves of my plans or not. We're separated. I'm planning to file for a divorce shortly."

That was true, wasn't it? How could she claim to want out of her marriage if she took no legal steps to end it?

She drew in a deep, calming breath. "Any business activities I choose to engage in are strictly my own concern, Meg. Surely you can understand that."

Megan's voice tensed. "We were all hoping that you and Dad might work things out—"

Grace had finally reached the point where she refused to allow herself to hope. She'd spent the past few months hoping, and after a certain point, the burden of optimism had become too heavy to bear. "There is absolutely no chance of a reconciliation," she said.

"But, Mother, why not? What happened? None of us understands what's going on. You and Dad always seemed so happy—"

"I don't want to talk about it." Grace heard her voice crack with ignominious despair. "Please, Meg," she whispered. "Don't ask me any more questions."

"No, of course not. Mother, I'm sorry, I didn't mean to upset you. Oh, heavens, Mom, are you crying?"

"No," Grace lied. "You know I only cry when I'm happy, or hopping mad about something. Look, let's not talk about my plans anymore. Let's talk about you. Have you done anything exciting lately?"

Meg gave a short laugh. "Gosh, Mom, I've been working too hard to have a social life. Let's see, I flew across to London to attend the gala benefit for the children's hospital on Thursday, and that's about as close as I've come this month to an exciting date."

"I'm glad you went. Was the gala a success?"

"A smash hit. The reviews for the play were wonderful, and we raised a lot of money for the hospital."

"That's terrific news. Did we reach our..." She stopped and rephrased the question. "Do you know if the targets the fund-raising committee set were reached? The goals I proposed—that the committee proposed—were rather ambitious."

"We exceeded the targets by a comfortable margin. The hospital's chief of staff was walking around the foyer afterward wearing a smile of dazed gratification. Everyone said the arrangements were wonderful. You received lots of compliments in your absence." Meg's voice softened. "You were missed, Mom, and not just by the members of your fund-raising committee."

Grace suppressed a pang of regret that she hadn't been there to see the culmination of several months' hard work, and to enjoy a gala night of celebration in the company of the twins she was so proud of. But she couldn't allow herself to get emotional over every loss from her old life or she would, quite literally, go mad. "I'm glad it was a success," she said. "Did you meet anyone interesting? There must have been dozens of eligible men around."

Megan gave an exaggerated sigh. "I take it that's one of your usual veiled requests for information about the state of my love life?"

Grace perked up. "How in the world did you guess?" she asked teasingly. "I thought I was being so subtle!"

"Sure you were. Like an oversized sledgehammer."

Grace actually laughed. "Okay, I'll give up on subtle and simply beg for information. I admit that I keep hoping to hear you've met some wonderful man who's worthy of you. Not just for your sake, although you're the sort of woman who would make a great wife, but for selfish reasons, too."

"I know, Mom, you're itching to plan my wedding. But I have to warn you that after my experience with Edward, I'm not exactly a prime candidate for another full-scale DeWilde wedding with all the trimmings."

"Planning your wedding would be fun, but that's not the only reason I wish you'd get married." Grace leaned against the back of the sofa. She kicked off her shoes and tucked her toes under one of the cushions, relishing a pleasant and unexpected feeling of relaxation. "I'm becoming selfish as I get older. Your father and I have reached the stage in our lives where we're flat-out jealous of all our friends who are grandparents. We want some grandbabies of our own to spoil."

As soon as the words were out of her mouth, Grace was appalled. Her subconscious mind had tricked her, linking her with Jeffrey again as if they were still a couple. It seemed that the moment she relaxed and dropped her guard, a new trap appeared on the path ahead, ready to spring closed and inflict fresh pain.

Megan would normally have rushed to point out that your parents' wish for grandchildren to cuddle was not one of the smartest reasons for embarking on the hazardous seas of matrimony. But she must have realized that Grace's reference to Jeffrey was an unwelcome slip of the tongue, because she tactfully glossed over the entire subject and went back to talking about the gala.

"Gabe came to the theater with a smashing new woman in tow," she said. "Leggy, gorgeous, hair to die for and a bundle of energy. Every man in the place watched her with his tongue hanging out. Come to think of it, you must know her, because you're the one who hired her for DeWilde's. Lianne Beecham. You remember her, I'm sure."

"Of course. So Gabe came with Lianne, did he?" Grace gave a brief chuckle. "Heavens, I wish I could have seen them together. I must say that when I was interviewing Lianne, the thought crossed my mind that she was exactly the sort of woman who was calculated to drive Gabe to distraction one way or another."

"You were right." Laughter colored Megan's voice. "At the moment, I'd say she's driving him to distraction just about every which way."

"I called Gabe a couple of times this week," Grace said. "I haven't heard back. I think he's decided not to return my calls."

"Oh, dear. I'm afraid he's really angry with you," Megan said after a tiny pause.

Grace had been so caught up in her own misery since she came to San Francisco that she was only just beginning to summon up enough objectivity to step back and analyze the situation from her son's point of view. "We always worked so closely together that I guess he's feeling hurt because I chose not to confide in him. He'll come around eventually when he realizes how difficult it is for parents to discuss their marriage with their children."

She spoke with more optimism than she felt. Divorce didn't just end a marriage, as she'd seen over and over again with her friends. Unfortunately, the fallout tended to be toxic and had an unpleasant habit of destroying the relationships of everyone touched by it. She prayed that her excellent rapport with her children would survive the ending of her marriage unscathed.

"I'm sure he will," Megan agreed. "He's a sensible person, so eventually he'll realize he's behaving like a total ass. There was one other thing, Mother." Meg had always been hopeless at deception. Her attempt to sound casual was so transparently forced that Grace knew immediately that her daughter was about to broach the real point of her phone call.

"What's that, honey?" Grace asked, playing along.

"We've had a couple of minor security problems here at the Paris store, and I have a suspicion that someone in middle management has sticky fingers."

"Oh, Lord, that's always such an unpleasant problem to deal with."

"Yes, it is. We need to hire an outside consultant to make recommendations for improvements to our security systems, and also to catch the thief, of course. Someone recommended a small company called Alliance de

Securité Internationale. The owner's a woman called Allison Ames, and I believe she did some work for the London store a few months ago. I wondered if you had any opinion about her and her company. The project I need her to work on is very sensitive, for obvious reasons. As you can imagine, we don't want to accuse an employee unless we're absolutely certain he or she is guilty."

Grace gripped the phone so hard that her fingers hurt. "Have you discussed this company with your father?" she asked, amazed to discover that her voice still functioned.

"Yes. He says that he has no professional knowledge of Allison Ames or the company. He reminded me he was in Australia, working with Ryder, when she completed her work with DeWilde's in London. He says he never met her."

Grace stared straight ahead, seeing nothing beyond the scarlet curtain of rage that had fallen in front of her eyes. She fought to keep control over her voice so that she wouldn't humiliate herself in front of her daughter. When love had vanished, pride and self-respect were all you had left. She was tired of weeping, Grace realized. Tired of mourning. Tired of regretting her mistakes. She didn't want pity from anyone. She wanted revenge.

"I'm not the person to ask," she said, astonished by the seeming tranquillity of her voice. "As merchandising VP for DeWilde's, my concerns were limited to questions of stock and display. If your father remembers nothing about Allison Ames..." Somehow she said the name without choking. "If your father has no comment, then the person to question would probably be Freddie Trevelyan. He's directly responsible for security in the London store and must have been responsible for hiring Ms. Ames's company."

"I'll talk to Freddie, then." Megan sounded uncertain.

"Personally, I'm a believer in using one of the large consulting firms," Grace said. "Nowadays, as you know, security is mostly a question of high-tech electronic systems, and I think the larger firms tend to have experts with a broader range of experience. But Ms. Ames may be an outstanding exception to the rule, of course. I wouldn't know."

Grace forced herself to exchange a few more pleasantries with her daughter before saying goodbye and hanging up the phone. She wasn't sure who was deceiving whom. Meg's story about needing to hire a security consultant might be true, but it wasn't the reason that she'd mentioned Allison Ames and Alliance de Securité to her mother. Grace would bet on it. Megan was merchandising manager for the Paris store, and she was no more involved in the routine administration of security matters than Grace had been.

The mere sound of Allison's name was enough to propel Grace into a state of full-blown fury. After spending most of her waking hours for the past two weeks staring listlessly into space, she was seized by a rage that felt almost refreshing in contrast to the debilitating inertia that had held her captive ever since she'd arrived in San Francisco.

Damn Jeffrey's lying soul to hell, she thought, pacing from kitchen to living room and back again. How dare he claim that he'd never met Allison Ames? The fact that the man she'd lived and slept with for thirty-two years had the capacity to indulge in such all-encompassing deceit made her question the very foundation of trust on which her life had once rested with such seeming security.

Grace paced from the living room to the bedroom to the room that would one day be a cozy den and through to the kitchen. The spacious apartment suddenly seemed too small to contain her fury. She stormed back into her bedroom, threw herself in the middle of the bed and reached for the phone. Of course it wasn't there, because she didn't have nightstands. Damn it, tomorrow she was going to buy nightstands. Somewhere in a city the size of San Francisco there had to be a pair of nightstands she could learn to live with. She hung over the edge of the bed and retrieved the phone from the floor, dialing the number of their London flat before she could wimp out and change her mind.

The answering machine clicked in. "This is Jeffrey DeWilde. I'm unavailable to answer the phone at the moment, but leave a message and I shall return your call at the earliest opportunity."

She knew he was there, could sense his presence at the other end of the line as clearly as if he were speaking to her. "Jeffrey, pick up the phone," she said. "Damn it, Jeffrey, do it—*now*."

"Grace, I'm here."

She closed her eyes when she heard the cool familiarity of his voice. The usual wave of pain started to wash over her, but she refused to surrender to it. "Are you alone?" she asked.

His voice chilled. "Yes, I'm alone. Do you care?"

"No." She willed her answer to be true. "What I do care about is my relationship with my children. I have no intention of allowing you to turn me into an object of derision in front of them, which seems to be your current intention."

"I've no idea what you're talking about, Grace."

"Then I'll spell it out for you, Jeffrey. I've just had a long phone conversation with Megan, and next time you're trying to scrounge work for your mistress, don't send her anywhere she's going to come into contact with my children. I won't have your sleazy little whore worming her way into my family. There, is that clear enough for you?" She brushed away her tears with the heel of her hand, determined not to let him hear a single sob. She was so sick of being torn apart by the intensity of her feelings while Jeffrey retreated deeper and deeper into dignified reserve.

"Allison isn't a whore—" Jeffrey stopped abruptly, but she'd heard the burst of protective anger in his voice, and it damn near killed her to accept that Allison Ames could rouse his emotions from their perpetual deep freeze, but she couldn't.

"This conversation is inappropriate and ridiculous," Jeffrey said, all trace of his anger suppressed.

Why not? Grace fumed. He was talking to his wife again. It was only mention of his mistress that had the power to inflame him.

"I gather from your wild outburst that someone at DeWilde's Paris has considered the possibility of hiring Alliance de Securité for a security check," he went on. "I assure you that I had no knowledge of such a proposal and certainly did nothing to promote or encourage it in any way."

"You're such a soul of rectitude, aren't you, Jeffrey. I wonder why I find it so damned hard to believe your protestations of innocence."

"Unless you have something useful to say, Grace, I have many other demands on my time at the moment and I need to curtail our conversation." With faint but discernible irony, he added, "You'll appreciate that I'm somewhat short-staffed at the office at the moment."

"I'm surprised you haven't hired a replacement for me already."

"I'm currently reviewing several interesting résumés."

"With Allison Ames to warm your bed and a new merchandising VP for DeWilde's, you'll be cozily squared away, won't you, Jeffrey?"

"What do you expect?" Surprisingly, she'd provoked him into another flash of temper. "I can't just sit around and worry about the fact that you chose to leave me and abandon your responsibilities to DeWilde's. Although you apparently find the concepts of loyalty and obligation difficult to understand, I have a responsibility to my shareholders and to the many fine people who work for DeWilde's."

"Oh, I understand perfectly, Jeffrey. How could I not? With my new store that I'm planning to open, I'm already knee-deep in obligations."

"What does that mean, precisely?"

She hadn't the faintest idea. She'd simply been engaged in another of their totally stupid sessions of parry and thrust, wound and retreat. "Which part of my statement didn't you understand, Jeffrey? I'm planning to open a new store here in San Francisco, you know that. Naturally, that requires me to enter into various legal contracts and negotiations."

"You can't possibly open a store," Jeffrey said. "How in the world are you going to get financial backing for such a major venture?"

"I thought I'd try a bank," she said sarcastically. "I'm quite sure that my brother will be able to give me some helpful introductions." Since her brother, Leland Powell, was the president and CEO of a corporation with vast holdings in real estate and several retail enterprises, the suggestion was credible.

Jeffrey gave a scornful laugh. "I think your brother has far too much business acumen to assist in finding loans for a venture that's bound to fail. You don't have the financial knowledge or the overall management skills to successfully launch a major new store. You have no way to raise the necessary capital, Grace."

It was the scorn in his voice that did it. "Of course I can raise capital," she said. "And if need be, I can provide the start-up capital myself."

"Impossible—"

"Not at all impossible," she said. "I plan to sell my stock in the DeWilde Corporation."

She had no idea what she'd been going to say until the words were actually spoken. The silence that greeted her statement stretched interminably, but she didn't question for a moment that Jeffrey was still on the other end of the transatlantic line.

Hah! she thought gleefully. She'd finally come up with a threat that pierced through the steel armor he'd wrapped himself in.

"The family's shares in the DeWilde Corporation are held in an irrevocable living trust," he said finally.

"The family's shares are in a trust," she agreed. "But mine aren't. Remember, your father was so thrilled when we got married that he made me a wedding present of what now amounts to five percent of the total stock in DeWilde's. For tax reasons, my shares were never included in the trust. I plan to sell them, Jeffrey, and use the money to start my own store here in San Francisco."

She had barely given the shares a thought since the day she received them from Charles DeWilde—until now. Suddenly, she realized that she wasn't joking, that she wasn't bluffing, and that she had the power within her grasp to exert some small measure of control over her life again. It was a heady, intoxicating sensation. "I plan to instruct my stockbroker to place my shares on the market ten days from now," she said with a coolness that almost matched her husband's. "If you would care to suggest an alternative source of capital for the down payment on my new store, please feel free to contact me. Anytime."

"You can't be serious!" In normal circumstances, the icy rage in Jeffrey's voice would have been terrifying. Today, lingering rage over his unfaithfulness with Allison Ames protected Grace from hurt.

"Is this some form of blackmail?" Jeffrey exclaimed. "Are you suggesting that I should bribe you with God knows what to prevent you from selling several million pounds' worth of DeWilde stock? You know that if you place your block of shares on the market, you'll exert an enormous downward pressure on the share price for DeWilde's."

Good. He was worried. She smiled. "That's exactly what I'm suggesting, Jeffrey. I'm sure it's a very worrying prospect for you."

He started to expostulate.

Grace hung up the phone.

CHAPTER TEN

THESE DAYS, when he thought about Allison Ames, Jeffrey couldn't quite remember what she looked like. He knew that she was blond and blue-eyed, and that she had a slender, trim body, but if he'd been asked to pick her out of a police line-up of women with similar coloring and features, he had a terrible suspicion he wouldn't be able to do it. Even in his current state of mingled fury and maudlin self-pity, it struck him as beyond ironic that he'd destroyed his marriage by having an affair with a young woman whom he would now find difficult to recognize.

He'd met Allison during one of his frequent business trips to Paris, a couple of months after Grace's humiliating admission that she'd married him not because she loved him but because she valued his name, his money and his position. Jeffrey supposed that some other men might have been able to handle such a confession with casual aplomb. He had been shattered. As far as he was concerned, Grace had undercut the very foundations of their relationship and rocked him to the center of his being.

Having spent the first five years of his life wondering why his father never came home, even though his mother insisted that he was well and safe, Jeffrey had grown up with a deeply rooted suspicion that he might not be worthy of love. The war hadn't been over long before he'd been old enough to recognize that his father's absence had been a matter of necessity, not of choice, and that his mother's daily claims that "Daddy" was alive and safe had been prayers, not statements of fact. Even so, there was a part of him that never overcame his early childhood fears.

By the time he finished university and acquired a reputation as one of Oxford's most eligible bachelors, his dazzling success with women had in some ways simply underscored his insecurity. He was smart enough, and perceptive enough, to notice that women were attracted to the DeWilde name and fortune almost as much as they were attracted to Jeffrey, the man. Being a mere human with no aspirations to sainthood, he took advantage of the offers of sex and guarded his emotions with fierce intensity.

Grace had seemed the glorious exception to the general rule. He'd met her while he was doing graduate work at the London School of Economics and she'd enrolled for a semester at King's, one of the other London University colleges. He fell head over heels in love at first sight, captivated by her bubbling energy, her artistic talents, the ease with which she made friends. In short, by all the things she was that he so markedly wasn't. After they made love for the first time, he knew that he would never want to marry any other woman. He took her home to Kemberly to meet his parents, and they were as captivated by her as he was. He proposed, on his knees, in the rose garden at Kemberly. Grace had accepted his great-grandmother's engagement ring, a sapphire surrounded by diamonds, with tears in her eyes and a kiss so tender he could still feel it in his dreams.

Fool that he was, he had never doubted that he and Grace were both making a love match from the day he proposed until the moment when he lay in his bed, with Grace in his arms, and listened to her say that she had married him because he was Jeffrey DeWilde, the rich and eligible bachelor.

Ever since that night, he'd been having difficulty sleeping. He always stayed at the Hotel Bristol when he was in Paris, and the staff there had become accustomed to his frequent late-night excursions. The night Allison came into his life, they simply nodded to him and murmured polite greetings when he came downstairs at one in the morning wearing sweat pants, a ski parka and sneakers.

He'd left the hotel, intending to take a brisk stroll through the nearby streets, hoping to exhaust himself physically so that sleep became inevitable. He'd barely reached the intersection with Rue de la Paix when he saw a woman, dressed much as he was, running toward him at a spanking pace.

What a crazy hour to be out jogging, he thought, watching her with detached admiration, enjoying the athletic fluidity of her movements. Gabe and Megan had both run on their university track teams, so Jeffrey was accustomed to estimating running speeds on sight. He calculated this woman was doing close to a seven-minute mile, which was almost competitive standard for some of the longer distance runs.

She was less than twenty yards away, her stride relaxed and easy, when a car turned out of the side street at cross angles to her, its headlights on full power.

Jeffrey could see her with perfect clarity in the beam of the car lights, but she was momentarily blinded. She blinked and lost her stride at precisely the same moment that a cat shot out of a side alley where it had been rummaging among the dustbins. Allison and the cat both met in midstride. The cat escaped unharmed, definitely using up one of its nine lives. Allison lost her balance and sprawled full-length on the pavement.

Jeffrey was at her side in seconds. She was cursing eloquently and creatively in American-accented English. He was surprised to discover she was American. She'd looked so at home, he'd assumed she was French. Besides, there was a certain indefinable Parisian chic to her appearance, even in a jogging suit.

Relieved that she hadn't been knocked unconscious, he introduced himself and offered his help. She insisted she wasn't badly hurt, but he could tell from the way she was rubbing her ankle that she'd given herself at least a mild sprain. She was covered in mud and grit, sneezing because she was violently allergic to cat hair, and annoyed that she wasn't going to complete her eight-kilometer run in thirty minutes, as she'd intended.

Jeffrey prided himself on his physical fitness, but he sighed a bit when he thought of the youthful energy involved in planning to run six miles in half an hour. He should introduce her to Gabe, he thought. They could run marathons together, and his son would probably enjoy the uninhibited vigor with which she expressed herself.

When she finally hauled herself to her feet with Jeffrey's help, she told him that her name was Allison Ames. She explained that she lived in Monte Carlo, but she was staying for the week with friends who had an apartment about four miles away.

"Come back to my hotel and we'll ask the concierge to call you a cab," Jeffrey suggested. "You can't walk to your friends' apartment with a sprained ankle." Unable to restrain his paternal impulses, he gave her a mild scolding. "You're fortunate something much worse didn't happen to you than a sprained ankle. It isn't safe for a young woman to be out running alone at this hour of night, not even in this part of Paris."

She smiled. Looking back, Jeffrey remembered that she had a lovely smile, and the perfectly straight teeth that only expensive American orthodontics could produce.

"It isn't safe for a young woman to accept invitations back to a man's hotel, either," she said, sounding amused rather than alarmed.

Horrified, Jeffrey had dropped the supportive arm he'd automatically placed around her waist. He quickly stepped back two paces. "My dear young lady, I assure you I had not the slightest intention of suggesting anything even remotely improper." As always when he was nervous or upset, his vocabulary became slightly old-fashioned, his way of speaking stilted and much too formal.

She flashed him another one of her nice smiles, her voice warm and self-confident. "Oh, well, in that case, I'm delighted to accept your offer of help. Thanks."

He was relieved that she didn't seem to be the sort of woman to read sexual harassment into the most innocent of actions, but he didn't risk holding her around her waist again. He extended his arm, offering help but not forcing it on her. Allison leaned her weight on his arm, and they'd stumbled along together. It wasn't far to the hotel—that was why he'd suggested taking her there—but they couldn't walk very fast because of her injury. To avoid an awkward silence, he'd explained that he lived in London but he often came to Paris on business. To reassure her that his intentions were strictly honorable, he also mentioned that he was married and had three children, two of them twins who were probably as old as she was.

Allison hadn't said much, no doubt because she was in more physical discomfort than she was willing to admit. Jeffrey admired the stoicism with which she endured the painful walk back to the Hotel Bristol. He also admired the fluent French in which she explained her predicament to the concierge once they got there. Guillaume had been all concern and insisted on showing *mademoiselle* to the ladies' powder room so that she could refresh herself before embarking on the cab ride home.

When Allison emerged from the ladies' room, Jeffrey was surprised to see how attractive she was once she was spruced up. She'd brushed her shoulder-length blond hair and washed the dirt from her face, revealing the fact that she had rosy cheeks and an absolutely perfect complexion. He also noticed that her eyes were a vivid blue, rather like Grace's. At the memory of his wife, he'd felt his mouth tighten and his smile fade. Thinking about Grace was as natural to him as drawing breath, but he resented the constant intrusion now that he knew the truth about her feelings toward him.

With one of the Gallic flourishes he reserved for favored customers, Guillaume had crossed the lobby to announce that the cab he'd summoned was now at *mademoiselle*'s disposal. Allison had thanked him in her perfectly accented French. Then she'd shaken Jeffrey's hand, thanking him, too. He'd been flattered by the obvious admiration in her gaze, the admiration of a woman for a man she found desirable. As she entered the cab, he realized that she'd probably come out without any money, and he borrowed two hundred francs from the concierge, giving it to Allison and refusing to take no for an answer.

"You don't want to wake up your friends," he said when she protested that there was no need for him to be so generous. "It's almost two o'clock in the morning. Please, I insist that you take it. Make a donation to your favorite charity if you feel you must pay me back."

Afterward, he wondered if it had been that casual gift of two hundred francs that triggered everything that followed. Would Allison have called the next day and invited him to dinner if she hadn't felt indebted to him for the loan of her cab fare? Would he have been smart enough to refuse her invitation if he hadn't been able to pretend that Allison was offering nothing more than an innocent thank-you for the loan of what amounted to less than twenty pounds?

He'd agreed to meet her at La Lune Ascendant in Montmartre, and had told himself that he shouldn't apply the standards of the sixties to behavior in the nineties. Asking him to dinner was no more than a courtesy, as far as Allison was concerned. After all, he reminded himself, she was younger than Gabe and Megan and undoubtedly saw him as a decrepit father-figure. He shouldn't read sexual overtones into a situation where none existed.

Looking back from the ruins of his broken marriage, Jeffrey admitted that if the two hundred francs hadn't provided him with an excuse to accept Allison's invitation, something else would have done. The fact was, he'd been ripe for an affair. His marriage had become a wasteland. His ego was bruised and aching. His sex life, once an incredibly beautiful part of his relationship with Grace, was now nonexistent. For the first two months of the new year, he and Grace had barely made love at all, even though a part of him desired her as much as ever. The final humiliation had come a couple of weeks before his encounter with Allison, when he'd tried to make love to Grace and hadn't been able to. "Temporary" impotence was not something that a fifty-five-year-old man could take lightly, because there was always the dreadful fear that "temporary" might soon slide into permanent. He added his inability to perform sexually to the long list of sins he was attributing to Grace.

Allison had made him feel young, potent and desirable. She'd also made him feel guilty as hell, even though he assumed that she was a young woman who was in the habit of enjoying multiple casual affairs. After two months of stolen weekends in Paris and midweek encounters in various discreet London hotels, he'd realized that she wasn't at all in the habit of having casual affairs, especially not with a married man. Appalled, he'd taken immediate steps to end their relationship. Which was when he'd made the even more shocking discovery that Allison wasn't sleeping with him because she enjoyed illicit sex with older men but because she thought she was falling in love with him.

It was odd, Jeffrey reflected, that a major part of Allison's appeal had been his assumption that she didn't care very much about him—the exact opposite of what he wanted from his relationship with Grace. About the only redeeming feature of his behavior during the entire affair had been that he'd broken off all contact with Allison the instant he realized her feelings were deeply involved. He'd even gone to considerable lengths to convince her that he was the sort of heartless, philandering bastard who didn't deserve a single moment of her regret.

The last, bitter irony of the whole situation was that Grace had discovered the name of his mistress and the details of where they'd been meeting on the very weekend that he ended the affair. She had been furious at his betrayal, whirling through their apartment, throwing things, crying.

Jeffrey, of course, had been his usual inarticulate self, incapable of explaining to her how he'd stepped onto the slippery slope that led to his unfaithfulness. The louder Grace had stormed and yelled, the further he'd retreated into stony, uncommunicative silence—until the fatal mo-

ment when his control broke completely and he told her
that he never wanted to see her again.

Which had led to the cosmically absurd circumstance
that in the very week when he broke off all contact with
Allison Ames and planned to grovel at Grace's feet, beg-
ging for her forgiveness, his wife had walked out and left
him. At his behest.

The gods, Jeffrey imagined, must definitely be laughing.

THE MEETING HE'D CALLED with his top managers that
morning had been surprisingly productive, Jeffrey con-
cluded, poking his head around the door of Monica's office to let her know that he was going out for a quick
lunch.

Ten days had come and gone, and so far his stockbroker was reporting that there was no sign of any large block
of DeWilde shares coming onto the market. Jeffrey wasn't
as reassured by this news as he might have been. These
days, he couldn't judge Grace's motives and plans any
better than a rank outsider. At best, he was afraid that her
decision not to sell her shares simply meant that she had
no immediate need for capital. At worst, he feared that
she was deliberately tormenting him, dangling the ever-
present possibility of their sale in front of him as a constant reminder of the power she retained to hurt both him
and DeWilde's.

He wasn't imagining Grace's feelings of enmity toward
him. A San Francisco attorney had recently sent him a
three-page letter, very brisk, very blunt and very American, outlining the terms of the no-muss, no-fuss Nevada
divorce Grace was prepared to offer him. Jeffrey hadn't
shown the letter to Ramsbotham yet, he'd been too embarrassed, but he hadn't needed a solicitor in order to in-

terpret the terms of the letter. Grace, it seemed, was willing to leave him with Kemberly and his shirt, possibly a pair of socks or two. Everything else, including the London flat, was to be hers.

In some ways, though, the letter had been a blessing in disguise. He could finally stop pretending to himself that tomorrow Gracie would come home. Energized by the knowledge that she was gone and DeWilde's was vulnerable, he'd steeled himself to expose the sorry state of his failed marriage to senior management and had told them bluntly that Grace was likely to use her block of company shares as a weapon in their divorce negotiations, or even as collateral to raise capital to finance her plans for a new store.

Gabe had been furious to learn of his mother's plans. If Jeffrey had wanted to find some tactic to alienate his son from Grace, he realized he could hardly have devised a better one. But, thankfully, his bitterness toward Grace hadn't yet corroded his sense of common decency to the point that he wanted to poison her relationship with their children. Grace had always been, and still was, a loving and wonderful mother. It pained Jeffrey that Gabe had decided to be so partisan, to place the blame for the breakup so totally and completely in Grace's lap.

The rest of management had, of course, taken the news less personally. They'd been surprisingly swift to come up with creative ideas to shore up the strengths of DeWilde's and to mitigate the effects that dumping such a large block of shares might have on the ability of the company to raise its own necessary investment capital.

Monica was already making arrangements for a conference call with Sloan DeWilde in New York and Ryder Blake in Sydney so that Jeffrey could update them on the situation and get their feedback on some of the ideas proposed at this morning's meeting. All in all, Jeffrey thought, this had been about the most productive day he'd had since Grace left him. Now that he'd finally accepted the sad truth that he wasn't going to wake up and discover Grace sleeping peacefully beside him, he had to stop wallowing in self-pity and get on with his job—which was the running of the DeWilde empire.

A surge of energy jolted through him, and he realized he had no desire to sit in a crowded restaurant and bolt down a meal when he wasn't hungry. It was another lovely spring day, after a week of showers and gray skies, so he decided to stroll along Bond Street and check the window displays of some DeWilde competitors before returning to the pile of paperwork waiting on his desk.

He was halfway through the arcade when he noticed a woman staring into the window of Asprey's, one of London's oldest and most prestigious jewelry stores. He recognized the rich chestnut color of Lianne's hair before he consciously registered who it was viewing the window display with such total absorption. Since the night Lianne had attended the play with his son, Jeffrey had been more aware of her presence in the office and had come to enjoy the occasional brief exchange of pleasantries with her. She was one of those sunny, extroverted people who almost always seemed to have something cheerful or interesting to say.

She was examining the display in Asprey's windows with the same vibrant intensity that she seemed to bring to every aspect of her life. It was almost, Jeffrey thought, as if she looked with her whole body and not just with her eyes. She was oblivious to passers-by, and it would have been quite easy to walk past her unnoticed. Jeffrey surprised himself by crossing over and standing next to her.

"What are you admiring?" he asked, without any other greeting. "The swan brooch? It's splendid workmanship, isn't it?"

"Not the brooch," she said absently, so caught up in what she was doing that she accepted his presence next to her almost as if they'd arranged to meet. "Look at the design of that emerald and diamond necklace at the side there. Now imagine that magnified about three times and twined around tiny silk orchids. Wouldn't that make a perfect bridal headpiece for a woman who's in her thirties and who's trying to find something romantic to wear for her wedding that doesn't look as if it was designed with an eighteen-year-old debutante in mind?"

He looked at the necklace, which years of training enabled him to say was of high quality workmanship and pleasing design. His imagination was definitely not up to the task of visualizing the stones magnified, reproduced in crystal and wound around silk flowers. "I haven't the faintest idea," he said, amused by his own inadequacy. "I'm afraid my creative talent is invisible even under the most powerful of microscopes."

She turned around and finally noticed—really noticed—who he was. "Mr. DeWilde!" She smiled at him as if she were genuinely pleased to see him. "I'm sorry. I wasn't paying attention, except peripherally. I have a hole in my collection where I ought to have two spectacular designs for older first-time brides, and I'm becoming marginally obsessive about what I'm going to do to fill the gap."

Jeffrey returned her smile. He suspected Lianne was the sort of woman whose smiles were always returned. He deliberately pushed away the thought of Grace, the only other woman he'd known with the capacity to make everywhere seem brighter just because she was there. He cleared his throat. "Delighted as I am to see one of my employees slaving away during her lunch hour, could I tempt you away from visions of bridal headgear and ask you to drink a cappuccino with me? There's an excellent coffee bar not five minutes' walk from here."

"I'm a coffee-holic, so I would love that. Thank you." Like Grace, she managed to sound enthusiastic without gushing.

"Did you enjoy the production of *Richard II?*" he asked as they fell into step together. "I thought they put on a pretty fair show myself. Outstanding direction from Sir Tony."

"Yes, I enjoyed it very much. I love Shakespeare's historical plays. Better than the tragedies, to be honest."

"Why is that? Do you know?"

Her forehead wrinkled. "I think it's because the histories are action-oriented, which suits me perfectly. I'm not good at dealing with hesitancy and indecision, which is what the tragedies all hinge on. Midway through Hamlet's umpteenth soliloquy wondering what he should do next, I'm sorely tempted to yell out that he should stop contemplating his navel and get a life."

Jeffrey laughed. "You have a point, but if that's the case, I wouldn't have thought that Richard II would appeal to you. He isn't exactly a model of decisive action."

"Oh, I don't know. I don't mind suffering with people who have real problems. Richard strikes me as noble and worthy, betrayed on all sides by men who are too thick-skulled and insensitive to see the pitfalls ahead of them. Henry Bolingbroke had tunnel vision. So he just charged forward and, of course, rode successfully over the pitfalls because he didn't even know they were there. And then his side won, darn it."

"It was probably better for England that they did. Henry made a good king."

"And Richard wasn't brutal enough to take charge of all those squabbling nobles, was he?" She looked momentarily saddened, totally caught up in the lives of people who'd been dead for approximately six hundred years. "There's absolutely nobody like Shakespeare for reminding you that life is frequently unjust."

"And invariably messy," Jeffrey agreed, opening the door to the coffee bar. "We're here," he added.

Lianne stopped on the way in to sniff a tub of violets on a street vendor's stall. "I love spring in London," she said as they sat at a table by the window. "On a day like today, I suffer from the very best sort of amnesia and totally forget how much I loathed all those dreary wet weeks in February and March."

"London's pleasant at this time of year, but the country is even lovelier. I'm going down to Kemberly this weekend, why don't you come and join me? I'm not a gardener, but even I can tell that the gardens are spectacular just now. I'll ask Gabe if he can drive you."

As soon as he issued the invitation, Jeffrey questioned whether he'd taken leave of his senses. Go to Kemberly this weekend? Where had that idea sprung from? Only a short while ago he'd been convinced that he would never be able to visit Kemberly again, that the reminders of Grace's absence would be too unbearably painful.

He wondered at what point he'd realized that the pain he felt was buried within his own psyche and would go with him everywhere. Which meant that a weekend at Kemberly was going to be no more—and no less—painful than a weekend spent anywhere else.

But quite apart from his own ambivalence, he wasn't at all sure why he was choosing to interfere in Gabe's per-

sonal life. After twenty-five years of rigorously refusing
to get involved in his children's love affairs, a policy which
had started when Gabe attempted to show his devotion to
a nursery school playmate by constantly taking her cray-
ons, this hardly seemed the appropriate moment for him
to be playing the role of matchmaker. Lord knew, he was
the last man in the world to pretend that he understood
what made two people into suitable mates for each other.
Just because Gabe had been stalking the hallways of
DeWilde's corporate offices like a bear awoken too early
from hibernation and unable to find food didn't mean
that Jeffrey had any reason to intervene. If Gabe wanted
to get together with Lianne, presumably he was more than
capable of making his own arrangements.

Their coffees arrived and Lianne stirred the milk froth
on hers with far more concentration than the task required. Jeffrey, whose sensitivity to other people's feelings was a great deal better developed than his ability to
express his own, realized that his invitation had thrown
her into a quandary.

When she finally lifted her gaze from her cappuccino,
he could see there was a little flush of color staining her
cheeks. "Thank you for asking me," she said. "But I'm
not sure if I should accept. I enjoy Gabe's company and
he enjoys mine, but I don't think he'd like to take me to
Kemberly. I think he might find my presence there
rather...intrusive."

Jeffrey decided he could make a reasonably good
translation of that cryptic response. At a guess, it meant
that Gabe thoroughly enjoyed having sex with Lianne, but
he'd made it plain to her that he wasn't thinking in terms
of marriage, commitment and introductions to his family. His son, Jeffrey reflected, was a fool.

He put down his cup. "My dear, Gabe isn't extending this invitation to you, I am. To put it bluntly, we're simply asking Gabe to be the chauffeur."

She smiled a little at that. "Well, when you put it that way, how could I refuse? Thank you, Mr. DeWilde. I'd love to accept your invitation to spend the weekend at Kemberly."

CHAPTER ELEVEN

SHE SHOULD NEVER HAVE told Gabe that she loved him, Lianne thought, staring at the hedgerows rushing by the car window without really seeing them. Even though she'd been scrupulously careful never to repeat her mistake, the damage had been done. Gabe hadn't been ready to hear anything about her feelings the night of the gala, and he still wasn't now, more than two weeks later. Unfortunately, when he'd taken her into his bed that night, her defenses had been so depleted by the stunning impact of their lovemaking that the fateful words had slipped out before she could stop them. Almost, in fact, before she'd realized their truth.

She stole a glance at Gabe's unrevealing profile and sighed. Her own face sometimes seemed to be a fast-moving TV screen of everything she was feeling, a window straight into her heart, whereas Gabe was a master of the controlled, reveal-nothing expression. Except, of course, that the very blankness of his features betrayed the fact that he was concealing emotions he didn't want to share with her, a deprivation that Lianne was beginning to find hurtful.

She couldn't fathom why it was that their relationship disturbed Gabe so much, but she knew his refusal to acknowledge their attraction for each other went beyond the standard reluctance of an eligible bachelor to give up his freedom and make a commitment. For some reason, Gabe didn't trust the chemistry that sizzled between them. Sometimes she almost had the feeling that he actively resisted the idea that the great sex they'd shared might develop into something more lasting.

For the past two weeks, the boundaries of their relationship had barely changed. They had discovered when Gabe got ready to drive her home after the night of the gala that his car had been towed from its illegal parking spot in front of his flat. Muttering curses beneath his breath—curses that Lianne considered quite mild, considering the circumstances—he'd summoned a taxi to take her home. As she started to step up into the cab, he'd pulled her back and held her close while he murmured how important the night they'd just shared had been to him.

Lianne believed he had been sincere, but from that moment until this he'd made no further mention of his feelings or how he viewed their relationship. Their frequent dates fell into a rigid pattern, carefully controlled by Gabe. Basically, they amounted to nights of blistering hot sex, preceded by formal outings where she and Gabe were invariably surrounded by other people.

He'd invited her to attend two plays and to accompany him to the opening of an art exhibition at a friend's gallery. He'd taken her to a rare concert given by Enya, for which tickets were almost unobtainable, and she'd twice joined him as his partner at fund-raising banquets for causes connected to the preservation of various historic buildings. She teased him that he harbored a secret desire for the whole length and breadth of England to be done out with flats and shopping malls disguised behind fake Georgian Revival facades. He'd grinned, only slightly shamefaced, and told her that every man was entitled to one eccentricity.

Lianne wondered why it was that when you fell in love with a man, even his foibles seemed endearing. She was enchanted by the fact that Gabe, who on the surface appeared every inch the international sophisticate, cherished a sentimental attachment to quaint thatched cottages and village gardens full of hollyhocks and snapdragons.

When contrasted with the memorable occasion of their first date, Lianne supposed she could say that their relationship had inched forward. Gabe had finally progressed from spending the entire evening glowering at her, as if daring her to have a good time, to the point where he now took obvious pleasure in her company and the ease with which she fitted into the circle of his friends. But she couldn't fail to notice that he never invited her to spend the evening at his flat, comfortably doing nothing, and that he always had some excuse as to why he couldn't join her when she suggested a Sunday morning at the zoo, or browsing through the Victoria and Albert Museum, or any other informal outing that would have required lots of one-on-one interaction.

This weekend had been shaping up as typical. She'd known for several days before Jeffrey invited her to Kemberly that Julia was going to stay with her brother's family for three days. Taking advantage of her friend's absence, Lianne had invited Gabe to come to the flat and share Chinese take-away food, followed by a night watching rented movies.

"I'll even let you have one of the bags of microwave popcorn that just arrived in my mother's latest care package from the States," she'd teased him. "Since you spent all those years in America, you must recognize that a movie isn't really a movie without popcorn, and I can supply the real thing."

He'd smiled and admitted that popcorn made even the worst movie almost bearable, but he hadn't agreed to come and spend the evening alone with her. Lianne could guess exactly how the weekend would have turned out if Jeffrey DeWilde hadn't forced the issue. At the last minute, Gabe would have found some concert, or dinner party, or charity ball that he needed to attend, and he would have asked her to accompany him. Anything so that he could see her, and have sex with her afterward, without venturing into a situation where there was the danger of long, quiet conversation and real intimacy. If she were forced to be honest and describe how Gabe felt about her, Lianne would have said that he liked her, but wished he didn't.

The sexual attraction between the two of them burned as fierce and strong as ever, but Lianne was beginning to feel the strain of sex that wasn't underpinned by emotional commitment. When Gabe had called at her flat this morning to pick her up, he'd made no effort to hide the desire that flared in his eyes the moment she opened the door. As soon as she confirmed that Julia had left for the weekend, he'd swept her into his arms and kissed her with a passionate thoroughness that left both of them aching and breathless.

They'd stood in the tiny entranceway, staring at each other in wary silence. Gabe might not be willing to acknowledge the stresses in their relationship but he wasn't a fool, and Lianne was sure he recognized them and knew that she was hurt by his elusiveness.

"We don't have time to make love," Gabe said finally. He was close enough that she could feel he was already aroused.

"No, we don't." Her denial carried not a shred of conviction, even to her own ears. It was one thing to wish that there was more than sex between the two of them, another thing altogether to deny the potency of their mutual attraction. She drew in a shaky breath. "Your father asked us to be at Kemberly in time for lunch. We need to leave right now if we're going to get there before one."

He bent his head, preparing to kiss her. "You've no idea how fast I can drive."

She turned away, avoiding his kisses but not moving out of his arms. Typical wishy-washy behavior when she was with Gabe, and utterly unlike her usual decisive self. "The speed limit..." she mumbled, furious with herself for wanting him, despite everything. Furious with him for assuming she was always available to fulfill his sexual needs. "The police come out in force on Saturday mornings."

Gabe looked at her, and his hazel eyes took on a lustful gleam. "I'll pay the speeding ticket," he said.

Arrogant bastard, she thought angrily. She steeled herself to say no. She knew she ought to refuse to open her heart and her body to him again until he was ready to take both halves of the package. But he swung her up into his arms and walked swiftly to her bedroom before she managed to summon up the necessary resolution.

His expression was savage as he looked down at her. "Damn it, Lianne, how in hell do you do this to me?"

"The same way you do it to me," she said, and for the first time there was a thread of bitterness in her words.

He didn't answer, just tumbled with her onto the bed, groping for the buttons of her sweater as she reached for the zipper of his slacks. Desire built so quickly, Lianne felt a flash of fear. How could she cope with the passion that blazed out of control at the mere touch of Gabe's lips on her breasts, or his fingers between her thighs? She'd never felt this way in her entire life, either about sex or about a man, and the intensity of her response scared her.

By the time Gabe entered her, she was wild, but so was he, driving into her with surging force. Lianne shook with every thrust. She struggled for breath, her rasping moans mingled with Gabe's as they raced toward the shimmering moment of release. Her nails scraped at his back. Her body arched off the bed, bowstring taut with anticipation. Above her, Gabe tensed, then plunged into her one last time. On cue, her body destructed into a thousand shooting stars of pleasure.

Gabe collapsed on top of her, oblivious to the world for at least a minute. Just long enough for Lianne to burrow her head into a pillow and fight back the betraying tears. She had been making love to Gabe. He had been having sex with her. She'd felt the deliberate withholding of his emotions in every fiber of her being. She wasn't sure how much longer she'd be able to tolerate the physical fireworks without any affection to give meaning to the dazzling display.

GABE'S VOICE BROKE the silence that blanketed the car, bringing her abruptly back to the present. "We're almost at Kemberly," he said. "The house sits on the crest of a slight hill, so you'll get a good view of it as soon as we turn the next bend in the road."

"I'm really looking forward to seeing it," Lianne said, putting aside the uncomfortable memories. "In fact, I'm looking forward to the whole weekend."

She was speaking the truth. Despite everything, it was wonderful to be out of town for a few hours, and she'd been enjoying the riotous green of the countryside ever since they left the motorway. She rolled down the window so that she could breathe in the good smell of fresh-

mown grass and the occasional sickly sweet waft of silage
for feeding to the dairy cows. She enjoyed living in London, and she relished the challenge of working in the
competitive European fashion market, but the real reason she had chosen to leave the States was because, as a
teenager, she had grown to love the English countryside,
and that love had never left her. Her secret dream was one
day to own a house or a cottage that had been built some
time before the dawn of the twentieth century.

Even so, even knowing how much she loved old houses
and old English manor houses in particular, she wasn't
prepared for the surge of emotion that flooded her as they
rounded the bend and Kemberly came into view.

Built at the crest of a rise, it was an early Georgian
mansion whose baronial owners had been too poor and
too profligate to indulge in endless modernizations. Consequently it had survived unscathed in its original flaw-
less state, avoiding the Victorian passion for fake medieval
turrets, the Edwardian craze for imperial embellishment
and the early twentieth-century penchant for stringing
telephone poles and electrical wires with a complete dis-
regard for aesthetics.

The design of the house was simple, a central core and
two angled wings, all facing onto a courtyard. The walls
of Cotswold stone were mellowed by age and further
softened by the rough, hand-hewn cast of the individual
stones. Tall, graceful Queen Anne-style windows were
teamed with incongruously wide Elizabethan sills, on
which sat window boxes filled to bursting with spring
flowers. The yellow and purple jonquils and hyacinths
appeared almost indecently brilliant, overflowing their
containers and splashing sensuous color against the pale
golden stone. Flagstone steps led down through formal
terraced gardens to a sloping lawn and a sheltering copse

of beech and sycamore trees. The sun, apparently determined that Lianne should see the house at its most spectacular, slanted across the tops of the trees and illuminated the front portico in radiantly clear light. To add the final touch of enchantment, a cuckoo called out, repeating his summons a half dozen times, as if in welcome.

Lianne looked at the perfection that was Kemberly, and the artist within her fell instantly and irredeemably in love. Speechless, she stared straight ahead, unable to move, while her overloaded senses drank in the sights, sounds and smells of the blossoming flower beds and picturesque house.

Gabe drew the car to a halt in the middle of the cobblestoned circular driveway. The slippery, uneven surface was probably an accident-in-waiting on a wet winter's day, Lianne thought wryly, but the cobblestones looked so wonderfully right that she could understand why the DeWildes had chosen not to replace them. Gabe got out of the car and came around to open the door for her. For once, Lianne scarcely noticed the careful way in which he avoided physical contact with her, since her gaze was riveted on the house. Gabe was still preoccupied with getting their overnight bags from the boot of the car when Jeffrey DeWilde came out and greeted them both with a smile that, Lianne saw, was a touch strained around the edges.

"Glad you made it in time for lunch," Jeffrey said, shaking her hand and giving his son a friendly pat on the shoulder. "Mrs. Milton's been cooking up a storm, she's so pleased to have people visiting here again. I trust you've both brought hearty appetites with you or she'll be disappointed."

He misses his wife, Lianne thought immediately, not sure how she had read that message behind the jovial words of Jeffrey's greeting, but quite sure that she had. Weekends, she supposed, must make Grace's absence more conspicuous, without the hurry and bustle of the office to disguise the loneliness. Jeffrey always seemed so self-possessed, it was easy to forget that appearances could be deceiving. In truth, the better she got to know Gabe, the more Lianne realized that a controlled facade not only could mask a tumult of emotion but usually did. Jeffrey's feelings, like Gabe's, were probably all the more powerful because they ran so still and so deep.

She felt sorry for Jeffrey and wished she knew him well enough to put her arms around him and give him a hug. Since hugs were out of the question, she compromised by returning his smile with all the friendliness she could muster.

"Thank you so much for inviting me here this weekend," she said to him. "Kemberly's cast its spell over me already. If the interior of the house is even half as beautiful as the grounds, you've won a slave for life, Mr. DeWilde. All you need do is promise me time at Kemberly, and your wish will be my command."

His eyes, so like Gabe's, gleamed with affectionate amusement. "Dangerous words, Lianne. I shall certainly remember them." He turned to his son. "Traffic must have been heavy. You're a little later than we expected."

Lianne felt the heat rush instantly to her cheeks, but Gabe didn't blink. "We were delayed setting out," he said coolly.

"Ah." The amusement in Jeffrey's gaze deepened. Appalled as she was to have her early morning activities so readily guessed at, and by her lover's father, no less, Lianne was almost willing to bear the embarrassment in exchange for the lightening she sensed in Jeffrey's mood.

"Mrs. Milton decided that Lianne should have the blue guest room," Jeffrey added.

Gabe finally smiled at Lianne and her stupid heart immediately skipped a beat. "You should be honored," he said to her as the three of them strolled toward the house, stopping from time to time to admire an especially colorful flower bed. "It usually takes at least a cabinet minister before the redoubtable Mrs. Milton is prepared to open up the blue room."

Jeffrey laughed his agreement. Then bleakness returned to his gaze. "Mrs. M. has been sadly deprived of guests to impress with her skills these past few months," he said. "If she had her way, you'd both be eating four meals a day, all served on antique china and tables smothered in starched damask tablecloths."

So the break between Jeffrey and Grace hadn't come out of the blue as Gabe assumed, Lianne thought. For the "past few months," it seemed the DeWildes' usual pattern of entertaining at Kemberly over the weekends had been disrupted. She had never for a moment believed that Grace had walked away from her marriage on a sudden whim, and Jeffrey's words seemed to confirm that there had been trouble in the marriage for some time before the final break.

"I'm honored, of course, to be on Mrs. Milton's 'A' list, but what's so special about the blue room?" she asked, hoping her question would banish the bleakness from Jeffrey's eyes again.

"Probably nothing." He chuckled. "Rumor has it that the Prince Regent was the first guest invited to the house after it was refurbished in 1826, and that he not only won three thousand guineas from his host playing whist, thus sending the poor baron into instant insolvency, but he also entertained the baroness in his bedroom that night, leav-

ing significant lingering doubt as to whether the son and
heir born nine months later was actually the progeny of
Baron Kemberly or a by-blow of the Prince Regent. I've
never been able to find any document that confirms the
legend, but all the locals insist that during their night of
passion, the prince commended the baroness on her
splendid new blue wallpaper and that subsequent ladies of
Kemberly always chose a blue decorating scheme for that
room in honor of the prince's compliment.''

"My mother likes to point out that if the Prince Regent had time to comment on the wallpaper, he and the
baroness couldn't have been having very much fun,"
Gabe said. He stopped abruptly, seemingly annoyed with
himself for introducing his mother's name into the conversation.

Jeffrey looked at him intently, then spoke with surprising mildness. "Your mother lived in this house for more
than thirty years, Gabe. She's been mistress of it for the
last twenty. You're not going to be able to come here for
the weekend and never mention her name or remember
her presence."

"No, of course not. I'm well aware of that." Gabe's
voice was colorless and his expression neutral. "This
house is the ultimate expression of my mother's personality. She loved it here." Without missing a beat, he
added, in the same bland tone, "If you're ready, Lianne,
I'll take you upstairs."

"Good idea," Jeffrey said, sending another assessing
glance in his son's direction, but deciding to make no
more personal comments. "Perhaps you could unpack
after lunch, though. Mrs. Milton is doing something
elaborate with puff pastry and would like us to eat as soon
as possible."

Gabe dutifully escorted Lianne upstairs, but left her as soon as he'd shown her into the blue room, which was as lovely as she'd imagined it would be, with furniture dating from the Regency period, an elegant Greek Revival fireplace and a captivating view. The windows faced the rear of the house and looked out over sloping lawns and a meadow bordered by a meandering stream. Sheep grazed on the far bank of the stream, and in the distance she could see a farmhouse and the spire of the village church. The scene was so idyllic it might have been the template for a Victorian print entitled Home Sweet Home.

The idyllic views were going to have to compensate for a lot this weekend, Lianne thought ruefully, hurriedly combing her hair and fixing her makeup in the modern bathroom that adjoined her room. It was almost as if seeing her here at Kemberly had brought all Gabe's ambivalent feelings into focus, to the point that he was having trouble being civil to her, much less loverlike. So much for her crazy, secret hope that being with her at Kemberly would make him start thinking in terms of commitment and permanence and all those other words he seemed to be avoiding with such fierce determination.

After a lunch that was as delicious and overabundant as he'd predicted, Jeffrey suggested a brisk tour of the gardens to walk off the effects of too much gooseberry pie topped with far too much Cornish cream. He did most of the talking during the walk, explaining the history of the house to Lianne, and how his family had bought it in a bad state of disrepair in the mid-thirties.

"My grandparents barely had time to finish the basic structural repairs when the Second World War broke out, and, sadly, they were killed during a bombing raid only months after I was born, so I never knew them, even though I was born here at Kemberly, and lived here until my father came home from the war."

"What happened after the war?" Lianne asked. "Didn't you continue to live here?"

"No." Jeffrey smiled. "My mother, Mary, is a very remarkable woman. She was the daughter of an English country squire, and she had the most traditional upbringing you could imagine. You'd have expected her to be enchanted with Kemberly, which is the quintessential English country house, and to spend all her time here, wearing droopy cardigans and trotting around with a wicker basket, snipping the heads off dead delphiniums and knitting booties for her grandchildren."

That description actually evoked a chuckle from Gabe. "You'll have to meet my grandmother," he said. "She's in her eighties, smokes like a chimney, using one of those long, jeweled cigarette holders like Marlene Dietrich, and she loathes the country with a fierce passion. She says only those people whom God has blessed with a twisted sense of humor could possibly want to live near cows and chickens. She has a flat in London and an apartment on Park Avenue in Manhattan, and she commutes across the Atlantic as the whim takes her."

"She's in New York at the moment," Jeffrey said, his mouth curving into a grin as he thought of his mother. "She says all the best plastic surgeons are in New York, and she's thinking of having a nose job."

"Fortunately," Gabe said, "she's having difficulty finding a doctor willing to perform elective cosmetic surgery on a woman in her eighties."

Lianne laughed, delighted at the affectionate pictures they were painting of an obviously remarkable woman. "How fortunate that her husband didn't insist on living in the country and making her play the role of lady of the manor," she said. "Your father must have been a very understanding husband."

"Superficially they weren't well-matched at all," Jeffrey told her. "My father, Charles, was hard-driving, work obsessed and very conservative in his manners and appearance. But in his heart of hearts, I've gradually come to believe he was just as much of a rebel as my mother. In typical British fashion, at least for those days, I was packed off to boarding school soon after my seventh birthday, and my parents joyfully removed themselves to London, where they bought a flat in Knightsbridge and lived a very sophisticated, glamorous life. Except during the long summer holidays, when they dutifully removed themselves to Kemberly for my sake. When Grace and I got married, my parents were delighted to find that we finally had a woman in the family who was longing to live at Kemberly. They formally deeded the house to us as a gift on our tenth wedding anniversary."

"So Megan, Kate and I grew up here," Gabe said. He shrugged his shoulders, a touch self-conscious. "It's crazy when you think of it. My mother's American, and Dad is the first generation in his family actually to be born in England, and yet I feel as if I have roots at Kemberly that stretch back forever."

"I can easily understand how that would happen," Lianne said. "I traveled around so much when I was a kid I soon realized it was feelings that bound you to a place, not how long you'd lived there, and certainly not where your ancestors came from." They'd been climbing a steep incline back toward the house, and she turned to catch her breath and look at the patchwork quilt of fields and village buildings behind them. Gabe turned to look with her.

"Despite your grandmother Mary's proclamation about cows and chickens, I imagine for most people it would be very easy to grow roots here," she said to him. "The past has barely been glossed over with a few modern touches, so you only have to dig a little way down and you can attach yourself to all the richness of Kemberly's history. I envy you your connection to this place, Gabe."

He was, as usual, maintaining a careful few inches between her body and his, because Gabe only ever touched her in passion, never in friendship. But as she finished speaking, he reached for her hand and slowly carried it to his lips, kissing the tips of her fingers with more warmth than he'd shown her in weeks of torrid sex. Silently, she looked up at him, her blood thrumming loud in her ears. What she saw in his gaze made her heart beat faster. Oblivious to his father a few yards away, he bent his head and brushed a slow, gentle kiss across her mouth.

Jeffrey continued to walk tactfully ahead, but Lianne was too conscious of his presence, and she reluctantly drew away from Gabe's embrace. "We'd better catch up with your father," she said, her voice sounding as shaken as she felt. She had just about learned to hang together and function when Gabe was offering her nothing but sex. If he started to offer her tenderness as well, her sanity was rapidly going to become a lost cause.

Gabe released her, but he held her hand in his and tucked it through his arm, walking with her in a silence that for the first time ever simply felt companionable. The spell Kemberly cast was truly potent, Lianne reflected, if it could mellow even Gabriel DeWilde.

They caught up with Jeffrey as he reentered the formal gardens. He was standing beneath a curved trellis that led into a walled and sunken garden with a stone-flagged lily pond at its center and rose bushes planted all around the edge.

"This is where I asked Grace to marry me," he said, walking slowly to one of the wooden seats, angled to give a pleasant view. "She brought this garden back from virtual ruin. Some of the roses she rescued are varieties that date from the eighteenth century and can't be found anywhere else."

"It's beautiful," Lianne said. "But everywhere here is beautiful."

"That's all Grace's doing. She transformed Kemberly from a cold barn of a place into a real home." Jeffrey cleared his throat, blinking rapidly. He gestured toward the arbor, deliberately drawing their attention away from himself. "I'm sure you can imagine what a spectacular sight this is in summer, when the dog roses are in full bloom over the walls and the trellis. Of course, at this time of year, the early buds are barely beginning to form."

Gabe paced restlessly around the paved perimeter of the lily pond, his eyebrows drawn back down into the scowl he'd only recently abandoned. Lianne sat next to Jeffrey. Acting on an impulse she didn't allow herself to reconsider, she reached out her hand and laid it over his. "She'll come back," she said quietly. "Nobody could build a home as warm and welcoming as Kemberly and then abandon it. Not permanently."

Gabe made an impatient sound. He skimmed a tiny pebble across the top of the lilies. "My mother did just that," he said harshly. "She upped and left, and flew to San Francisco, abandoning my father, and Kemberly and anyone else who happened to be in the way of her new, self-appointed path to fulfillment."

Jeffrey stared at the rich black earth of the rose beds. Slowly, his fingers curled around Lianne's, accepting the clasp of her hand. "No," he said at last. "That's not quite what happened." He drew in a long, unsteady breath. "Grace left because I drove her away."

Behind her, Lianne felt Gabe freeze into shocked silence. When nobody spoke for several seconds, she said tentatively, "You could always ask her to come back, Mr. DeWilde."

Jeffrey gave a wintry, self-mocking smile. "No, I couldn't," he said. He removed his hand from Lianne's clasp, but swiveled on the seat to meet her gaze. "I'm a man without much courage. And like a lot of cowards, I suffer the consequences of my own fears. I forced Grace to leave because I was afraid of her power to hurt me. Which is rather like chopping off your arm because your finger is bruised." He watched a dragonfly land on a lily leaf, and his voice shaded into deeper irony. "To my profound amazement, I'm discovering that a missing arm hurts more than a bruised finger."

"I don't believe you're a man without courage," Lianne said quietly.

"Thank you," Jeffrey said. "But that's because you're one of those people who is fortunate enough always to see the very best in others. I used to find that tiresomely naive. Now I consider it a major strength." He stood up, brushing nonexistent lint from the immaculate creases of his twill slacks. He looked at his son. "In some ways, Gabe, you're too much like me. Don't make a fool of yourself by amputating your arm because you're afraid that one day—years from now—you may have a bruised finger."

"What point are you trying to make?" Gabe asked, his voice clipped. "I've never been good at solving riddles."

Jeffrey's mouth twisted into a faint smile. "Then I'll make my advice crystal clear. You, Gabe, are currently behaving like a blithering idiot. I will therefore point out that you're not me, and Lianne isn't Grace. If the two of you get married, you're not doomed to repeat your parents' mistakes. Or our successes, for that matter."

Having reduced both of his listeners to openmouthed silence, Jeffrey nodded courteously to Lianne and swung on his heel. "I have some paperwork I need to catch up on, so if you'll excuse me, I'll leave Gabe to entertain you. Dinner tonight is at seven-thirty. I've asked a few of our neighbors to join us, so I'll see you both then." He walked off, his stride lithe and energetic, but his shoulders hunched and his hands thrust deep into the pockets of his tweed jacket.

Lianne stood and watched him leave, her face burning with embarrassment. Gabe came to stand in front of her. Surprisingly, he didn't look either annoyed or embarrassed but rather amused. "My father has the most infuriating capacity for hitting the nail squarely on the head," he said.

"Which particular nail were you referring to?" Lianne asked with unusual tartness. "The fact that he called you a blithering idiot?"

"Especially that." Gabe put his arms around her waist, drawing her slowly toward him. "But more specifically to the fact that I've spent the past several weeks running away from you because I was too much of a coward to do what I really wanted to do. Which is to tell you how much I love you, and ask you, please, to marry me."

Her breath constricted in her throat, but she turned away, uneasy at his instant capitulation to his father's bidding. "Gabe, you don't have to do this. We're a hop, skip and a jump away from the twenty-first century. This may come as hot-breaking news to you, but it's been a hundred years or so since dutiful sons proposed marriage because their fathers told them to."

"Now you're being foolish," he said. "Totally absurd, in fact." He drew her back to the seat and sat down, taking her into the shelter of his arms and dropping a light kiss onto her hair. "Of course I'm not asking you to marry me because my father told me to. I'm in love with you, Lianne, crazily in love. That's why I want to marry you."

"You've never expressed the slightest interest in marrying me until one minute ago."

He hesitated for a moment. "These have been a rough few weeks for me, Lianne, watching the breakup of my parents' marriage. The truth is that my feelings for you got badly mixed up with the way I was feeling about their separation." He shrugged, self-conscious at revealing his uncertainties. "Most of the time recently, I haven't been sure what I felt about anything. Somehow, it never seemed to be quite the right moment to suggest getting married."

"I can understand that," she said. "But I have the impression something a lot more personal was going on between us than just the generalized backwash of your parents' situation. Sometimes when we're together, I get the feeling that you're actively struggling not to like me. This morning, for example, in the car. You hated the fact that you were bringing me to Kemberly. I could feel it as clearly as if you'd said the words out loud."

"Well, my father was right about a lot of things just now, including the fact that I was scared. I didn't hate the idea of bringing you to Kemberly, I was scared of it."

"But why? Scared of what? I've never thought of myself as an intimidating person."

He drew in a deep breath. "I was scared by how much you remind me of my mother," he admitted. "Not in looks, but in personality. You have all her exuberance, her creativity, her capacity for grabbing life by the throat and getting the best out of it. I always think of myself as being more like my father, with my emotions held on such a tight rein that I'm often in danger of choking myself to death. Seeing you here—seeing how completely you fit in..." He stumbled to a halt and started over. "It seemed to me that if my parents couldn't make a go of their marriage, the two of us would be tempting fate if we tried. We'd be juggling problems that were so similar to theirs, and if they couldn't succeed, how could we?"

"And a few words from your father could make you change your mind, just like that?"

"Not in the way you're imagining," Gabe said, failing to hear the quiver of anger in her voice. "My father is normally a very private man, and I think the reason he told us as much as he did about the breakup of their marriage was because he wanted me to see that I've been misjudging my mother. He wanted me to realize that she didn't wake up one morning and decide to fly to San Francisco on a whim, that there were all sorts of complicated undercurrents at work that contributed to the breakup."

"And because your mother didn't precipitate the split with your father, now you've decided that it's safe to ask me to marry you? That because Grace didn't behave in the way you feared, now you can trust me to be a good wife?" Lianne's entire body was shaking with the force of her fury. She scrambled to her feet. "Thank you, Gabe, for asking me to marry you. The answer is no. I'm not interested in being some psychologically twisted substitute for your mother."

She pulled away from him and ran toward the house, but he caught up with her and dragged her around to face him. "It isn't you I don't trust," he snarled. "It's myself."

"And your father's suddenly inspired you with a burst of confidence in your own judgment?" she demanded with biting sarcasm.

"Yes, damn it, yes! He made me realize that I can't bear the thought of spending the rest of my life without you, and to hell with the problems, real and imagined. I want to marry you because I love you, damn it! Because life with you is a rainbow of color and without you it's nothing but gray shadow."

"Very poetic," she said. "It's a great act, Gabe, but it's too late for protestations of undying affection. I don't want to marry you."

He slammed her against the wall, palms flat on the bricks, imprisoning her between his arms. "Then live with me in sin, I don't care. But don't try to tell me you're ready to give up this." He slanted his mouth across hers, his kisses searing, almost cruel.

No, she didn't want to give up the sex. But she didn't want to marry a man at his father's bidding, either, however well-meaning Jeffrey's interference had been. "You're right, Gabe," she said wearily. "Sex with you is fabulous. Gives me a real high. So when you next want sex, call me. I'm available. But I'm not going to accept any more invitations to concerts and plays and charity balls. And I'm especially not going to accept invitations to spend the weekend at Kemberly. Let's not pretend there's anything more to our relationship than there really is."

He looked confused, angry, unsure of himself, light years from his usual cool self. "You told me two weeks ago that you loved me."

"Yes, well, some things are better left unspoken. Or forgotten once they've been said."

He stepped away from her, but only far enough to reach into the inner pocket of his jacket and remove a small, dark blue box with the familiar DeWilde logo stamped in gold on the lid.

He held it out to her. "I bought this the morning after we made love—after the gala," he said. "I've been carrying it around with me ever since, trying to find the words to go with it."

Lianne didn't move, so he took her hand and dropped the box into her palm, curling her fingers around it. "It's probably too late," he said. "But I wish you'd open it."

She looked down at the ring box, almost unable to believe what she was seeing. This had to have been Gabe's own idea, nothing to do with what his father had just said. Throat tight, she pressed the tiny gold latch and watched the lid spring open.

Nestled in a bed of velvet, with the traditional puff of peach satin as a backdrop, was the Victorian ring she'd admired on the day she started work at DeWilde's.

Slowly, she drew the ring out of the box. The tiny diamonds at the heart of the golden flowers sparkled in the sunlight. "How did you know I liked this ring?" she asked, voice low, not quite even.

"Harry Pierce, the salesman, told me you liked it." He cleared his throat. "I wish you'd keep it, Lianne, no strings attached, of course. It suits you perfectly, and I'd like to think of you wearing it."

The workmanship was exquisite. Even so, it had probably been one of the least expensive rings in the entire

DeWilde store. Lianne's heart turned over with love when she looked at it and knew that Gabe had had the sensitivity to choose something so absolutely right for her. "You'd better put it on," she said, holding out her left hand.

Gabe perked up a bit at that. "Er...which finger?" he asked.

"You choose," she said softly.

"That's easy," he murmured. He slid the ring onto her engagement finger, then carried her hand to his mouth and pressed a burning kiss at the place where the band met her skin. "I love you, Lianne. More than I know how to express. If you marry me, I promise that I'll do everything in my power to make you happy."

She touched the ring, smiling at him, her eyes misty. "Actually, Gabe, you just did a pretty good job—of expressing yourself, and making me happy."

He grinned, still faintly self-conscious. "Yes, well, I heard you can always buy a woman's affections with diamonds."

"Or with great sex," Lianne said. "You should keep that in mind for future reference."

He took her into his arms, crushing her against him. "Then I've got it made," he said. "How many men can you hope to find with their own private supply of cost-price diamonds and the best damn sex outside of the *Kama Sutra?*"

"Not many," she said, her breath catching. "I'm sure there can't be many."

CHAPTER TWELVE

*3:00 P.M.: INSPECT possible office space with Rita Shan-
non.* Tossing her purse and car keys onto the kitchen
counter, Grace made the entry in her calendar and un-
derlined it. Rita Shannon was her newly hired assistant,
and she was already proving herself invaluable, a hard
worker with creative energy to spare. And Grace certainly needed competent administrative help. She was
getting inundated with work, meetings and commit-
ments—and it felt terrific!

She poured herself a glass of ice water and drank
thirstily. Inspecting potential sites for her new store was
hot and tiring work, but she was loving every minute of it,
despite the fact that she was no closer to finding something suitable than she had been ten days ago. Today,
she'd been shown a building that was ideally located.
Unfortunately, it was almost derelict, but she supposed it
might, with extensive renovation, be made viable as an
upscale bridal store rather than the failed health club it
currently was. She would take her architect to look at it
tomorrow and see how much money they were talking
about to do the job properly. She was determined not to
ruin her concept for the new store by skimping on the up-
front expenditures.

She checked her answering machine, which was
crammed with messages from three different real estate

agents, an interior design architect who had heard rumors of her plans to open a store, her bank, her brother, and even one from Kate, who for once didn't seem to be working back-to-back shifts and wanted to meet for dinner.

Grace wrote down the messages, smiling as she turned the pages of her calendar and saw that every day for the next couple of weeks had at least one meeting scheduled. She smiled again, even more happily, when she turned to September and saw the red-letter notation for September 21.

Gabe and Lianne's wedding.

Three months almost to the day and her beloved Gabe would be a married man. Among the many changes his engagement had produced was the minor miracle that Gabe was speaking to her again. He'd phoned personally to tell her the wonderful news that he and Lianne Beecham were engaged, and although he hadn't initiated any more conversations, he'd at least answered the phone on the two occasions during the past month that Grace had called him. If she could just get him to accept the fact that her plans for a bridal store in San Francisco would have no impact on DeWilde operations...

Realistically speaking, convincing Gabe that she had no plans to undercut DeWilde's was likely to be a gradual task, and in the meantime, the days were marching inexorably toward September and his wedding. They really didn't have enough time to arrange the perfect ceremony and reception, but with a little bit of hard work and cooperation from all the parties involved, Grace thought she should be able to pull off something spectacular enough to do justice to the occasion. If she'd hand-picked the woman she wanted Gabe to marry, she couldn't have come up with anyone more perfect than Lianne, and she wanted the ceremony that celebrated their union to produce memories both Lianne and her son would treasure for a lifetime.

Humming, Grace walked into the bedroom, casting an approving half glance toward the sleek lines of her all-in-one headboard and nightstands. The hideous phone conversation with Jeffrey last month had proven liberating in the end, cutting her loose from the paralysis that had gripped her in the first few weeks of their separation. Riding high on a burst of fury, she'd rushed right out and spent a small fortune on furniture, which was still being delivered on an almost daily basis.

The memory of her painful conversation with Jeffrey—the last one she'd had, since he'd chosen to remain totally silent on the subject of Gabe's engagement—was no more than a minor irritant, a sore spot she could comfortably bandage over. These days, she could sometimes go for hours at a stretch without giving her husband so much as a passing thought. She assumed that one day in the not too distant future, she'd discover that she had survived an entire twenty-four hours without thinking of him at all. And that would be the day on which she finally worked up the courage to file for a divorce.

She tossed her linen jacket over the back of the swivel rocker in the corner of her bedroom and dropped her earrings into a ceramic pot on the top of her dresser. Having lived most of her adult life surrounded by antiques, she'd decided to make a complete break with the past and furnish her San Francisco apartment with the latest in contemporary, high-tech style. So far, her bedroom was the only room for which all the furniture had been delivered, and she loved every piece of it. Moreover, the alien and glossy freshness of her apartment was inspiring her with a cornucopia of ideas for the new store.

In her mind's eye, she was already building an image of her store, and she saw display areas with lots of soaring glass and polished chrome, softened by intimate display nooks and specialty boutiques decorated in warm, feminine colors, so that brides trying on wedding gowns would be able to visualize themselves against both soaring, public spaces and the intimacy of their honeymoon suite.

Oh, yes, Grace thought, kicking off her high-heeled sandals and walking toward the bed, her San Francisco store was going to become an immediate landmark in the retailing industry. And it would owe nothing, absolutely nothing, to the stuffy, antique splendor of DeWilde's. The concept would be entirely hers, all Grace and nothing of Jeffrey. Definitely not even a smidgeon of Jeffrey.

She sat cross-legged in the center of the bed and reached across to press a command button on the electronic keypad built into her nightstand. A small door in the headboard slid open, and a shelf projected itself forward electronically to offer her the telephone. When the shelf was fully extended, a little spotlight illuminated the dial. She grinned with childlike pleasure as she lifted the receiver, wondering in amusement how any furniture designer ever came up with the idea that customers would pay money to have their phones glide in and out on a useless electronic tray, and knowing full well that she'd fallen for the lure and would never again be entirely happy with a bedside phone that didn't have its own secret niche to slide into at the push of a button.

It was already ten-thirty at night in London, but Grace assumed Lianne would still be up. Pulling her checklist of wedding questions out of the bedside drawer, she dialed the number of Lianne's London flat. So far, the list was depressingly clean, unsullied by a single checkmark indicating task accomplished, which was worrisome, to say the least. She mustn't forget to ask about bridesmaids, Grace thought, scribbling a notation as the phone started to ring. Sometimes choosing the right bridesmaids' dresses could be more difficult than finding the perfect wedding gown....

"Hello." A sleepy, distracted voice finally answered the phone.

"Lianne? This is Grace. How are you, my dear? I hope I didn't wake you."

"Grace? Oh, how nice to hear from you. No, you didn't wake me. It's...um...only ten-thirty."

"Good, I'm so glad I managed to reach you. We have so much to talk about, and with the eight-hour time difference, it's difficult to catch you at home." Grace crossed her legs and tucked a pillow behind her back, getting comfortable. "I'm longing to hear all your plans for the wedding. Gabe really didn't seem to know anything when I spoke with him last week, but then men never manage to cope very well with wedding plans, do they. I remember Jeffrey was absolutely useless when we were trying to decide—"

Damn! She'd been doing so well in the Jeffrey department today. She broke off sharply and began again. "Well, let's get down to the most important question first. Have you decided yet whether you're going to be married in town or at All Saints in Kemberly?"

There was a long pause before Lianne replied. "Actually, Grace, my parents seem to feel that it would be a very good idea if Gabe and I got married at the Unitarian church they attend in Benton's Inlet. They like the minister a lot and they think I'll like him, too."

"Benton's Inlet? In Michigan?" As soon as she spoke, Grace realized that she'd said Michigan as if it were located somewhere between the dark side of the moon and the planet Jupiter. "Well, of course I realize that the bride's family traditionally chooses where the wedding is going to take place, but Gabe has so many friends in London, and I'm sure you do, too. Not to mention all our friends, people we ought to invite because of their connection to DeWilde's..."

"My parents have a lot of friends, too."

Grace drew in a deep breath, appalled at her tactlessness. "Of course they do, how thoughtless of me. A fall wedding in Michigan will be just lovely, I'm sure. Your mother and I had a long chat on the phone the other day, and I remember that she told me Benton's Inlet is right on the shore of Lake Michigan, which must make for a very pretty setting. And if you and Gabe want to get married on this side of the Atlantic, naturally I'm delighted."

"Well, we still haven't quite decided exactly what we want to do," Lianne said. "As you pointed out, most of our friends are here in London, but my relatives nearly all live in Michigan, and they really want to come and see me get married. Plus my mother is worried about my grandparents. My grandfather is eighty-six years old, and his wife is eighty-seven. My mother knows the plane journey to England would be too much for them, but if I get married here, they'll insist on making the trip. Which is a bit of a dilemma."

"I can see how it would be. But rather a nice dilemma in a way. How splendid that your grandparents are still alive."

"Yes, my father's mother is alive, too, but she's in much better health than my mother's parents. I'm very fortunate." Lianne's voice sounded hollow.

"Well, if you and Gabe decide to tie the knot in Michigan that will make travel plans a lot easier for Kate and me!" Grace was determined to look on the bright side.

"Don't book your plane tickets yet," Lianne cautioned. "Gabe and I are still discussing all the various pros and cons. There's a lot to take into consideration."

Grace bit her tongue and managed, with heroic effort, not to point out that with only three months to go, she and Gabe needed to stop "considering" and make a decision one way or the other. Lianne was a dear, sweet girl, but she obviously didn't grasp the time constraints they were working against. Three months was scarcely more than the blink of an eye when you were trying to plan a formal wedding. In fact, it would be impossible if it weren't for the DeWilde connection and the contacts Grace had within the industry. Until the church had been selected, no arrangements could be made for the reception. And until the venue for the reception had been decided upon, no caterers could be selected. And without caterers, no menu could be finalized. Not to mention the thousand other details that would have to be taken care of—the band, the flowers, the photographers, the video people.

And then there was the urgent need to get invitations engraved and addressed in plenty of time for busy people to clear their schedules and plan their travel itineraries. Especially, Grace thought, if guests from England and France were going to have to get themselves to an obscure place like Benton's Inlet. And how about Ryder Blake in Australia? Gabe would probably want Ryder as his best man, and with his hectic work schedule, Ryder would need to know whether he was supposed to be flying to the States or to England.

However, she had always sworn she would never turn into one of those dreadful, bossy mother-in-laws, Grace reminded herself, much less one of those mothers who was so busy organizing the wedding to her own taste that she forgot about minor details like the wishes of the bride and groom. She decided that a tactful change of subject was called for.

"Have you chosen your dress yet?" she asked. "This is a good year in terms of style and workmanship, isn't it? The manufacturers seem to be deemphasizing the glitter and paying more attention to subtle details like the cut and fall of the dress."

"You're right, the selection was great." Lianne finally began to sound enthusiastic. "I had a hard time making my final choice, but I'm really pleased with the one I picked in the end. It's quite a simple design, ivory satin with long sleeves and a scandalously low neckline."

A bubble of the bright laughter that Grace always associated with her daughter-in-law-to-be finally warmed Lianne's voice. "I'm going to buy one of those new superbras that they're advertising everywhere and see if I can't walk down the aisle with some real, honest-to-God cleavage beneath my modest lace veil. That'll be a real wedding present to myself."

Grace laughed. "I shall remember to take special note of the cleavage. I'm sure it will be spectacular! Please have one of your bridesmaids take a picture when you have your fitting and send it to me by express mail. I can't wait to see exactly what you've chosen. And, Lianne, I'd be thrilled if you'd allow me the very great pleasure of buying your dress for you. Think of it as a little extra wedding gift from me."

There was a moment of tense silence before Lianne responded. "Grace, thank you, you're so kind, and I do appreciate your generous thought, but...um...Jeffrey has already offered to pay for my dress and I accepted."

"No problem," Grace said, managing—she hoped—to make her response sound light and carefree. "You'll simply have to indulge me when I next come over to London and we'll buy something wonderful for your honeymoon. Where are you going, by the way? Or is that a secret?"

"It's a secret. Although I will tell you that I vetoed Gabe's first suggestion of a yak trip through Kathmandu." Laughter returned to Lianne's voice. "I suggested he should stop striving so hard for originality and start thinking more along the lines of in-room hot tubs and twenty-four-hour room service. He came up with Las Vegas. It took him a couple more tries, but I think he's finally managed to get it just right."

Grace refused to remember her own honeymoon in Rome, with hot, blissful days exploring the wonders of the ancient city, and cool, blissful nights discovering the wonders of making love to Jeffrey. She wouldn't think about the afternoon, sipping espresso in the Piazza San Bartolomeo, when Jeffrey had bought a slightly wilted rose from a street vendor and handed it to her with a shy, self-conscious smile. And she'd made the astonishing discovery that she was falling head over heels in love with the man she'd married for all the wrong reasons.

Her honeymoon in Rome was more than thirty years in the past, the love she'd shared with Jeffrey dead and forgotten. These days, her husband didn't care enough about her to pick up the phone to talk about plans for their only son's forthcoming marriage—

Grace ruthlessly cut off her descent into self-pity, knowing from bitter past experience that it was a most self-destructive path to take. "Well, it's been great talking to you, Lianne, although I can't exactly say we finalized any plans." Grace tried not to let even a trace of impatience color her voice. "I'll look forward to hearing from you as soon as you and Gabe make up your minds exactly where you're going to have this great event."

"Yes, of course. I'll be sure to call."

"When you next see Gabe, give him my love, won't you?"

There was an infinitesimal pause. "Yes, I'll tell him. Er... when I see him."

Oh, Lord, Grace thought wryly. *Gabe's there with her, which is why she sounded so sleepy and distracted when I called.*

"Well, I must run," she said, deciding it was definitely time to get off the phone. "My schedule is jam-packed for the rest of the day, and it must be getting toward your bedtime."

"Yes." There was a tiny catch in Lianne's voice and Grace had a sudden, embarrassingly vivid image of what might have caused it.

"Nice chatting with you, Lianne," she said quickly. "Goodbye."

LIANNE HUNG UP THE PHONE and rolled over in bed, swatting with mock annoyance at Gabe's marauding fingers. "Your mother guessed," she said accusingly. "It was extremely embarrassing. She guessed you were in bed with me."

Gabe nibbled delicately on his fiancée's earlobe. "Did she? Somehow I don't think that will be the first hint she's had that we're not going to our marriage bed in a state of virginal purity."

Lianne sighed. "Honestly, Gabe, the way things are going right at the moment, I'm beginning to have serious doubts about whether we'll ever make it to our marriage bed."

He sat up, his smile wiped away in a single instant. "What do you mean? Are you suggesting that you don't want to marry me after all?"

She shook her head. "No, of course not. How could you even think that? But, Gabe, you've been so busy at work, I don't think you realize what's going on. This wedding ceremony is turning out to be a nightmare of major proportions. I honestly don't know how we're going to get through it."

"How so? What's the problem?" He grinned. "I've heard a rumor that DeWilde's is a really good bridal store, with contacts to help you take care of every detail in planning the perfect wedding."

She didn't crack even a small smile. "It isn't one problem, it's dozens of problems, and none of them the sort that can be solved by DeWilde's or any other store. Your mother isn't talking to your father and vice versa, and either one could file for a divorce at any moment. That's just for starters. Then there's Julia, my best friend, the person in the world I most want to have as my maid of honor. She's in love with you, Gabe. There's no point in trying to ignore that fact any longer."

"Are you sure?" he asked, frowning. "Honest to God, Lianne, I never said a word about marriage to her, never even hinted at it. And she always seems perfectly cheerful whenever we happen to meet. You know, like a friend, a good friend.''

"She's way too cheerful, that's the problem. She's lost half a stone in the past two weeks, and she smiles with such desperate determination every time she sees us together that I want to cry, even if she doesn't.''

He took her hand, lacing her fingers with his. "I'm really sorry if I've hurt Julia. I sure as hell wish I hadn't. But I'm in love with you, and we can't decide not to marry just because it upsets Julia. That makes no sense at all.''

"True. But I'm going to go all through the service knowing that my best friend's heart is breaking, and that I'm putting her through several hours of unrelieved torture by asking her to watch us get married.''

"You couldn't ask someone else to be your chief bridesmaid?''

Lianne shook her head. "I've thought about it, but that would be worse. At least now she still has her pride. If I don't ask her to be my maid of honor, she'll know exactly why I didn't, and it sort of forces everyone to confront truths it would be much more comfortable to keep covered up.''

"Yes, for once I don't think honesty is the best policy. You're right—it's a problem,'' Gabe said.

Lianne grimaced. "You ain't heard nuttin' yet. We've barely started on the list of problems. There's the whole issue of my family. My mother and father have discovered approximately two hundred aunts, uncles, cousins and miscellaneous relatives who are going to be mortally wounded if they can't come and dance at our wedding. Which they can't afford to do unless we have the ceremony in Michigan.''

"Well, that's easily solved. We'll get married in Michigan."

"Gabe, I could hear your mother grinding her teeth to stop herself from having apoplexy when she heard that might be where we would have the ceremony. My parents are thinking picnic tables in the church hall, and your parents are thinking caviar and champagne, followed by a four-course dinner catered by England's finest chefs."

"The picnic sounds just fine to me."

"Does it? What about all our friends? They're here in London. I don't think they want to fly to Michigan for a barbecue. As for your sister Kate, she was excruciatingly polite when I called and asked her to be one of my bridesmaids, but I know she was secretly worrying about how in the world she was going to find time to fly to London. Or Michigan, or wherever the heck this wretched ceremony is going to be."

"You've left out Megan," he said, settling back against the pillows and beginning a languid tasting of the hollows at the base of her neck. "What's Megan's complaint to add to this litany of pending disaster?"

"Nothing," she said. "Megan is so relieved your mother has another family wedding to plan that she's ecstatic. She's hoping everyone will lay off for a few months and stop trying to fix her up with some man or another. She thanked me profusely for taking the spotlight away from her."

"There you are, then," he said. "At least we're making one member of the family happy."

"That leaves about 295 people in the other column."

"Then I guess this is where you draw in a very deep breath and accept that you can't please everyone."

"Not even ourselves?"

"You always please me," he said, his voice deepening. "I'll do my damnedest to return the compliment." He rolled over and captured her hands, holding them high over her head so that he had better access to her body. "Mmm," he said, tasting appreciatively. "You know, I can understand how the vampire legends got started. There's something so incredibly erotic about a woman's throat. Not to mention her breasts and her—"

"Gabe, damn it, you're not listening to me!"

"It's hard to lick and listen at the same time."

She pushed him away, surprised to discover that she was a hairbreadth away from tears. "Gabe, this isn't funny! What are we going to do? By the time this wedding finally takes place, nobody is going to be speaking to anybody! Probably including me to you!"

Gabe sat up, pulling her into his lap and cradling her head against his shoulder. "I'm sorry, sweet, you're really serious about this, aren't you."

"Of course I'm serious. Gabe, this is the sort of situation that tears families apart, creates feuds that last into the sixth generation and leaves the bride and groom so exhausted that they take the first two years of their marriage to get over the horrors of the wedding."

"You exaggerate, my love. I'm sure it wouldn't take us a day over six months. We have such great communication skills."

She smiled weakly. "Gabe, what in the world are we going to do?"

He put his hand under her chin, tipped back her head, and kissed her gently. "Don't worry," he said. "The important thing is that we both know we want to spend the rest of our lives together. It shouldn't be impossible to solve the problem of how we actually get married."

When he smiled at her, she could believe that he was capable of anything, even devising a way to marry her without hurting the feelings of either set of in-laws. She sighed and nestled closer to him. "Sometimes that DeWilde arrogance of yours comes in really handy. You sound so self-confident, I almost believe you."

He kissed the end of her nose. "You should believe me. Trust me, darling, this is all going to work out just fine, you'll see."

EPILOGUE

THE DOORMAN STOPPED GRACE as she hurried toward the elevators after a day filled to bursting with appointments, meetings and discussions with lawyers. "Mrs. DeWilde, a package has arrived for you. We put it in the fridge in our storeroom, so it would keep cool."

"Thank you," Grace replied absently, her thoughts split almost evenly between tomorrow's meeting with one of her brother's bankers and the fact that neither Gabe nor Lianne had seen fit to call her in almost two weeks. She was trying to hold on to her patience, but their failure to fix on a place for their wedding was progressing well beyond inconvenient and moving into downright inconsiderate. It was too late to phone England tonight, but first thing tomorrow morning she was going to call Gabe and read him the riot act.

The doorman came out from the storeroom carrying a large wicker basket, wrapped in cellophane and tied with long streamers of silver ribbon. "Can you manage it, Mrs. DeWilde? There's nobody else covering the door or I'd carry it upstairs for you."

Grace took the basket and hefted it in her arms. "I can manage, thanks. Fortunately, it's not too heavy." She poked apart the cellophane wrapping while she waited for the elevator. "Mmm . . . Dom Perignon," she said, seeing the magnum of champagne nestled in a bed of fake white straw. "Not to mention a box of chocolate truffles and a carton of imported Italian sugared almonds. It all looks very expensive." She smiled at the doorman as he held open the elevator door for her. "Somebody's sure anxious to make a good impression. I wonder what they're trying to sell me?"

The doorman grinned. "Whatever it is, take your time deciding. That way you may get another basket of goodies."

"Great advice," Grace said as the elevator doors slid closed.

Her apartment was blissfully cool and quiet after the hot, noisy day. Grace set the gift basket on the center island in her kitchen, along with her purse, and untied the streamers of silver ribbon. Pushing aside the cellophane, she reached for the enclosed gift card at the same time as she pressed the playback button on her answering machine. Listening to the first message, she slit open the gift card, which was unusually large and bulky. And probably came complete with attached sales pitch, Grace thought cynically.

The gift card didn't come with a sales pitch but with a letter. Grace started reading. The second phone message never made it past the first three or four words. With a strangled gasp, she hit the pause button on her answering machine and stared in blank disbelief at the letter. Blinking as if faulty vision were the problem, she read through the lengthy note one more time. It was still signed by Gabe and Lianne. It still said the same incredible things.

Choking back several choice expletives, she grabbed the bottle of Dom Perignon and stormed into her bedroom, shedding shoes and clothes as she went. She ended up undressed as far as her slip, perched in her favorite spot in the middle of the bed, breathing hard, the bottle of champagne nestled at her feet.

She grabbed the phone, dialing London without even stopping to think. "Don't leave the answering machine to pick up," she muttered. "Come on, Jeffrey. I need to speak to you. I really need to speak to you."

"Hello."

"Jeffrey." Her entire body slumped in relief. "Jeffrey, thank goodness I caught you at home. I just got back to my apartment and there was this totally incredible package waiting for me from Gabe and Lianne—"

"Champagne," he said. "And chocolates. Also *confetti*—the traditional sugared almonds at Italian weddings. You must admit that they made their announcement in grand style."

"Good grief, Jeffrey, I can't believe you're sounding so calm!"

"You should have caught me six hours ago when I came home and found my gift basket! You have to remember that I've had a little longer than you to get used to the idea. In fact, I've been expecting your call for the past several hours."

Belatedly she realized that in London it was 2:00 a.m. "Oh, Lord, Jeffrey, I'm sorry to phone at such an ungodly hour, but I had to talk to you. I can't believe it! They've eloped, damn it! Eloped!"

"To Gretna Green, according to the helpful little note they enclosed with my basket of goodies," Jeffrey said dryly. "I'm sure they gave you the same fascinating piece of information."

"How could they?" Grace wailed. "Jeffrey, we would have given them such a beautiful wedding, and instead they decide to run off and get married in some poky little registrar's office in Gretna Green, for heaven's sake!"

"I know. It's monumentally inconsiderate of them. I would have strangled Gabe for you, my dear, but unfortunately, he wasn't available for strangling. And by the time he and Lianne get back from their honeymoon in the Scottish Highlands, I dare say we'll be foolish enough to forgive them."

"Oh, Jeffrey!" Grace hovered somewhere between tears and laughter. "For a family that has a world-famous name for fulfilling wedding fantasies, we don't seem to be doing too well with our own children, do we. First Megan gets left at the altar. Now Gabe and Lianne elope. I shudder to think what Kate will come up with—"

"Better that Megan got left at the altar than that she ended up married to the wrong man. And in the long run, the important thing is that Gabe and Lianne love each other, not whether they got married with a supporting cast of hundreds to watch them."

"I suppose so. But I did so want them to have a special day to remember."

"I'm sure this has been a special day for them," Jeffrey said quietly. "Anyway, Gracie, the deed is done. All that's left for us now is to wish them happiness."

"Damn it, Jeffrey, would you stop being so...so mature about all this? He's our son, our only son. I know it's selfish of me, but I so badly wanted to stand next to you in the church at Kemberly while he and Lianne promised to love and care for each other—" Grace stopped abruptly, appalled at how much she'd unwittingly revealed in that unthinking remark, not only to Jeffrey but also to herself.

Her husband was silent for several long moments. "Well, I suppose we shall have to make our own impromptu, long-distance celebration as best we can," he said at last. "I haven't opened my champagne. Why don't you get your bottle and bring it back to the phone. Then we'll pop the corks, each pour ourselves a large glass, and toast Gabe and Lianne together."

"I already have the bottle of champagne here on the bed with me," Grace said.

"You're sitting on the bed?" Jeffrey asked, his voice suddenly strained.

"Yes." For some odd reason, a wave of heat washed over her. She swallowed, moistening her dry throat. "Old habits are hard to break."

There was another long pause. "Yes, I've discovered that." Jeffrey cleared his throat. "Do you have a glass, or just the bottle of champagne?"

He knew her too well, Grace thought, knew that she would have stormed to the phone clutching the champagne and—inevitably—forgotten to bring a glass. It was almost as if he were in the bedroom with her. "I don't have a glass, but I'll get one," she said. "The start of our son's marriage deserves to be toasted with something more elegant than a swig from the bottle."

She grabbed one of her new crystal glasses from the dining room and came back to the bed. She picked up the phone. "I'm ready. I have everything now."

"Then open the bottle of champagne and pick up the phone when you've poured yourself a glass."

The cork shot up toward the ceiling with a satisfying pop. Grace poured herself a glass and picked up the phone. "Jeffrey? Are you there? I have a full glass."

"I'm here," he said, "Dom Perignon in hand. And I offer a toast to our son, Gabe, and Lianne, his new wife. May they spend a lifetime together in love, health and happiness."

Grace was suddenly afraid that she was going to cry. "I'll drink to that," she said huskily, and took a quick sip of champagne. "To Gabe and Lianne."

She put down her glass and waited, breath squeezed so tight in her lungs that her chest ached, but Jeffrey didn't ask how she was or what she'd been doing with herself all day. Perhaps he was afraid to, she thought sadly. Perhaps, on a call celebrating the start of Gabe's marriage to Lianne, he didn't want to risk introducing the bitter debris of their own failures.

Finally, he spoke. "Grace, thank you for calling. I'm glad we were able to share a glass of champagne together on such a special occasion, even if it was at long distance."

"We did make three super kids, didn't we, Jeffrey? Whatever else we messed up, we managed to get that just right."

"Yes, we did," he said softly. "We managed to get that just right."

He didn't say anything more, and this time it was Grace who broke the silence. "Well, I know it's late for you, Jeffrey—"

"Yes, it is rather late, and with Gabe leaving so unexpectedly, I'm going to have a hell of a day tomorrow. Good night, Grace. Take care of yourself."

"Good night, Jeffrey. Sleep well."

She hung up the phone and stared unseeingly at the bottle of Dom Perignon. Finally, she squared her shoulders, picked up her glass and tossed back the rest of her champagne in a couple of quick gulps.

"Here's to us, Jeffrey," she whispered. "Here's to us."

WEDDINGS BY DeWILDE

continues with

THE RELUCTANT BRIDE

by Janis Flores

Available in May

Here's a preview!

THE RELUCTANT BRIDE

"For heaven's sake, Jeffrey," Grace said into the telephone. "You could have warned me, you know. I hardly knew what to say when that detective appeared on my doorstep."

Jeffrey was being his officious best, pointing out, "I did send you a memo, Grace."

"I detest memos, as you're very well aware. I realize things are a little...strained between us at the moment, but don't you think you could have given me the courtesy of a phone call?"

"I didn't know when Mr. Santos would arrive."

"While *I* didn't even know he existed."

"We were all surprised. When that tiara showed up in New York...well, you can just imagine what we all thought."

Grace could, indeed. The theft of six pieces from the world-famous DeWilde collection had been a carefully guarded secret, but now that one of the jewels had appeared, the pretense had been shattered. Apparently, there was no disguising the fact that the tiara was the real thing. Once word got out, questions were bound to be raised.

Which was why Jeffrey had hired a private investigator.

"I know how your family values privacy, Jeffrey, but it was unsettling enough to find out that a piece of the collection had suddenly surfaced. To be unexpectedly confronted with an investigator was almost as disturbing....."

Jeffrey sighed. "This isn't really about the investigator, is it, Grace?"

"Well, of course it—" Grace stopped. "No, you're right. It isn't."

"Then what?"

"The truth is, I'm so *tired* of fighting about every detail regarding this reception we're supposed to be giving for Gabe and Lianne."

"It's not my fault that you're so far—"

"Don't say it," she warned. "You've made it crystal clear how you feel about my relocating, *and* my opening a store."

"Ah, now we've really come to the crux of the problem, haven't we."

"Have we? You have no right to try and stop me, Jeffrey. I'm not competing with you in any way."

"The board sees it differently." He paused. "But I caution you to remember one thing—"

"And that is?"

"The corporation will do everything necessary to protect itself."

Absolutely irritated by now, Grace sighed wearily. "Well, fine, Jeffrey. At least we're on the same wavelength about one thing. Because I assure you, I'll do everything I can to guard my own interests."

HARLEQUIN®

Don't miss these Harlequin favorites by some of our most
distinguished authors!
And now, you can receive a discount by ordering two or more titles!

HT #25663	THE LAWMAN by Vicki Lewis Thompson	$3.25 U.S. ☐/$3.75 CAN. ☐
HP #11788	THE SISTER SWAP by Susan Napier	$3.25 U.S. ☐/$3.75 CAN. ☐
HR #03293	THE MAN WHO CAME FOR CHRISTMAS by Bethany Campbell	$2.99 U.S. ☐/$3.50 CAN. ☐
HS #70667	FATHERS & OTHER STRANGERS by Evelyn Crowe	$3.75 U.S. ☐/$4.25 CAN. ☐
HI #22198	MURDER BY THE BOOK by Margaret St. George	$2.89 ☐
HAR #16520	THE ADVENTURESS by M.J. Rodgers	$3.50 U.S. ☐/$3.99 CAN. ☐
HH #28885	DESERT ROGUE by Erin Yorke	$4.50 U.S. ☐/$4.99 CAN. ☐

(limited quantities available on certain titles)

	AMOUNT	$
DEDUCT:	10% DISCOUNT FOR 2+ BOOKS	$
ADD:	POSTAGE & HANDLING	$
	($1.00 for one book, 50¢ for each additional)	
	APPLICABLE TAXES**	$_____
	TOTAL PAYABLE	$_____
	(check or money order—please do not send cash)	

To order, complete this form and send it, along with a check or money order for the
total above, payable to Harlequin Books, to: **In the U.S.:** 3010 Walden Avenue,
P.O. Box 9047, Buffalo, NY 14269-9047; **in Canada:** P.O. Box 613, Fort Erie, Ontario,
L2A 5X3.

Name:_____

Address:_____ City:_____

State/Prov.:_____ Zip/Postal Code:_____

**New York residents remit applicable sales taxes.
   Canadian residents remit applicable GST and provincial taxes.   HBACK-JS3

Look us up on-line at: http://www.romance.net

SILHOUETTE... Where Passion Lives

Order these Silhouette favorites today!
Now you can receive a discount by ordering two or more titles!

SD#05890	TWO HEARTS, SLIGHTLY USED	
	by Dixie Browning	$2.99 U.S. ☐ /$3.50 CAN. ☐
SD#05899	DARK INTENTIONS	
	by Carole Buck	$2.99 U.S. ☐ /$3.50 CAN. ☐
IM#07604	FUGITIVE FATHER	
	by Carla Cassidy	$3.50 U.S. ☐ /$3.99 CAN. ☐
IM#07673	THE LONER	
	by Linda Turner	$3.75 U.S. ☐ /$4.25 CAN. ☐
SSE#09934	THE ADVENTURER	
	by Diana Whitney	$3.50 U.S. ☐ /$3.99 CAN. ☐
SSE#09867	WHEN STARS COLLIDE	
	by Patricia Coughlin	$3.50 U.S. ☐
SR#19079	THIS MAN AND THIS WOMAN	
	by Lucy Gordon	$2.99 U.S. ☐ /$3.50 CAN. ☐
SR#19060	FATHER IN THE MIDDLE	
	by Phyllis Halldorson	$2.99 U.S. ☐ /$3.50 CAN. ☐
YT#52001	WANTED: PERFECT PARTNER	
	by Debbie Macomber	$3.50 U.S. ☐ /$3.99 CAN. ☐
YT#52008	HUSBANDS DON'T GROW ON TREES	
	by Kasey Michaels	$3.50 U.S. ☐ /$3.99 CAN. ☐
	(Limited quantities available on certain titles.)	

TOTAL AMOUNT	$
DEDUCT: 10% DISCOUNT FOR 2+ BOOKS	$
POSTAGE & HANDLING	$
($1.00 for one book, 50¢ for each additional)	
APPLICABLE TAXES*	$
TOTAL PAYABLE	$
(check or money order—please do not send cash)	

To order, complete this form and send it, along with a check or money order for the total above, payable to Silhouette Books, to: In the U.S.: 3010 Walden Avenue, P.O. Box 9077, Buffalo, NY 14269-9077; In Canada: P.O. Box 636, Fort Erie, Ontario, L2A 5X3.

Name:_____

Address:_____City:_____

State/Prov.:_____ Zip/Postal Code:_____

*New York residents remit applicable sales taxes.
Canadian residents remit applicable GST and provincial taxes.

SBACK-SN3

WAYS TO *UNEXPECTEDLY* MEET MR. RIGHT:

♡ Go out with the sexy-sounding stranger
your daughter secretly set you up with
through a personal ad.

♡ RSVP yes to a wedding invitation—soon
it might be your turn to say "I do!"

♡ Receive a marriage proposal by mail—
from a man you've never met....

These are just a few of the unexpected
ways that written communication
leads to love in Silhouette Yours Truly.

Each month, look for two fast-paced, fun and
flirtatious Yours Truly novels
(with entertaining treats and sneak previews
in the back pages) by some of your favorite
authors—and some who are sure to
become favorites.

YOURS TRULY™:
Love—when you least expect it!

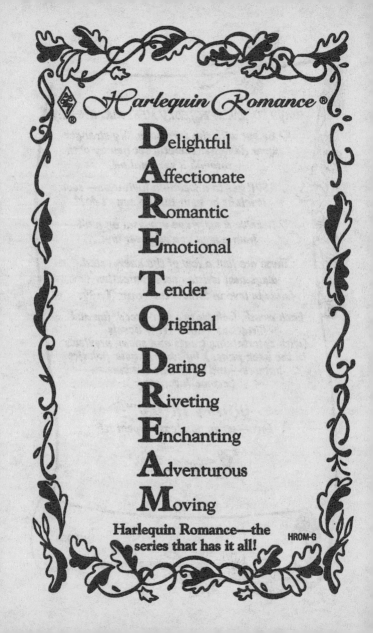

Harlequin Romance ®

Delightful

Affectionate

Romantic

Emotional

Tender

Original

Daring

Riveting

Enchanting

Adventurous

Moving

Harlequin Romance—the
series that has it all!

HROM-G

SILHOUETTE® Desire®

Do you want...

Dangerously handsome heroes

Evocative, everlasting love stories

Sizzling and tantalizing sensuality

Incredibly sexy miniseries like **MAN OF THE MONTH**

Red-hot romance

Enticing entertainment that can't be beat!

You'll find all of this, and much *more* each and every month in **SILHOUETTE DESIRE**. Don't miss these unforgettable love stories by some of romance's hottest authors. Silhouette Desire—where your fantasies will always come true....

Harlequin® Historical

If you're a serious fan of historical romance,
then you're in luck!

Harlequin Historicals brings you
stories by bestselling authors, rising new stars
and talented first-timers.

Ruth Langan & Theresa Michaels
Mary McBride & Cheryl St. John
Margaret Moore & Merline Lovelace
Julie Tetel & Nina Beaumont
Susan Amarillas & Ana Seymour
Deborah Simmons & Linda Castle
Cassandra Austin & Emily French
Miranda Jarrett & Suzanne Barclay
DeLoras Scott & Laurie Grant...

You'll never run out of favorites.

Harlequin Historicals...they're too good to miss!